As I trolled through the audience's psychic communion I accidentally touched Rick's mind. It was brimming with rapturous power as he poured himself into the crowd, giving them everything he had.

I floated on his blissful tide for a moment before I noticed a subtle shift in the grand harmony. Strange minor notes emerged and began to dominate. Slowly the sharing moved along an odd, discordant scale I had never heard before.

Rick's body began to shake and quiver: every muscle stood out as though carved. His lips were drawn back in a horrible grimace. His very head seemed to swell.

I looked into my brother's mind, and screamed.

People around me began to erupt into flame as though they had each been doused with kerosene and touched by a struck match. The human torches filled the night sky with the stench of burning flesh. Black smoke obscured the stars. The shrieks. Oh, God, the shrieks were terrible, deafening, worse than the worst nightmare.

My brother was still on stage, still on his feet, but he was staggering, collapsing to knees and elbows, cradling his head in his hands. Alanna was on stage, too, running toward him. But it was all happening so slowly, so very slowly. I could see her dark hair bobbing in the wind as though it were weightless. But she was taking so long to reach Rick. Hurry, I thought. Help him!

Mutant

Legacy

KAREN HABER

A Byron Preiss Book

BANTAM BOOKS
NEW YORK • TORONTO • LONDON • SYDNEY • AUCKLAND

MUTANT LEGACY

A Bantam Spectra Book / January 1993

ISBN 0-553-29671-X

Published simultaneously in the United States and Canada

Bantam Books are published by Bantam Books, a division of Bantam Doubleday Dell Publishing Group, Inc. Its trademark, consisting of the words "Bantam Books" and the portrayal of a rooster, is Registered in U.S. Patent and Trademark Office and in other countries. Marca Registrada. Bantam Books, 666 Fifth Avenue, New York, New York 10103.

PRINTED IN THE UNITED STATES OF AMERICA

RAD   0 9 8 7 6 5 4 3 2 1

For Byron

*(For aid, assistance, editing, and/or
general encouragement,
a special thank you to
Lou Aronica, Janna Silverstein, David Harris,
John Betancourt, Pat LoBrutto, Jim Burns,
Carrolly Erickson, Jerrold Mundis, Rosalyn Greenberg,
Bonnie Carpenter, Nancy DeRoche, Sandra Stephenson
Lembo,
and, always, Bob.)*

INTRODUCTION

WE HAVE REACHED the fourth and last volume of Karen Haber's saga of the secret mutants in our midst. The mutants, secret no longer, have moved steadily into the mainstream of American life since the time of Volume One —*The Mutant Season*—which saw the election of the first mutant senator, Eleanor Jacobsen.

But now we are a couple of generations onward from that point. The threat of the emergence of a supermutant with virtually invincible powers—every normal human's paranoid horror story brought to life—came and went, apparently, with the exposure of Victor Ashman's superabilities as a pathetic hoax in *The Mutant Prime*. But then—in the third book, *Mutant Star*—we discovered that a *genuine* supermutant existed after all, unbeknownst not only to his own people but even, for a long while, to himself.

Six years have gone by since the violent climax of *Mutant Star*, when the troubled and tormented supermutant Rick Akimura, in full possession of his immense powers at last, exploded in a frenzy of wild wrath, bringing grief to his family and posing a monstrous problem for the world of normal humans. Intoxicated by the realization of the scope of his abilities, Rick seemed about to run amok; but Julian, Rick's fraternal twin brother, had at the last moment been able to recall Rick to his senses and send him into an exile of atonement.

Now, though, Rick is beginning to stir in his desert solitude. The final act in the tale of the mutants' emergence from self-imposed obscurity is about to begin.

SINCE MEDIEVAL TIMES, when the genetic anomaly that created the mutant clan first appeared, this tribe of people equipped with virtually miraculous extrasensory powers had taken care to remain out of sight of the world of normals, fearing that their mutant abilities would awaken the envy and fear of the majority population and call down merciless persecution upon them. But as the age of witch burnings and pogroms retreated into history, the mutants—cautiously, even timidly—allowed themselves to edge forward into sight.

Their own scripture tells it:

> And when we knew ourselves to be different,
> To be mutant and therefore other,
> We took ourselves away,
> Sequestered that portion of us most other,
> And so turned a bland face to the blind eyes
> Of the world.
> Formed our community in silence, in hiding,
> Offered love and sharing to one another,
> And waited until a better time,
> A cycle in which we might share
> Beyond our circle.
> We are still waiting.

In the introduction to the second of these four novels I compared the emergence in the early twenty-first century of mutants into the mainstream of American life to the emergence, nearly a century earlier, of such political figures as Martin Luther King, Jesse Jackson, and other leaders of the black drive for racial equality. (I did point out that the parallel was a very approximate one, since the goal of the black civil-rights movement was *equality of opportunity*, whereas the mutants were in fact an advanced form of the human species, not merely equal but essentially superior, and so were faced with the overwhelming task of persuading the far more numerous normal-human population to accept them for what they really were, not simply to allow them the political rights that were due by Constitutional guarantee to any member of society.)

But the two volumes of the series that tell the story of the Akimura brothers provide us with a very different parallel to the course of human history as we know it: for now that the mutants are out in the open, they want to use their powers to heal and comfort the world's suffering people, whether they be mutant or nonmutant. The kind of healing they will offer, though it has no overt religious content, will inevitably come to take on something of a religious coloration. And so what we begin to see is something analogous to the emergence of early Christianity in the first years of the Roman Empire.

Jesus lived and died during the reign of Tiberius, second of the Roman emperors. Through the decades that followed, Christianity became a powerful underground movement, persecuted and suppressed wherever it ventured into the open. But as the centuries passed, and Christianity was widely embraced throughout Asia Minor, Greece, and even Rome itself, the Empire's attitude toward this subversive religious movement gradually evolved, and finally, early in the fourth century A.D., the emperor himself—Constantine the Great—was willing to claim membership in the Church. He had seen a miraculous vision in the sky— the Cross—bearing the legend, *In Hoc Signo Vinces*—"In This Sign You Shall Conquer"—and that seems to have been decisive in his conversion (which probably also had more worldly political motives).

An edict of Constantine's issued in the year 313 proclaimed full toleration of all religions and restitution of wrongs done to the Christians by his imperial predecessors. Laws aimed at Christianity were repealed; Sunday was made a public holiday; and, less than fifty years after Constantine's death in 337, Christianity had become the official religion of the Empire. The astonishing metamorphosis from secret sect to dominant spiritual and political force was complete.

In the four novels of the mutant saga we see something similar beginning to happen. The hidden, wary mutants of medieval times give way in the more tolerant twenty-first century to ones who will openly admit their powers, and we see the first election of undisguised mutants to public office. And now with the advent of Rick Akimura we observe a far more startling development—the beginning of a mighty quasi-religious movement, built around what is essentially a mutant messiah, that will sweep not only the mutant society but move into the world of normals as well.

But this parallel with ancient Christianity, like the other one, is only approximate. Jesus worked some miracles, the gospels tell us, but here we have a whole *race* of miracle-workers. The extrasensory powers of even the most timid and self-effacing mutant are far beyond the mental capacity of any normal. And though it is possible for a normal to be sympathetic to the mutants, even to fall in love with one and marry one, conversion to mutancy is altogether impossible. A Roman emperor could and did become a Christian, but no amount of willingness will turn a nonmutant into a telekinete or a telepath.

Still, some sort of rapprochement between the two branches of humanity is possible, leading to an end to the fears and misunderstandings that have divided them—when the proper leader is at hand. Or perhaps the job will take *two* leaders—one with the charisma of a messiah, and the other—well—

This is his story.

—Robert Silverberg
Oakland, California
January, 1992

. . . Man is not enough,
Can never stand as God, is ever wrong
In the end, however naked, tall, there is still
The impossible possible philosopher's man,
The man who has had the time to think enough,
The central man, the human globe, responsive
As a mirror with a voice, the man of glass,
Who in a million diamonds sums us up.

—Wallace Stevens

1

I CAN STILL SMELL the city burning. I know that it was reduced to ash and the cinders blown away on the wind forty years ago. But that peculiar smell, part melting plastic, part burning flesh, arises from the ghosts of the ruins to assault me at odd moments.

My name is Julian Akimura and I am the head of what some people call the Church of the Better World. It is not a job I particularly wanted but I have grown accustomed to it in much the same way that one's foot, by forming calluses, adjusts, with time, to a tight shoe.

The church squeezes me, squeezes my life, and in response, in virtual self-defense, I've grown a tough, protective hide: cool, calm Dr. Julian whom nothing rumples. Underneath, I seethe, I boil. If not for my duties and their numbing pleasure . . . but I won't think about that, not now. No one sees. No one knows. And the only one capable of piercing my defenses is gone.

"Dr. Akimura?"

The voice, a sharp contralto, slides between me and my visions, neatly severing me from the past. I blink and peer out the window where the city sits, immaculate, untouched, white spires reaching for the china-blue sky.

My familiars range around me in this well-appointed meeting room: elite members of the administrative upper tier of Better World, the house that Rick built. We are having a meeting: the priests and priestesses of management like meetings. They enjoy sitting around the polished sandstone table, sipping green Mars Elixir from faceted crystal cups, and making policy while I pretend to listen.

"Dr. Akimura?" It was Barsi, director of Therapeutic Services, speaking. Lovely Barsi, former Hindu, my dark-eyed, devoted Brahmin acolyte, calling my attention back to the business at hand. "As you know, we're still undecided about the deployment of certain Better World funds."

"Refresh my memory," I said.

She gave a quick, sidelong glance to Ginny Quinlan, chief financial officer, a sharp-featured blonde who wore her hair short and slicked back. Had Ginny put her up to making the proposal, knowing my obvious fondness for Barsi?

"Well," Barsi said, "we already have sufficient funding for the outreach programs and service missions. Many of us feel that we could use some of the money elsewhere. We might find it useful to, say, buy a controlling interest in TexMedia. We know that it's in a vulnerable position and we could get it at a good price."

"Wait a minute," I said. "Useful? To whom? And what good would a third-rate vid company do B.W.? Are we planning some new programs that require more production facilities? And if we are, why haven't I heard about them?"

Another quick glance exchanged between the two. What was going on here?

"You needn't worry," Ginny said quickly. "We were merely thinking of expanding our broadcasting range. We want to attract as many members as possible."

"Why?" I said. "Because of their need for help or your desire to swell our already overflowing coffers?" I could see the dollar signs in her eyes. It was the same old argument we had been having for almost twenty years: expansion of the corporation versus meeting the needs of the members. "Expansion? We already own one vid company. Excerpts from *Rick's Way* are read, dramatized, and discussed every night around the globe. What more do we need?"

Barsi, beside me, took a deep breath and plunged. "Julian," she said, and her tone was more direct than I had ever before heard it. "You might as well know that we feel Better World needs to move more, well, aggressively. Money has been piling up—*Rick's Way* sells out every printing, and we think it's time to move forward. Invest it in some of the off-world mines and so forth. Increase our returns. Prepare for future contingencies."

"Make more money? Don't we have enough? We shouldn't be thinking about investments, we should be thinking about helping the poor and needy."

"You know we are. But we can do more. So much more. We're getting into a rut. If we don't move forward, we'll decay."

"Surely you don't have to be told that there are all kinds of programs in place," Ginny said. Her husky alto rasp was harsher than usual, the vibrato almost shredding her words. "We provide hot meals, medical care, remedial education, family counseling. In every major city where we have a center we offer all these services. Don't accuse us of depriving anyone."

Quickly I took up my sword in the familiar battle and said, "If we're doing so much and so well, why are there still so many people in need?"

The B.W. cenobites exchanged uneasy glances—obviously, the old man was proving less pliable than usual. Dammit, they would never have tried something like this when Betty Smithson was alive to ride herd on them. But she had died six months ago, and since then, the children had been getting into mischief.

Don Torrance, city manager, spoke up. "Dr. Akimura, no one is saying there isn't always room for improvement. Perhaps what we mean to say is that there are different ways of addressing needs, of providing services, of helping people."

"I'm listening."

He smiled, aiming for charm but overshooting. "We've been considering a plan to expand a portion of Better City's recreational facilities in order to provide activities for visitors. Perhaps even construct a museum/information center and accommodations for overnight travelers. We see it as a way to more aggressively reach out to the community."

"Reach out aggressively?" I said. "What the hell does that mean? Do you want to seize a city? Kidnap a czar?" I was furious now, face heated until I was dripping sweat, hands shaking. "Have you all forgotten what we do here?

We are a healing organization. We help others. Not ourselves. We don't build amusement parks. We don't put up tourist hotels."

That should have settled them. Occasionally I've had to play rough in the past. But what was this? Each face, every one of them, was set, scowling, stern, unrelenting. They were not giving way, neither bowing nor scraping.

Ginny and Barsi were conferring in guarded whispers. I saw private discussions taking place around the table as though I were not even present, as though I were dead already, safely immured in the legend of Better World and nicely silent. But not yet, by God. Not just yet.

"We feel," Ginny said, "that we should employ these funds now, while the market is accessible. It will only enable us to do more later. You shouldn't trouble yourself about these things, Dr. Akimura. Trust us. We can handle them."

It was a palace revolt.

"You can't do this," I thundered, pounding the table. "I won't allow it. My brother did not create Better World and I have not devoted my life to preserving it so that a bunch of restless administrators could play games with the stock portfolio."

"We didn't mean to upset you," Barsi said, oozing conciliation. But I could read her mind, and what I saw I didn't like. They would placate me now and later, behind my back, proceed as they wished. A bloodless coup. The head wouldn't even realize that it had been separated from the body.

"That's right," Ginny chimed in. "If you really feel strongly about this and don't think we should invest the Better World funds, then of course we won't do it."

All around the table heads nodded, faces smiled. Liars. Hypocrites. Did they all really think I was so old and unaware of their motives?

"Fine," I said. "Let's leave everything in place then, shall we? Oh, and Ginny, from now on I'd like to see quarterly reports of the Better World portfolio."

She stared at me, caught off-guard. "Of course. But you might find them tiresome. There's a great deal of paperwork and I don't know if you can handle—"

"Quarterly reports," I snapped. "Right away." So my suspicions were correct: Ginny had already begun to deploy the money. I could hear her dismayed thoughts loud and clear.

He's going to be difficult.

Yes, indeed, my dear Madame CFO. At least I certainly intended to make every attempt at it.

The meeting ended quickly after that with smiles all around and a great show of false fellowship. Barsi even offered to escort me back to my quarters but I shook her off.

"No, my dear. The old man wants to be alone." And for a moment, a precious, regretful moment, I gazed upon her lovely dark face. She wore golden bells that hung from her ears and her dark braids like metal flowers. I had come very close to loving her, in my way. Despite her sudden betrayal I found myself warming to her yet again. But no. "I'll see you in the morning."

ALONE IN MY ROOMS I realized that I needed help—reinforcements. And quickly. Very soon now, the administrators would seize control of Better World and run it as they saw fit: as a corporation in the business of self-perpetuation rather than the service of others. I couldn't hold them off alone. But I couldn't let it happen. It would make a mockery of everything I had worked toward, and my brother before me. It was unbelievable: once again I was being forced to fight for control of this blasted, sainted organization.

Rick, are you laughing?

At night when the bare branches rub against one another groaning like a poorly strung violin I think I can hear your laughter in the trees.

Memory plays tricks on an old man and the ghosts of past days waver before my eyes like old-fashioned projected movies. My parents wave from a faded frame. And there's Narlydda, a gifted artist, and her husband Skerry, my true father. Killed by my only brother, Rick. Yes, that's correct. The Desert Prophet was a murderer who committed that most Grecian of crimes: parricide. But that truth is hidden safely in the past along with my ghosts. I've seen to that.

No one is alive now to remember it. No one but me. And Alanna.

And now I must turn to her. My half-sister, daughter of Narlydda and Skerry. Of all my ghosts she is the only one with substance. We have not spoken in years. But I remember her number easily and put through a call on my private, shielded line. Her message field answers: Alanna disdains simulacra.

"Help me," I say to the orange, glowing screen. "You are the only one, Alanna, the only other who remembers . . ."

THE YEARS SPIN BACKWARD and I recall them all too clearly. Daylight came and went, the seasons moved through their ritual dance for six long years after Skerry died, and never in all that time did I receive word from Rick, whom I had sent into exile. Not that I expected it. At first I had felt incomplete without my twin, an emotional amputee. But with time I grew accustomed to that phantom ache, and Rick faded, faded until he was transparent as a specter, almost disappeared.

The Mars Colony that multinational forces had established in the middle of the century was a huge success—and, after the New Delhi spill, very popular with refugees. I half believed that Rick had joined the outflux to the red planet and for a time I took a certain pleasure in imagining him pitting his remarkable skills against that harsh, alien world, forcing it to yield to his will and the need of the colonists. That was in 2062, I think, or 2063—toward the end of the nine-year drought in the Western Hemisphere. A year of food riots, it was. At first there were so many hungry people. And then so many dead. It was a haunted year, and I was only slightly surprised when I received a letter from one whom I had come to regard as a ghost. It came in a creased, stained, old-fashioned postal envelope stamped with an address, some P.O. box in Portales, New Mexico.

The message inside was simple: "Come, Julian. I can be reached here. Join me." The paper was yellow, almost antique in texture, and the message was the echo of some old, old dream. It was not so much a request as a summons, unsigned. But that didn't matter. I knew who had sent it.

For days I pondered it, touched the paper, realized that Rick had sent me something tangible so that I could not dismiss him lightly. But I was not ready to deal with him. Despite the temptation to respond I forced the notion away from me and buried the letter—and my brother—deep within a file drawer safely out of sight and mind. Stay away, Rick, I thought. Stay safe, and keep us all safe.

A week later I was at Mass. General consulting on a case when I received the summons from Joachim Metzger, Book Keeper of the newly merged Mutant Councils.

"We have located your brother, Dr. Akimura. Please come at once."

This time I moved: canceled meetings, sessions with clients, social engagements, and hopped the shuttle to California. Would Rick be there, unchanged, full of life and anger and danger, shaking his fist at the world?

The meeting hall was as I remembered, somber greens and browns stenciled along the redwood-paneled walls. A hundred pairs of golden eyes turned to gaze as I walked in. But none belonged to my brother. He wasn't at the meeting, nor anywhere in sight, and for a moment I was relieved. He was still just a shadow at the back of my memory, a tingle at the base of my neck.

Joachim Metzger sat at the center of a long platform that had replaced the original Council table. He was a big, ruddy man with a square jaw, generous fleshy folds beside his wide mouth, and a head of curling white hair that fell almost to the shoulders of his purple Book Keeper robes.

"You said something about knowing my brother's whereabouts—" I began.

"Dr. Akimura," the Book Keeper said. "We know exactly where he is."

I didn't expect that. This Metzger was disturbingly direct. There was no way to dodge his probing golden gaze. "Where is he?" I said.

"In New Mexico."

"How do you know?"

"His mental footprint is distinctive," Metzger said, and a faint smile played across his face.

"Well, then you've found him," I said. "Is that what you dragged me across the country to tell me?"

13

Metzger wasn't smiling anymore. "Of course not. If he was just sitting in the middle of New Mexico, minding his own business, we wouldn't have bothered to contact you at all. Unfortunately, he's not. In fact, that's the last thing he's doing."

"Meaning?"

"Dr. Akimura, we fear that your brother is building some sort of cult."

"A cult?" I couldn't have been more amazed if he had told me that Rick had decided to run for President of the United States. "What are you talking about?"

"We've had reports of a so-called miracle worker wandering around New Mexico."

"That's all?" I almost laughed. "There have always been crazy stories about holy men wandering around in the desert. It's a favorite archetype."

"That may be, but this archetype is doing things that only Rick Akimura could do. And people are flocking to him."

"Are you sure?"

Metzger nodded without losing a beat. "The first we heard of him was over a year ago—something about a hermit who was working miracles among the ranchers. Somewhere near White Sands. Next we began to hear about a poltergeist. A kindly one."

Now I did laugh. "A friendly poltergeist? And what did this nice ghost do?"

"Started stalled skimmer engines. Broke ice in the wells. Redirected dust storms. One man was saved from an angry bull that had him cornered in a pasture: he was lifted right up and over the animal as it charged."

"So," I said. "One old man on an isolated ranch was saved by a miracle. At least, that's what *he* says. More likely he had a touch of home brew before he went for a walk in the meadow. And because of that tipsy old man I asked for leave and came rushing out here?"

"There's more—that was just the beginning," said Metzger. "The stories have been pouring in of missing horses and sheep miraculously returned, of lost hikers who felt their feet being guided to safety, and even of a diverted landslide in the Sangre de Cristo mountains."

I shifted uncomfortably in my seat. That sounded like Rick all right, but I wasn't eager to publicly confirm Metzger's theory without more evidence. "Any passing telekinete who cared to could have pulled most of these stunts," I said.

"And would any passing telekinete have been able to teleport a nonmutant little girl to a hospital after an accident? Or stop a freak flood? Smother a lightning fire in the woods?"

"What's your source for this?"

"A friendly reporter. Watch this."

The lights dimmed and a wallscreen came to life as a tape of vidnews began flashing headlines: "Lost Child Found Alive in Desert by Charity Group," "Good Samaritans Save Starving Family," "Do-Gooders Build Desert Cult," "Wilderness Guru Holds Transcendental Meetings," and "Thousands Join New Mexican Cult."

Next, we saw a group of people wearing blue and green jumpsuits wading into an angry mob of field workers who were threatening to torch a farm collective. The scene shifted and the same group was there when a megatanker turned over in the Gulf of Mexico.

Among them there was a trim, muscular figure who wore jeans and a work shirt. He had a brown beard and wore a black, western-style hat. He was obviously a telekinete, for he held out his arms and seemed to right the ship, forcing the oil back into the tanker's hold. But his features were unclear—he could have been anyone, anyone at all.

The next image was more startling: the same bearded man stood in the center of a huge auditorium. A spotlight picked him out of the darkness and made him seem to glow with his own vibrant power. All around him people had joined hands, closed their eyes, and bowed their heads. They were smiling, all of them, with a quiet ecstasy that unnerved me.

Within the Mutant Council chamber the reaction to this scene was explosive.

"He can't do that!"

"It's against everything we believe. Only Book Keepers may hold a sharing."

What's he up to? Why doesn't he come to us if he wants to conduct a sharing?

Hush, Joachim Metzger told the assemblage. *Be silent and watch.*

A plump, red-haired woman two seats away from me broke in. "Book Keeper, he seems kind of harmless. I mean, all I'm hearing about this group is that they do good deeds. What's so terrible about that?"

"Nothing terrible at all," Metzger said smoothly. "In fact, his intent is admirable. But his group shows signs of growing beyond a personality cult. He already frightens people with his powers. If his organization gets too big, it could create a wave of terror, a backlash against all mutants."

I jumped to my feet. "Hold on now. Don't you think that's kind of paranoid?"

He gazed at me a moment and I saw pity in his glance. Then he addressed me privately through mindspeech.

Dr. Akimura—Julian, please—sit down. We haven't taken a vote yet. We intend to remain neutral as long as possible.

Rick should just be left alone, I told him. *He's acting out a terrible penance.*

Some of us know that. And we feel for your brother. Truly, we do. But the threat to all mutants from a backlash is just too great.

Do you really believe that, Metzger?

Regardless of what I personally believe, officially, I must endorse this policy of investigation. I represent the combined Mutant Councils.

And if you all judge Rick and his cult to be wrong, what then, Book Keeper? What then?

Then he will have to be stopped. Humanely, of course. But I'm sure that, given time, he will cooperate with us. I remind you that we have a greater responsibility to society. Rick is seen as a renegade. And the Mutant Councils believe there is nothing worse than a renegade, especially one with enhanced skills. If nothing else, he at least must donate his plasm to our geneticists—and his sperm to our sperm bank, too. If he cooperates in these areas, perhaps we will agree to leave him alone. But please, watch the rest of our vid report.

Still furious, I took my seat as, onscreen, the scene changed to show parched land and low hills. I saw a mock-adobe building in front of which stood a buffed and polished vid reporter with red and black striped hair and a matching stretch suit. As I watched, she knelt down and began talking to a thin little girl with blond hair and green eyes.

"Now, sweetheart," the reporter said. "Tell us again what happened to you in the desert."

The little girl nodded mechanically, as though she had been carefully rehearsed. "We were going fast, real fast," she said in a soft, high voice. "The skimmer fell down off the road, on its side. Daddy bumped his head and didn't move. So I got out of the car."

"Why?"

"Because I was scared."

"Then what happened?"

"I was crying. And then he was there."

"Who?"

"The man with golden eyes."

"And what did he do?"

"He picked me up in his arms, said, 'Close your eyes,' and threw me into the air."

"And where did you land?"

"Near a bunch of policemen. In Albuquerque."

The vid clip froze, faded, and another replaced it. A reporter eagerly told us all about the wonders of a flash flood that had been held back "by magic" in northern New Mexico—I seemed to remember hearing about the incident months ago. In turn, this clip was replaced by one describing a fire set off by lightning that had threatened to destroy several miles of forest in the foothills of the Sangre de Cristo mountains. Mysteriously, the blaze seemed to have extinguished itself.

"Teleportation?" I said aloud. "Turning back raging flood waters? Forest fires snuffed? I've got to admit that it sounds like Rick. That is, if any one person was really responsible for these acts. Which I doubt."

Metzger stared at me as though I were the village idiot. "*You* may doubt it, Dr. Akimura. But people are beginning to make shrines and leave offerings in the New Mexican wilderness."

"Offerings? What do you mean?"

"Food. Money. Liquor. And that, in turn, is bringing a lot of hungry scavengers out into the desert. The New Mexico State Police are complaining about that. Meanwhile, certain groups of Pueblo Indians have begun holding a dance in honor of what they're calling the desert spirit. That draws tourists and the press. And a flock of so-called pilgrims has grown up around him. Not only do they support him, they protect him as well, keeping out investigators and busybodies. We've been trying to break through the privacy shield around him for several months without any luck."

"The curious will go away eventually."

"I wish I shared your confidence," Metzger said. "But we think this is only the beginning of a very serious problem."

"I fail to see the problem."

"Keep watching the screen."

Now the scene switched to an arid landscape, obviously southwestern, possibly New Mexico. I saw a noisy demonstration, people screaming and flailing as police tried to restrain them. The crowd—predominantly Hispanic with some Indian and Anglo mixtures—was massed outside of a two-story adobe building. As I watched, frightened faces peered out the windows, then vanished within.

There were holosigns proclaiming Rick as the Antichrist, a mutant menace, and demanding his arrest. Some of the protesters even carried crosses that they waved before them like weapons. They looked angry, angry and frightened.

But something about the entire scene was a bit peculiar, everybody seemed just a little too well prepared and rehearsed, as though they had been primed by some director, perhaps some religious group. It was easy to see why Rick might scare the caretakers of the remains of organized religions. After all, there had been a gradual falling away from the altars of worship over the last hundred years. Now a magical mutant was drawing attention and admiration, possibly even homage, from truly desperate folk who might otherwise have sought out traditional sources of spiritual solace. And if there had been defections from the hardcore flocks, the priests and elders who oversaw their remaining congregations would no doubt be alarmed, even envious.

Better to try to nip this thing in the bud, if possible. But they were foolish. They didn't see that their very efforts would enflame public interest in Rick and draw media attention right to him.

The scene shifted again to a kaleidoscope of interviews: the head of the American Medical Association demanded to see Rick's credentials for healing. A purse-lipped nonmutant woman wanted to know why the mutants had been withholding their miraculous powers for so long. A therapist begged Rick to teach him his healing techniques. A desperate man appealed to all mutants, any mutant, to reach in and heal his little boy. An old woman wanted the army to arrest Rick or to investigate him right away.

"As you can see," Metzger said, "your brother is creating quite a fuss. He's frightening and confusing the nonmutants. He should be stopped before this gets out of hand."

"Yeah," said a bald-headed mutant. "Who are all those people out there working with him? Maybe he's gathering some kind of crazy private army."

Another chimed in with mindspeech. *Arrogant, he was always arrogant. He's no better than before.*

The outcry spread.

"He's dangerous. Do something about him."

He's ignored all of our summonses.

"The brother. Send the twin to see him. That's the one he'll listen to."

"That's hardly likely," I said. "He never did before." I was prepared to refute all arguments, to refuse to get involved, when my treacherous conscience spoke up, using my mother's voice: "You're wrong, son," she said. "Rick did listen to you once before. Six years ago. When you told him to go away."

And I had sent him away, hadn't I? At the time I thought he would be gone for good and thank God for it. Why hadn't he stayed lost, stayed a ghost, safe in the past? Rick in the flesh was too dangerous, too unpredictable. The part of me that was an adult rebelled, resisted, wanted nothing to do with this problem. But guilt weakened my resolve—*I* had sent my own brother into exile—and the part of me that was still nine years old and a good boy gave in.

"All right," I said to my inner and outer persecutors. "All

right, Book Keeper. I'll go to New Mexico. Yes, I'll go to see my brother."

NEW MEXICO IS NOT a balmy place in winter. The desert is sere, cold, and empty. A chilling wind rustles through the dried chamisa before sneaking up inside the back of one's jacket. The tri-city area of Albuquerque, Santa Fe, and Taos was filled with too many people gone native or trying to get there. A brief exposure was all it took to inoculate me against any desire for turquoise, serapes, or silver belt buckles set with holograms that rippled through traditional Navajo patterns.

I rented an old skimmer jeep and set out for Torrance, site of Rick's first supposed miracle. The heater was slow to kick in and my breath made white plumes in the air before me.

Rick, I thought. Where are you? Will I sense you before I see you? Does the old twinsense still work after so many years of idleness?

In the badlands halfway between Torrance and White Sands, the vegetation is sparse, the wind wicked, and the population thin. Jolting along the rutted pavement in my rented jeep, I passed one unnamed town that was little more than two streets meeting in a T intersection. Ten miles beyond that I saw the first shrine. At least, that's what I think it was.

A primitive structure of weathered boards and scrap wood nailed and wired together, fitted out with bright metallic paint and pieces of mirror, it looked like a five-year-old child's first creation in arts and crafts. A white, half-burned candle sat, flame extinguished, in the middle of a pile of pears, oranges, and tattered bits of paper.

Notes? Pleas for succor? Requests for intercession?

I killed the engine and got out of the jeep. The first note was illegible, words weathered into a creamy blue smear. But the second had been laser-printed, and although the type was faded it was still legible: "Praise God. You were the answer to our prayers. Bless you and keep you. With love and deep gratitude, the Mendez family."

The next was handwritten in indelible ink: "To the Desert Prophet, whoever you are, wherever you are, you saved my life and I'll never forget you. Someday, somewhere, I will find you and somehow repay you. Thank you, thank you, thank you. Ricardo Aroncio."

Appended to it was some childish scrawl: "Dear Desert Angel, please make my sister Rosa's leg stop hurting."

A chill unrelated to the temperature of the air danced up my spine and down again.

Who was the writer petitioning? Jehovah? Buddha? Shiva? And why out here in the middle of nowhere?

I got back into the skimmer and slammed the door. A mile down the road I came across another shrine. No child's craft, this. Someone had spent money and time on the slim cylinder. Its matte-gray surface held a holographic message that scrolled patiently and then rescrolled, rainbow letters wavering in the thin sunlight. The content was simple: "Thank you, our benefactor, whoever you are, for the gift of your goodness and your aid. Samuel is mending. Without your help he would have died. We invite others who have been touched by your grace to join us. Fax: 5050-758-1478."

It was a Taos exchange. Taos was five hours up the road but I decided to find these people and learn why they had spent so much money erecting a sign in the wastelands to somebody they didn't even seem to know.

Taos was once a small town dominated by a square plaza where locals watered their horses and later parked their automobiles. Of course, that plaza is now the centerpiece of a multilevel civic center built to accommodate the needs of the two hundred thousand people who live in the greater Taos metropolitan area. I think there's even a brass plaque somewhere to indicate where D. H. Lawrence once used the bathroom.

The jeep was too old to have a dashfax so I parked it and used a public kiosk. I sent a note explaining that I was researching the desert phenomenon and received a quick reply from Betty Smithson, wife of Samuel. We agreed to meet in the bar of the Taos Hotel. The original hostelry, which dated back to the nineteenth century, had been enshrined within the sparkling new 150-room inn. A state-of-the-art air system pumped the scent of old leather into the lobby and two Native Americans wearing bright woven jackets (and doubtless paid by the management to add local color) occupied tables near the door of the ultra-rustic bar. I was surprised when the red-bandannaed barmech produced a hypo cleverly disguised to look like a farm implement. I didn't much fancy pressing what appeared to be a rusty trowel against my arm but it was better than being asked to drink from a trough. The alcohol took the chill off and perked me up considerably.

Betty Smithson was a tall, muscular woman of around fifty with faded good looks that reminded me of an overexposed vid. Her blondish hair was almost white and her pale blue eyes were vivid in a very tan face. She wore a sturdy brown jacket, jeans, and only one silver bracelet. Her handshake was strong.

"So you saw one of our signs?" she said. "I haven't thought about those old things for a while."

"One? How many did you put up?"

"Twenty between here and White Sands, about two years ago."

"Isn't that a bit expensive?"

She shrugged. "We're fifth-generation ranchers. We've been very lucky."

"It was an impressive sign, no doubt about it. But why did you put it up to begin with?"

She gave me a sharp look as though I had startled her. "But I thought you knew! Didn't you fax me about the desert miracles?"

"Well, yes, that's what I'm here investigating—"

"Oh, I misunderstood. I thought you'd had a similar experience. I'm not interested in talking to reporters." She stood up and headed for the door.

I hurried after her. "Wait, please, Mrs. Smithson. I'm genuinely interested. And I'm not a reporter. I'm a doctor."

She paused, turned. "Show me some credentials."

I flashed my hospital ID holo at her.

Her eyes widened. "Akimura? Is that really your name? Well, why didn't you say so? You must be Rick Akimura's brother. He said he had a twin. No one else knows, of course." She leaned closer, confidentially. "He won't even tell anybody his last name. I'm the only one who knows. Forgive me, Dr. Akimura. I didn't mean to be rude—I had no idea who you were. I guess I'm afraid of being treated like one of those nuts on the evening news."

"Please, let's sit down and talk about it." I gestured toward two deep leather chairs in a dim corner. After a moment's hesitation she sat.

"Now, about that sign," I prompted. "Why did you say you put it up?"

"Well, we had to, didn't we?" Her tone was matter-of-fact, as though people routinely paid small fortunes to have holosigns erected in the wastelands. "After all," she said, "he saved Samuel when that skimmer nearly crushed him. As it was, Sam got a fractured pelvis. Even with the drugs it took him months to heal."

I leaned closer. "And who was it, this man who saved your husband?"

"But I thought you knew. It was Rick. He had golden eyes, just like yours, so I knew he was a mutant. Took Sam to the hospital as quick as you could imagine. Quicker. I've never seen anything like it."

Despite misgivings about intruding on her privacy, I ventured a quick telepathic probe. But all I saw was a blurred dark-haired figure, indistinct, and some peculiar mental static, rare in a nonmutant.

"He hardly said a word," she said. "When that skimmer started to fall off its hoist he was just right there. Don't know where he came from. But now that we've found him, we'll help him all we can."

"We?"

Her voice took on a steely timbre. "That's right. We've formed a group. We call ourselves Better World—B.W. for short. I'll tell you, Dr. Akimura, I didn't ever have much use for what you might call faith. Never thought much of it. But frankly, this has changed my mind about hope. Trust. And everybody else this man has helped feels the same way. This is something good, Dr. Akimura. I don't really know how else to explain it." She stared at me and her eyes were bright with inner fire. "For two winters we'd been hearing stories out here of a ghost who kept helping folks with their problems. Well, I don't think there ever was any ghost. I know it was Rick. Had to be. And all of us whom he's helped, we wanted to thank him. So we joined with him to help him reach others." She paused, then added, almost shyly, "He *is* your brother, isn't he?"

I forced a polite smile. "He may be, Mrs. Smithson. I don't really know yet. That's why I'm out here to begin with." Inwardly, I was rattled. If a woman as sturdy as Betty Smithson could find an epiphany in the actions of this ghostly desert mutant, how many other people might join her? Soon there would be shrines sprouting next to every chamiso bush from here to the border. And an army of true believers. Had the Mutant Council been right about Rick drawing a private army around himself for comfort and protection? "I certainly appreciate your honesty," I said. "But perhaps you should be careful whom you confide in. For your own sake."

"Oh, I'm no blabber," she said. "I agreed to meet you because I'd hoped you would join us. I see now you can't do that. Yet. But you seem to have an open mind. I don't think the others would have objected to my talking with you." She glanced down at her watch. "It's getting late. Why don't you come along with me and see for yourself?"

2

WE DROVE UP ROUTE 522, past Lobo Peak and Carson National Forest, and were almost in Questa by the time I saw the holosign advertising Better World. We turned right, drove past a grove of blue-gray junipers, and into the sprawling Better World compound.

The air was already sharp with cold and the wintry sun cast long purple shadows over a complex of buildings nestled into the foothills of the Sangre de Cristo mountains. Clay-colored walls intended to resemble adobe rose for three stories to a flat, tiled roof. A silver holosign on the front of the building proudly proclaimed Better World in bright, slanting letters. It had been designed to look like a huge Navajo belt buckle.

I took another lungful of chilly air and followed Betty Smithson through the wide carved wooden doors into the main building. She removed her coat and I saw she wore a blue suit that nearly matched her eyes. A Better World logo was embroidered on the back: a golden circle drawn around the blazing New Mexican sun motif. The design reminded me uncomfortably of Mutant Unity pins I'd seen long ago: a golden circle that enclosed a staring golden eye.

Her eyes searched mine for a moment. "We're just in time for the evening meeting." She made a gracious and proprietary gesture that took in the entire building. "So what do you think of our center?"

I glanced around. The entry hall was cast in striped tiles,

white and black, with red lanterns hanging from a central beam in the ceiling. The floor was a soft resilient ceramic, red and white with black accents that reminded me of old Navajo weavings. The place had the look of a brand-new hospital. But not the odor, at least. I was astounded by the scale of the place.

"Mrs. Smithson," I said. "Forgive me for asking, but how can you afford all this?"

Her smile was a bit smug. "Donations. Oh, don't look at me that way, Dr. Akimura. We don't solicit money. Never have. But that doesn't mean we don't accept gifts. And people seem to want to give and give. We just bought a bankrupt business park and had a few changes made to suit us."

"These donations sound very . . . convenient."

Her smile dimmed, then disappeared. "I don't see anything wrong with that. And neither does Rick." She paused. "But you haven't answered my question yet."

"Well, I think it's really very nice," I said, and stamped my feet to get some circulation in them. "In an antiseptic kind of way."

"What do you mean, antiseptic? The design incorporates elements of traditional Native American design but it's meant to be functional." She seemed about to say something else when a door slammed down the hall and a brief snatch of rhythmic music danced teasingly on the air.

"They're getting started earlier than I'd thought," she said. She looked relieved, even grateful for the distraction, and began to walk toward the music, quickly outpacing me. "Come on, Dr. Akimura. Just leave your coat here."

When I hesitated she shook her head impatiently. "You don't want to miss all the fun, do you?"

I shed my heavy parka and hurried after her through the red door and into a huge, multitiered partial atrium whose back wall was paneled in weathered, carved wood. It was filled with people on every level dancing, singing, eating, and drinking. Champagne bubbled from a green ceramic fountain shaped like a prickly pear cactus as a mechband laid down a steady, infectious tribal beat.

Below us on the main floor a tall redheaded woman was dancing with a dark-skinned man half her size. Next to them, a man and woman with matching high cheekbones and short bleached hair gyrated to their own private rhythms. The place was packed. Some of the dancers were Hispanic, others of Asian ancestry. All wore Better World jumpsuits in varying colors: red, blue, pink, brown. There were no mutants in the room except for me and I felt strangely conspicuous, blinking at everybody with my alien golden eyes.

"I'm surprised that they're not playing Beethoven," Betty said. I noticed how her voice rose, swelling with authority. "That's Rick's favorite, you know."

By the time we had worked our way down two levels to the floor of the ballroom, the music had stopped, red inflatable chairs had appeared, and the revelers were seated in a loose semicircle several rows deep. Betty and I took two aisle seats in the back.

Hush.

It was a mental command that seemed to resonate throughout the timbered hall. A man had appeared at the center of the room, his face calm, eyes closed. He had a neatly trimmed beard and his dark hair was pulled back and tied at the base of his neck with a rawhide cord. Despite his amiable expression there was a look about him of wariness and mystery, as though he had been in the desert a long, long time.

"Rick?" My voice half caught in my throat and came out as a strangled whisper. I didn't want to believe it. Didn't want Rick to be here. And yet, my own brother, my twin—

He was spare and tanned. His skin looked as though he had spent much time outdoors in bright sun and dry air. We were the same age, of course, but Rick now seemed to be nearly ten years older than I was. His nervous mannerisms had vanished. This was a different Rick. He was sitting quietly, almost expectantly, on the simple wooden seat at the center of the room. He seemed like a man who was accustomed to waiting.

To my amazement joy flooded through me, sharp and bright, almost painful in its startling intensity. Tears filled my eyes. I was about to call out, to hail him, when my brother mindspoke again and the crowd stilled.

We have gathered here for the purpose of sharing our

resolve. We have been gifted and now we wish to extend our hands to others. He raised his hands. *Come. Join with me now.*

I nearly gasped: Rick was giving the ritual invitation for a mutant group sharing. But there were no mutants here besides him and me. Why was he doing this?

A pulsing wave of mental energy enfolded us in a mind-numbing blanket. I could not speak, could not think.

You are not alone. You will never be alone again. Together we have purpose. Together we have meaning. We are a community in service to the larger community beyond these walls. Together we give. Together we are one.

The words shimmered and echoed in every mind there. A group sharing—Rick was holding a group sharing! I couldn't believe it. My brother was no Book Keeper. And this was not a Mutant Council. It was a blatant flouting of tradition and it scared me. What was he doing? The entire group looked eerily blissed-out: eyes closed, lips moving as they silently mouthed the words Rick mindspoke to them. The gathering had the feel of an ecstatic séance. And within the groupmind I sensed the same mental static—amplified a hundred times over—that I had encountered with Betty Smithson. Perhaps it was a residue of Rick's effect upon nonmutants, but I was only guessing. I didn't really know what it was.

Rick arose and paced before us, apparently mulling over what he had to say. For at least five minutes there was complete silence. Itches prickled under my jeans and between my shoulder blades but I could not move. Beside me, Betty Smithson was calm and still, caught by Rick's spell.

Finally, my brother turned to face his audience again.

I know. I know that each of us has been so alone in the prison of his own head that any company, any place, was welcome. I know what it is to ache for companionship. To yearn for comfort without any hope of finding it. I know how silence and solitude can turn the strongest of us weak with longing and regret. I have been in the silence and with the longing. I have been alone and I know its every shade, its every mood. And all of you do, too. But here no one is alone. We share and are shared. You need not be alone ever again. Share with me. Be with me. Together we shall help others. And in so doing, we shall help ourselves.

That's it. No have-tos. Just be good to yourselves and each other.

A wave of rising, pulsing pleasure rose, overwhelming me with orgasmic intensity. Rick had to be stimulating our pleasure centers—but how? I moaned and gasped with the rest of the group until, finally, Rick released us.

For a moment there was stunned silence. Then, with thunderous applause, the meeting broke up. People hugged, laughed, and wandered off into the twilight.

"What did you think? Wasn't that wonderful?" Betty Smithson's reserve and formality had melted away. She looked radiant—as though years had been peeled from her age—and she was bubbling with energy. Obviously, the sharing had reinvigorated her. If that was the way Rick ended each meeting, no wonder she was hooked. Who wouldn't be?

"Let's go see your brother. Rick," she called. "Look who's here!"

He turned, removed his hat and twirled it loosely in his hand, smiling a half smile. "A pleasure, Doctor. You must have gotten my note." He didn't seem even remotely surprised to see me.

I froze, studying the unfamiliar yet familiar lines of his face.

"Rick, my God, I can't believe it! Is it really you?" I threw my arms around him, pounding his back in delight. He hesitated only a moment, then gave me an awkward bear hug. Betty Smithson stood by, beaming. Then she tactfully slipped away and we were alone, together, for the first time in six years.

I was still reeling from the shock of seeing him and I felt his arm tighten across my shoulder to brace me. "What are you doing here?" I said. "I thought you'd gone to Mars."

"I did, for about five minutes. That's all it took to convince me that New Mexico was a verdant paradise by comparison." His voice was huskier than I remembered and he squinted now as though he found most light too bright.

"Rick, I never expected to see you again."

"I know."

Even now, years and miles distant from our reunion, I'm caught up in the emotion of that moment. All the dizzying ambivalence I associated with my brother comes swirling back to confuse me. The love—and the anger. Gods, how I miss him! And how thankful I am that he is gone.

"Little brother," he said. "It's really good to see you. Been a long time. I hope you've come ready to work."

I stared at him, nonplussed. "What do you mean?"

"We've got lots to do."

"Like that sharing I just participated in? Do you mind telling me just what the hell was going on in there?"

"A little mind linkage, that's all."

"You're not supposed to be holding a group sharing for nonmutants."

"Not supposed to?" His casual tone grew sharp. "According to which supreme authority? Did you come here to quote me chapter and verse from the Book? Don't be a jerk, Julian. I'm not hurting anybody."

"No? Do these people know you're influencing their moods and emotions? Perhaps toying with their very personality structure? We're still not certain just what effect a group sharing has on nonmutant participants."

"Then if you don't know, why worry? Get off my back, little brother. Mutants have been hoarding these abilities for years. And how did it benefit them or anybody else? I make these people feel good, and better than good. What's wrong with that? They deserve it. My God, if I had known that you were going to be such a tightass I would have sent you straight back to your hospital and your nice, safe rule book."

Within five minutes of greeting we were already back into our old antagonistic pattern! I couldn't believe it. I glared and my brother glared back at me until footsteps in the hallway broke into our private dispute.

Two B.W. staffers in green jumpsuits straggled toward the front doors: a tall, big-boned blond woman and a slight, slender man wearing a stained brown cowboy hat.

"Good night, Rick," the blond said. "Thanks for reminding us. We need not be alone."

"We share and are shared," the man piped up. "We will never be alone again."

They giggled like teenagers and clasped hands.

Rick waved carelessly to them as they passed. "Good night, Rod, Kate."

"Don't you see?" I said when we were alone again. "Now they're quoting the scripture to you." I paused, expecting an angry response.

Instead, Rick sighed and rubbed his eyes. "Look, I don't want to fight with you, Julian. Let's get something to eat, okay? I know a decent Mexican restaurant in town. We can talk there."

"I'll drive."

"Don't bother." He touched me gently on the shoulder.

I felt a wave of dizziness and nausea as the walls began to slip and spin. The floor dropped away. I fell and fell, hurtling through black space, an airless void. Blood pounded in my ears. My mind gibbered like a chimpanzee in a space capsule. I couldn't breathe, I was being flayed and shattered, I was being crushed between planets—

3

"**H**ERE WE ARE," Rick said.

We were sitting in a booth in a long dark room whose only illumination was the crylights flickering on every table. The air was filled with spicy aromas and tinkling guitar music. Holograms of piñatas dangled from the ceiling, strange dark shapes that seemed to move slowly in the overheated air, spilling open and then retracting each shower of gold, over and over again.

My head stopped spinning. It took another minute for my stomach to settle down.

"Fun, huh?" my brother said.

"Not what I would call it, exactly." I punched up a hypo from the tablemech and, hands shaking, pressed it against my arm. The shot of alcohol steadied me. "Next time warn me, will you? Otherwise I can't vouch for my stomach on the return trip. That was a wild ride."

He grinned. "You get used to it." Despite his jaunty good humor he looked worn and pale. I regretted my hasty outburst of moments ago.

"Rick, what's happened to you?"

"Do you want the whole tale, unabridged and uncensored?"

Eagerly, I nodded.

My brother leaned back, took a deep breath, and launched into the story of his six-year odyssey.

He had roved through the West, stopping here and there

at tiny outposts and small towns. Inevitably, his presence drew the curious, the helpful, and the intrusive and he was forced to move on. He lived this way for nearly a year before he came to New Mexico and stayed.

Food and water had never been a problem: he could summon what he needed. And shelter was easily solved as well. But he had no way of dealing with the dreadful loneliness, not even with the help of his superior mutant skills.

His time was spent scavenging, roaming over the badlands looking for abandoned skimmers and other machinery with which he could tinker to build screenbrains. These he used to power three-dimensional sims that were programmed to keep him company and to monitor news vids. He stole tapes of the music of his beloved Beethoven. And for a while, he time-hopped through his visions. That distracted him and allowed him, briefly, to have the illusion of reentering society. But these were pale shadows, not very different from vids. He could neither participate in what he observed nor be seen as anything more than a ghost.

In lonely desperation he began to cast his farsight upon the town fifty miles to the north. The folk who lived there had become accustomed to the presence of a hermit in the hills and from time to time they left out food and tools for him. In turn, he provided protection for the town whenever it was needed, pushing back a hailstorm, frustrating a greedy developer, even shoring up the crumbling walls of the town hall. He cared for the townspeople affectionately, even possessively, but stayed away, watching them from the distance with obsessive hunger. Until the day that he found the little girl and the wrecked skimmer.

Once he had saved her he decided that there was no turning back. He would take the risk of human encounter and range over New Mexico a bit to see where else he could help out. In his travels he came upon the Smithsons and others like them. Before he knew it there were shrines being set up along the roadsides and vid ads pleading for him to reveal himself. Finally, one afternoon, he summoned his nerve, walked up the slate walk of the Smithsons' ranch, and rang their doorbell.

"Rick," I said. "Aren't you worried?"

He levitated a toothpick from the holder on the table and

inserted it into his mouth. With studied casualness he said, "About what?"

"This little group that worships you so much."

"What's wrong with it?"

"Can't you see what's happening?"

"What do you mean, Julian? I don't see boogeymen under every chair. I'm not a pessimist. That's the antithesis of what I'm trying to do here. But I look around me and all I see is crap. People going hungry everywhere. Technology outstripping our ability to make use of it. Governments and religions getting far too big and becoming even more unresponsive. They're in business just to perpetuate their own authority. They don't answer the needs of the people. Not their *REAL* needs."

"How do you know?"

His eyes glowed. "Because I can hear and see what people think. What they want. What makes them tick like a bunch of sad clocks. There's way too many unhappy people out there, Brother. I always knew it, always felt it. I was one of 'em. But now I want to do something about it."

He leaned closer. "I'm going to heal them, Julian. I know how to reach in, to take the hurt away, to make it better. I've got to do it, little brother. *Got to.* You're a healer. You should understand. Just imagine a cleansed society, Julian. People without their pain, their envy, or their anger. I've seen it, you know."

"In your visions?"

He nodded. "It can happen. We can make it happen!"

What he said sounded elegant and noble but the fanatic light in his eyes frightened me. I knew how dangerous saints could be, especially if they were also supermen. "But, Rick," I said, "what if people don't want you reaching into their heads—"

"Their pain distorts their thinking. They'll thank me for it later. Most people don't know how to look out for their own best interests anyway."

"I can't believe what I'm hearing. You're just going to heal people whether they want you to or not? What about personal privacy? Your followers may not care about it, but don't you?"

"Once I heal them they'll be grateful for what I've done."

I made one more try to reach him. "Rick, you can't just reach inside people's heads without their permission."

"Why not? The more people I heal, the better."

"Is that what you hope to accomplish by holding these souped-up sharings for nonmutants?"

"Sure. The mutants have hoarded their skills long enough. Their healing powers belong to everybody, not just a select group of golden-eyed elitists. Besides, all I'm really doing is making some therapeutic linkage and goosing a few pleasure centers."

"That's all? Rick, do you realize how dangerous it is to monkey around with people's minds? Do you really want to encourage this cult?" My voice was getting loud, too loud.

Instead of looking annoyed, Rick seemed amused, almost condescending. "Julian, how can I think anything other than what I'm doing is fine? Why should I? Don't you spend years working with your patients trying to imbue them with the kind of attitude that I already have? Besides, who said it was a cult? Not me. I want it to be a service organization."

"Your own private Lions Club? Rick's Brothers and Sisters of Mercy?"

"Why not? Do you see anybody else doing anything even half as useful? Maybe I could actually do some good. Atone for old sins." Now he was less amused, openly challenging. "You were the one who told me to do that, remember?"

"Creating a nut cult isn't exactly my idea of making amends for murder!"

I was sorry for the words as soon as I had spoken them. But it was too late. I sat there braced for the explosion. But it never came.

Instead, Rick gazed at me thoughtfully and his voice, when he spoke, was sad rather than resentful. "You still can't forgive me, can you? I'd hoped that you, more than anyone else, could. But I guess I'm being stupid." He leaned toward me and his tone changed, took on an almost pleading note. "So much time has passed, Julian. So many things have happened. I've been atoning for my crime, really, I have. And that's what I'll devote the rest of my life to doing. I promise you."

For a moment we were both silent. I was upset and confused. Why couldn't he have just stayed out in the desert and left me alone? I was more comfortable helping other people tame their personal demons than struggling with my own anger, ambivalence, and regrets. I gazed across the table at the messianic stranger wearing my brother's face and wondered who he was.

He broke the silence. "Y'know, I've followed your career, Julian. You've done well."

I sat up, surprised. "You have? How?"

"I've got my ways. Oh, yeah, I kept tabs on one or two people. Saw you making strides, getting your medical certification and all that. I was glad for you. You're a talented, successful therapist. Just as you wanted to be."

But be careful what you want, I thought. "So," I said, "are you suggesting that the doctor who helps others heal their old wounds should heal himself of the past? Encourage you in this wild plan? I'm sorry, Rick. It's not that easy. I can't let go of what happened, at least, not as easily as it seems you have."

"Don't be stupid, Julian." His eyes flashed with a fragment of his familiar old rebellious spirit. "I carry Skerry's death around with me like a brand, inside, always burning." His voice turned hollow. "Whenever I close my eyes I can see him lying there and hear Alanna crying." He paused and his expression softened. "Have you talked to her?"

My stomach knotted. Alanna was someone I didn't want to discuss with him. With him, especially. "Once or twice over the years. Narlydda took it pretty hard. Alanna had to take over managing her affairs."

An odd smile twisted his mouth. "Just what she most dreaded having to do." He shook his head ruefully. "When I make a mess, I make a good one. Did she ever marry?"

"No."

"Any lovers?"

"I don't know." I was getting irritated now. "Why? Thinking of looking her up?"

"No. No. All that's behind me now. It's none of my business, I know. I was just curious, that's all."

I punched the mech's button and it spat out the bill. But as I reached for my wallet, Rick waved me away. "It's taken care of."

"What do you mean?"

"These folks know me and the food is gratis."

"How nice." The uneasiness came sneaking back, sliding down my spine vertebra by vertebra. "And how do other people pay you off?"

"I don't ask for payment, Julian."

"Just devotion? Worship?"

He looked positively nonplussed. "Why are you so hostile, little brother?"

"Oh, come off it, Rick. This is a dangerous situation. I can see that even if you can't. Things could get completely out of control here. And knowing you, they probably will."

"I know what I'm doing."

"Do you? Or are you just driven by guilt?"

That stung him. "Save your damned head-shrinking for your patients, Doctor!"

"Rick, listen to me. You've got to give this up. Please. Disband Better World and go away—go back to Mars." I was willing to beg, even bribe him.

"Leave? When I've finally found the way back?" Rick glared at me, and for a moment he was the brother I remembered, quick to flare, quick to forgive. But the moment faded. "No, Julian, I've paid in my own time and sweat and tears so that others may be spared their pain. I'm here for them now. They don't know it yet. But they will."

His crazy words struck me with the force of physical blows. "Rick, you don't know what you're saying."

"It couldn't be clearer to me."

"Hitler had a plan, too, you know. He thought he was helping people, too."

Anger smoldered in his eyes now. "Look, either help me or butt out, Julian. I began this without you and I can maintain it without you."

"But—"

"You came looking for me. Well, you found me. You're welcome to stay. But I won't listen to your cockeyed analogies. I know what I'm doing."

"You may think so." Fear had transmuted into fury, making me completely heedless of what I said. "But it seems to me what you've got here are all the symptoms of a massive psychosis. I think you need help, Rick."

"And maybe I don't give a damn what you think."

We glared at each other. Only Rick could get me this angry, so angry that I could barely hear the thin, high voice of sanity whispering at me to calm down. I had to get away from him, away from his strange visions and crazy mission.

"Julian, wait—"

The door slammed on his words and I was out in the freezing night. My breath made thick, almost opaque clouds of moisture. I stumbled along on the icy pavement, cursing the Mutant Council and all its skulduggery.

A full moon lit the plaza with cold blue light and for a moment it was almost peaceful. But a high squealing sound cut through the air, getting louder, setting off a fusillade of barking from the neighborhood dogs.

A silver skimmer rocketed around the corner, lights off, motor whining, and headed straight for me.

Julian, get back!

Rick's mindspeech was loud and coercive. But before I could act the skimmer bore down on me. I was trapped against a wall. Everything slowed, slowed, almost stopped. Each beat of my heart, each lungful of breath, every eye blink took an eternity. I was going to die. Right here and now. It was absurd.

I felt faint, lighter than air. Then I realized that I *was* lighter than air—I was floating high above the plaza, shocked into awareness by the freezing cold. Far below, I saw my brother moving swiftly across the plaza. But he hadn't been there a moment ago, had he? The skimmer had come to rest against the building and Rick was pulling the occupants out of the car: two teenagers, a girl and boy, drunk and giggling.

"Hey!" I called. "Rick, let me down."

My brother whirled. "What? Oh, sorry."

I floated to the pavement like a leaf in the wind.

"I was distracted by trying to keep these two damned fools from killing themselves. And you," Rick said.

With a groan the boy was quickly and extravagantly sick over his girlfriend's green leather boots.

"You gork!" she cried. "Those are my sister's best boots!"

"That's gratitude," Rick said. "If you're not careful it can get all over you. Now why don't you two tell me who you are?"

"You're not the police," the girl said. Defiantly she tossed a hank of dark hair over her shoulder. "Billy, we don't have to tell him anything."

"I don't think Billy is going to be able to say anything for a while," I said.

Billy turned and puked on the skimmer's silvery fender.

"Not on the skimmer!" the girl cried. "You scurfy jerk, I told you not to drink so much."

Rick snapped his fingers and pointed at her. "Hey, I know you."

She gave him a frightened look. "No you don't."

"Oh, yes I do, girlie. You're Mayor Stewart's daughter, aren't you? And I know she's out of town. Is that Mommy's skimmer?" He chuckled. "I'll bet it is. Since when do fourteen-year-olds get driver's licenses?"

"I'm not fourteen," Billy said, wounded. "I'm nearly sixteen."

"Uh-huh," Rick said. "Well, you almost didn't make it to sixteen, friend. Still might not if you don't get your head on straight. I'm going to do you a favor this time and help you clean this up. But next time I might not be around, and you wouldn't enjoy becoming part of the local architecture. Believe me."

Billy said nothing. He glared at Rick defiantly.

Rick nodded and in a flash the skimmer was clean. The girl's boots sparkled in the lamplight.

"I need an address," Rick said.

The girl frowned and looked at the ground, away from his probing gaze. "Three forty-two Morning Star Road," she said.

"Get in the skimmer."

She hesitated.

"Get in," Rick said again.

This time they obeyed, slamming the doors.

"Good night, kiddies."

The car was gone. I gazed through where it had been and saw the frost-rimmed terra-cotta walls of the plaza. It was quiet, eerily quiet in the plaza. Even the dogs had stopped barking.

"Jesus, Rick. You transported that entire skimmer."

"Yep. And I'll bet old Billy's decorating the inside of it right about now. If he has anything left in his stomach." Rick chuckled and for an eerie moment he was the image of our biological father, Skerry.

"If you hadn't stopped them—" The words backed up in my throat.

"Yeah," Rick said. "Dead. Those two, maybe you. Damn fools." He spat out his toothpick. "I can't protect everybody from themselves all the time. I wish I could."

I owed him my life. In wonder and a little fear I stared at my brother, and a wave of awe swept over me, so powerful that for a moment I felt light-headed. Rick had saved us, saved those two kids and me. He didn't want praise, didn't want thanks. What he had just done was as natural for him as it was for me to breathe.

I had thought that I knew my brother, knew him in that private, intimate way that only twins enjoy. But he was stranger and greater than I had ever suspected. Unique. More powerful than I'd dreamed. The rules that applied to others couldn't apply to him, and I had no right to ask that. I never would again. But I said none of these things for fear of sounding like a fool. Instead, I just reached out and squeezed his arm.

Rick turned tired eyes toward me. "How's your digestive tract?"

"It wants to go home and get in bed." I managed a weak smile.

"Hang on, then."

With a deep breath I told my stomach to behave, and nodded.

Blackness swallowed us.

I STAYED THE NIGHT at Better World: my quarters were Spartan, bare wood floors with scatter rugs, a few pieces of rustic furniture, but the bed was comfortable and I slept better than I had in years.

Rick seemed to think I had come to stay but I quickly dispelled that idea the next morning. He was outside, working without a jacket, seemingly untroubled by the wintry air.

"I thought you said it was cold out here."

He grinned. "Out there, yes. But I'm nice and cozy, thanks to a little bubble of air I brought along from inside."

"I should have guessed." Envy pricked me for the ease with which my brother could master his environment. "I've got to get back, Rick. I just took a quick leave to come out and see if you were really here."

He gave me a keen, knowing look. "You didn't just come out here to see me, did you, Julian?"

"Well, I—"

"No, don't bother trying to find a good cover story. I know—the Mutant Council sent you, didn't they?"

"Rick, it's bad manners to eavesdrop on somebody else's thoughts." I felt my cheeks heating up with embarrassment.

"I wasn't eavesdropping, little brother. Just making an educated guess. And from the color of your face, I guessed right. I knew that bunch of golden eyes would send somebody sooner or later. They've been trying to get hold of me for some time now. But I'm not interested in going to them. They're welcome here if they want to help out."

"Maybe you should go see them."

"And do what? Offer myself up for their convenience? Become their errand boy? No thanks. What good did they ever do anybody? They're just a bunch of misers, Julian. Stingy with their mutant skills when they could be helping millions of people. And should be."

"They might make trouble for you."

"Anything they want to dish out I can take. But you tell them that it's a bad idea to antagonize me, Julian." He left the threat hanging between us.

"I thought this was the new, improved Rick."

He gave me a half-smile. "Yep. But I'm nobody's fool. And as someone a whole lot smarter than me once said, you can afford to be gentle only when dealing from a position of strength." He held out his hand and grasped mine firmly. "I'm sorry to see you go, little brother. There'll always be a place for you here. But tell those golden-eyed bastards that if they don't want to help me out, then they had better stay away."

4

I WENT BACK TO THE Mutant Council with the bad news. A special meeting had been called, and the grand meeting hall was almost full. From across the room I noticed a striking woman: high cheekbones, the skin stretched tightly across them. Dark, curling hair provided the perfect frame for delicate features that might have been sculpted from porcelain and coated with a thin celadon glaze. Alanna, my half-sister, here. I hadn't seen her in years. Why was she in attendance? Before I could reach her, or even use mindspeech to greet her, Joachim Metzger convened the meeting.

"You were right," I said. "It's hard to believe, but my brother *does* have an organization out there," I said. "It's called Better World. And he has pledged it to community duty. He seems to think the mutants have been rather lax in their public service and he's trying to make amends. Unfortunately, it's like trusting a child with liquid explosives." There, I'd said it. I believed it, too. But I didn't feel good about turning against my own brother, not one bit.

"If this is so, then he must be stopped," Metzger said. "Before something truly dangerous occurs. We have had barely a hundred and fifty years of emergence and many nonmutants are still not comfortable with us. We simply can't afford the risk."

"Risk of what?" a woman's voice called out fiercely. "Too many happy, pain-free, well-adjusted people? What's wrong with that?" The voice sounded familiar, and when the speaker rose to her feet, I saw that she was Alanna.

"Julian, how can you be so disloyal?" she cried. "Perhaps you're jealous of Rick. Hasn't he suffered enough? Paid for his crime enough?"

"I can't believe you're defending him," I said. "He killed your father."

"Yes. And you exiled him for it."

"I don't deny that. Otherwise he would have gone to jail. Or hurt more people."

"So instead you put him into his own private prison, with you as turnkey. Well, Julian, when is his sentence up?" Her golden eyes glittered with anger. "I think what Rick is doing is admirable, wonderful. His work could be of great benefit, not just to society in general, but to mutants in particular. The Mutant Council should support Rick Akimura's Better World organization and offer to participate. Perhaps we could offer guidance to him—he might accept it as long as we were cooperating."

I turned on her furiously. "Don't be ridiculous, Alanna. Rick would never accept guidance in any form, from anyone. What are you saying?"

"I'm not denying that trying to work with Rick is a calculated risk," she said. "But it's one worth taking. Don't condemn Rick. Don't turn your back on him. Help him. My father would understand what he's doing. Not only that, he would approve."

There were muffled chuckles and I saw several gray-haired mutants smiling.

"Why shouldn't we support Rick's program of outreach to the nonmutants?" Alanna said. "What's wrong with it? In fact, I think it might be an even better means of bridging the gap between us."

"We have programs in place—" Metzger said.

Alanna cut him off. "Are we so calcified in our behavior? So immobilized, so ritualized that we can't share the riches of our mutant gifts with those who don't have them?"

All around the room people were nodding their heads. Alanna was tremendously persuasive and she might just be able to swing a vote in favor of Rick. But she was wrong—I knew she was. Rick was still impulsive, dangerously unpredictable, and uncontrollable. With the best of intentions he could do dreadful damage. He had to be stopped.

"What are you trying to do," I demanded. "Create an excuse to reestablish your ties to Rick, now that you know where he is?"

She glared at me and I knew that I had hit home. I didn't enjoy doing it but I had to use any weapons I could to destroy her argument before she won everybody over.

"Don't you wonder why he didn't contact you, Alanna? Why he didn't summon you? Are you certain that you want to force yourself upon him now?" I knew I was being cruel, going perhaps too far, but I couldn't help myself. I was too afraid of the threat that Better World represented, and I had to try to stop my brother, even if that meant making an enemy of my sister.

Alanna gave me a look that both damned and dismissed me. Then she turned to face the Book Keeper. "I offer my services to spearhead a task force to contact Rick Akimura. I could represent mutant interests while participating in his organization and guiding it."

"Do you think he will accept your interest and suggestions?" Metzger asked.

"It's worth a try, isn't it?" Alanna said.

"And I say we must stop him entirely," I cried.

Metzger leaned forward. "What you say makes sense to me, Dr. Akimura. You know my feelings. But I must poll all here and see what they think." He closed his eyes and I felt the brief touch of his mind as it reached out past me, across the crowded meeting hall into every mind there.

"Hmm, as I feared," Metzger said, and chagrin was evident in his voice. "We are almost evenly divided. Therefore we can't endorse either of your proposals."

"This is a terrible mistake," I said. "We mustn't delay our efforts."

"I couldn't agree with you more," Alanna said. "I'll go to New Mexico right away." She gave me a look of malicious triumph. The battle lines had been drawn between us and we both knew there was no retreating.

THE AIR WAS COOL AND DRY, and a welcome breeze set the yellow acacia blooms dancing in my parents' yard. The January weather in Los Angeles was unusually warm, a gentle treat after the sub-zero days and nights of Boston. I finished my coffee and left the cup for the mechmaid to clear.

My mother sat across from me, lounging restlessly against the big blue pillows on the webseat. As meticulous and chic as ever, she wore a red stretch suit and her hair was cut in an asymmetrical curve that revealed glittering emerald earrings.

"So, Mother, should we talk about it?" I said.

She gave me a wry half-smile. "I was sort of hurt, you know. I thought, somehow, that Rick would get in touch with me, first. But I suppose that you're the logical choice."

"I don't know about that. I'm the one who sent him into exile, remember?" I stared at a perfect pink rose bobbing in the warm breeze.

"When did he call you?" my mother asked. There was an unfamiliar tremulous tone to her voice that I didn't care for.

"He didn't. He dropped me a note." My mother said nothing, merely toyed with her coffee cup. She was beginning to make me nervous. "When is Dad coming home? I'd love to hear his opinion of what Rick is up to."

"A little before noon."

"And what does he think?"

"He says it's the usual crackpot reports from the provinces. You know Yosh."

She had begun to refer to him as Yosh rather than "your father" in the months following Skerry's death and it had become a habit with her. It saddened me that she still had trouble with that. Never for a moment had I considered Skerry my father in any but the biological sense. Yosh's calm guidance had seen me through childhood fevers and fears, adolescent storms, and even some of the peculiar rites of manhood. In terms of love, and every other emotion, in the only terms that truly mattered to me, Yosh was and always would be my father.

"And what do *you* think?" I said.

"Well," my mother said. "At first I ignored these rumors of miracles in the desert. At least I did until that little girl was saved. But then I knew. It had to be Rick."

"And you approve? Of this entire crazy Better World group he's got going?"

She nodded briskly. "Of course I do. And we *have* to go there, Julian. Right away."

"Oh, sure, Mom. I'll just quit my practice and we'll leave Dad a note so he knows he has to fix his own dinner."

"I don't understand your attitude, Julian."

"And I sure as hell don't get yours." I stared at her, amazed. "Have you forgotten who Rick is? And what he is?"

"I don't care." Her knuckles were white where she held the coffee cup. "Listen to me, Julian. He's paid his debt. I want to see my boy." She reached out and grasped my hand in a punishing grip. "Oh, Julian, don't you see? If we don't join with him now we might lose him forever. This is our one chance."

"I'm not so sure you're right. Or that losing him forever wouldn't be the best solution for all involved." I extricated my hand from the clamp of her fingers.

"How can you say that? He's your brother. Your twin."

"Mom, he's a proven killer."

"You know that was a mistake! He never intended to kill Skerry. He just wanted to be left alone with Alanna. Everything just happened too quickly for him on Ethan Hawkins's damned space station—Rick barely had time to get accustomed to his mutant skills. Everybody was jumping on him. Besides, that was six years ago. He's grown up since then, I'm sure of it. And I very much doubt that he's hurt anybody since."

Her defense rankled me. She had always been quick to protect Rick. Two nulls in a pod. "Mistake or no," I said, "Skerry's still dead, isn't he? And Narlydda has never recovered from that. If Rick can do so much damage purely by accident, just imagine what he could do if he set his mind to it."

She stared at me, shocked. "I can't believe you would say that about him."

"Mom, I love Rick as much as you do. But I'm not kidding myself when it comes to his nature. He's reckless and unstable. And that's a bad combination, especially when you add superior mutant skills to the brew. I'd just as soon he stay out in the desert for good. For his sake as well as ours."

"Have you talked to Alanna?"

"Briefly." I hadn't yet told her what had happened at the Mutant Council. "I don't think we're exactly on speaking terms these days."

"You shouldn't just let family ties unravel."

Just one big happy family, I thought. Or thinking will make it so. I took a deep breath and said, "Mom, she may be my genetic sister but she grew up with Skerry and Narlydda. I wish I could feel closer to her. But it's not possible." Especially now.

"Don't be ridiculous. If you kept in better contact, you'd feel closer. And you'd know that Alanna has forgiven Rick. She told me so herself." Mother nodded. "I knew that she would. She still loves him."

I felt a sudden pang at her words, at the thought of Alanna still in love with Rick and rushing to his side. Well, hadn't I accused her of just that? And how did I really feel about my beautiful half-sister? I didn't want to probe that area too deeply for fear of what I might find. "Mom, I might as well tell you. Alanna and I had a falling out over Rick."

"That's foolish. If Alanna can forgive him, why can't you?"

"There's nothing to forgive."

"Stop playing head games with me, Julian. You know how much you resent him for the mess he made. But do you really want to bury him in the desert?"

Before I could answer, my father walked in. He was wearing a loose-fitting black sweat suit and a brown leather jacket over that. There were more lines at the corner of his eyes than I remembered and his long hair was touched with gray.

"Julian."

We shook hands gravely. He sat down next to me and patted my shoulder. "So Melanie has conjured you up from the land of Eastern Standard Time."

"Dad, you don't agree with Mom that she should go to New Mexico and join Rick, do you?"

A look flashed between my parents, opaque and unreadable. "I don't know, Julian," he said. "I don't want to be the heavy here. But I certainly wouldn't be happy if she went."

"Which," my mother said, "translates into no."

My father frowned. "It seems like a foolish waste of time to me to go running around New Mexico. If Rick wanted you there, wouldn't he ask you to come?"

"Better a cult of strangers than his own family?" Mother glared at me. Then she included her husband in the indictment. "I can never forgive myself for turning away from him."

This was becoming a familiar refrain. I stood up. "Look, Mom, let's skip the mea culpas, okay? You didn't do anything to him—*we* didn't do anything. He did it. He did it all."

"Don't we have any responsibility?" Melanie said. "Aren't we all guilty of Skerry's death?"

Dad cut in. "Don't be so melodramatic, dear. I get plenty of that at the symphony."

"I don't think we're guilty of anything except excess guilt," I said. "I refuse to blame myself for what happened to Rick. And I'm still convinced he's unstable and dangerous. Which is why I'm doing everything I can to stop him —and this crazy Better World group—before it creates trouble for everyone."

For a moment no one said a word.

My mother broke the silence. "My God," she said, shaking her head. "I can't believe you would turn against kin, your own brother. Honestly, Julian. You're so stubborn sometimes. You remind me of my father. He refused to bend, to accept change, and his attitude caused the family —and himself—a lot of pain."

"Do you think I enjoy doing this?" I said, and tears came to my eyes. "Turning against you? Against Rick? Do you think I would do it if I felt I had any choice, any other choice at all?"

"Why not leave it alone, son?" My father's voice, as ever, was gentle.

"I can't, Dad." My voice shook, embarrassing me. "I wish I could. But this group that Rick has formed could be dangerous. I had hoped you would see that and support my side of this. But regardless of what you think, I have to do what I believe is best."

"Even if it destroys Rick?" my mother asked.

"Even if it destroys him."

She closed her eyes. When she opened them a moment later I saw tears glistening against the gold. "I love you, Julian. But if you hurt Rick, don't come back here."

"Melanie!" my father cried.

"Mom, you don't mean that—"

"I do. I'm sorry, Julian. I hope you'll fail."

"And I hope that you'll change your mind." I grabbed up my jacket and started toward the door.

My father caught me outside as I got into my rental skimmer. "She doesn't know what she's saying. Give her some time to get accustomed to what's happening."

I hugged him fiercely, feeling gratitude and love. "Dad, I hope so."

"You can reach me at the symphony during the day," he said. "Or leave a message on e-mail at night." He smiled a sad smile, the mender, the bridge-builder. "Stay in touch, no matter what."

BOSTON WAS A WELCOME SIGHT, even with its snow and chronic garbage strikes. I settled back into my counseling practice and allowed the gentle friction of regular routine, hospital rounds, and familiar faces to abrade my memories of family strife. Time passed, weeks, then months, and my clients made the expected degree of progress and regression, that endless therapeutic two-step.

It was a morning early in April, with the first hint of spring in the air and swelling purple buds dotting slender tree limbs. Boston, in April, seems to take a deep breath and come back to life, casting off its winter somnolence. The hiss and mutter of skimmers cutting through slush is exchanged for the sound of wheels against dry pavement, birds twittering in the morning sunlight, and children shouting their high-pitched exultation that spring has come once again.

I began dreaming of blue skies and water dotted by sailboats, of walks along the Charles in purple twilight, and red tulips waving from window boxes.

I was in the midst of a particularly busy day, reviewing a complex case on which I was consulting when Joachim Metzger came to see me at my office. He arrived sans retinue, in a plain blue stretch suit. He could have been a traveling rep for a drug supply house.

"Just the two of us?" I asked.

"I thought perhaps it would be easier if we met alone," he said. "One on one."

Metzger had a reputation as an ambitious man who favored the company of politicians, mutant and non. I could see why: he looked like a politician with that thick head of white hair and regal stature. He smiled broadly but I knew well enough that an engaging persona often hid implacable determination. Rumor had it that Metzger planned a career in politics. I had never before met a mutant who had entertained post-Book Keeper ambitions.

I invited him into my sanctum sanctorum. "Please, sit down," I said, indicating the plushly upholstered sofa. "Would you like something to drink?"

"Coffee, thanks. Black."

I opened a small brown cabinet beside my desk. The coffeemech extruded a quikform mug and filled it, and I passed it to the Book Keeper. "If you had called first," I said, "I might have had donuts as well."

Metzger chuckled, but his smile faded as he got down to business. "About Rick—"

So that *was* why he had come. Of course. "I can't believe that you couldn't muster a vote to censure Better World," I said.

Metzger looked distressed. "Yes, I know. But I have to be very careful. I'm supposed to be an unbiased facilitator, not a dictator, Julian." He spread his hands upon the table. "Try to understand. I represent the oldest established faction of mutants in the world. We number at least two million on the Eastern Seaboard, three million throughout the country, and another million on the West Coast. It's no secret that the majority of the Eastern Council members are plenty conservative. But that's not true of every mutant: the Western Council has a tradition of liberalism that I must respect. However, what your brother is doing horrifies and alarms me." His voice rose on the last word and now I caught a glimpse of steel behind the velvety bonhomie. "He has no authorization from us and he ignores the best interests of the mutants in favor of his own wild ideas.

He even chased away a delegation from the Western Council. Refuses to communicate with any of the designated mutant authorities. We would like to work with him. Peacefully. But he rejects our every overture."

His implication was clear and I began to be frightened, both for my brother and all mutants. But I had to stay cool and pretend to be the pacific Dr. Akimura. "I know it's frustrating. But threatening Rick won't bring him back into the fold."

"Who said anything about threatening?" Metzger was suddenly the genial, well-met fellow again. "We're not threatening him, not in the slightest. In fact, we'd be happy for him to join us, even now. We've sent him repeated entreaties, but he's refused every one while he pursued his own course."

"But I thought he was willing to cooperate with the Mutant Council as long as it was on equal terms."

"That's not good enough," Metzger said. "He must recognize our authority. By refusing to do so he's forced our hands into opposition. Which is where you come in."

"I'm afraid I don't understand what role you foresee for me in all of this."

"It's simple, really." His voice took on a pedantic tone. "If your brother were keeping a lower profile, just rescuing cats from trees or lost kids at county fairs, I'd say bravo. God knows we need more people interested in helping others. But your brother is getting too big for his own good. Or ours. It's only a matter of time before he does something wrong and brings down the wrath of the entire society upon the heads of the mutants. So you must publicly oppose his actions at every opportunity."

"You know I don't trust what Rick is doing," I said. "In fact, I hope to send him a personal message about my feelings, between the lines. But I'm not entirely comfortable with speaking out publicly against him, especially if he's sincere in his intentions. And, frankly, Metzger, you sound a trifle paranoic to me. After all, the age of pogroms is long past."

Metzger bristled as though I had just kicked him. "We remember, Julian. We must. You young guys think that we're safe because we've made it through almost a century without violence. But it can happen again at any time. We're never safe. Never. Which is why we must always be on guard."

"Surely you're not suggesting that Rick be hurt?"

To Metzger's credit he looked genuinely uncomfortable. "Of course not. Of course not. That's the last thing I want. We're talking about organized opposition here, not violence."

"I see."

"Julian, I want to offer you a leading role in this."

"Why not you?"

"It might splinter the entire mutant community if I'm seen actively opposing what a large segment seems already to support."

"You mean Alanna's faction?"

He nodded. "You know, of course, that Rick has not accepted her, either."

"What?"

"She was turned away from Better World when she arrived. I hear she's currently in Taos, attempting to reach your brother by any means possible."

"Interesting. So he doesn't want her, either."

"Just you, it seems."

I was heartened by that. Perhaps Rick was attempting to make a real fresh start. But I mistrusted his intent enough to agree with Joachim Metzger that he had to be stopped. Briefly, I wondered if Metzger was truly opposed to Rick's cult on the grounds that it could hurt the mutants en masse or whether he was more concerned that Rick's ascendancy might damage his own political plans. Regardless of his motivation, he was apparently on my side.

"You know," he said, "I originally contacted you because I hoped you would have some suggestions for how to bring your brother to heel. But I see it's not quite that easy. Nevertheless I'm sure we could work together, Julian."

I stared at him, deeply ambivalent. In the same conversational tone of voice in which he might have invited me to a cocktail party Joachim Metzger had asked me to betray my own brother. Yet hadn't I decided to do just that?

As I struggled with a momentarily unruly conscience Metzger pressed home his point. "You know that your brother puts us all at risk. Performing public sharings with nonmutants. What's next? A vid ministry?" The Book Keeper made a grimace of distaste. "Do you know that we have had complaints from all over: the pope, from the Mormons, even the Episcopalians? And my contacts in government tell me that he is being watched. Closely."

"You don't have to recite chapter and verse to me," I said. "The threat is clear enough. Rick's actions put us all at risk." And, I thought, forced me into odd alliances. "I'll cooperate as long as we get one thing clear."

"What's that?"

"I refuse to allow any knowledge of my biological relationship to Rick to be revealed. I won't do that to my parents. If word of it gets out, then I'm out, too."

Joachim Metzger gave me a long, searching look. "Very well, Dr. Akimura," he said, finally. "It will be as you wish. You will be a spokesman for the mutants without any mention of family ties. No one outside of the Mutant Council knows who Rick really is. Your secret will remain safe."

5

Back in those days I didn't know Joachim Metzger very well and what I did know I didn't much like. But how often do wartime allies like each other? So I shook his hand and sealed our compact against my brother and against Better World.

A soft, three-chord chime interrupted my memories and brought me hurtling back to the present.

My message sim spoke in its gently asexual voice: "Forgive me, sir, for the intrusion. But you have a call."

"Who is it?"

"Alanna."

I hesitated. I hadn't expected her to call back so quickly. Was I ready? Of course not.

"Put her through."

My half-sister's face appeared, ivory skin with just a touch of celadon, curiously unlined. Her dark hair was upswept, held in place by a thick green ribbon. She looked ageless, untouched by the years.

"Julian." Her voice, at least, had grown deeper, throatier. "It's been years since we talked. How long?"

"I never bothered to count."

"Why break the silence now?"

"I need your help."

"So you said. But what's happened?"

"I'm not comfortable explaining it over the phone."

"Don't you have a privacy shield?"

"Yes, but I don't trust it."

"You've gotten paranoid, Julian." Yet she was the one who looked suspicious and regarded me without trust.

"Can we meet?"

"Where? I won't come to Taos."

"Albuquerque, then."

"Why don't you come out to the West Coast?"

"No good. Too many people would come with me."

"Can't you just slip away?"

I laughed at the thought. "These days I can scarcely get enough privacy to go to the bathroom by myself."

Alanna hardly blinked. "I don't see why I should make a special trip to New Mexico. You know I only come out there once a year and I'm not due for months."

"It's only a half-hour shuttle ride," I said. "If you like, I'll buy your ticket."

"Thank you, I can afford my own fare."

"Then you'll come?"

"No. Can't it wait until my regular appearance?"

"Alanna, I need you. Right now. You're the only one I can turn to. Now will you—goddammit—come and see me?"

For a moment her eyes widened in surprise at my vehemence. Otherwise, her implacable mask didn't shift. But the urgency of my request seemed to have gotten through to her. "All right, Julian. All right. I'll come."

WE AGREED UPON NEUTRAL TERRITORY: the private conference room at the old Albuquerque Inn on the edge of Old Town. I could shake off Barsi's faithful watchdog protectiveness for a trip to the Old Town antique shops as long as I promised to check in regularly.

I went with misgivings, with irritation and fear simmering: a volatile stew. Alone, I blinked in the sunlight, as disconcerted as a vampire caught far from his coffin at daybreak.

The traffic whizzed past, far too noisy and much too fast. The shrieks of children playing set off a steady, throbbing ache above my left ear. Yes, it was the messy, discordant, uncontrolled world running its rampaging course around me. Momentarily I longed for my B.W. hideaway and its thick, protective walls.

I reserved the room—using a pseudonym, of course. It would never do for word to get around that one of the elders of Better World had emerged into the realm of lesser mortals without his handlers.

The room was cozy as conference rooms go: a domed adobe fireplace with holo fire tape and carefully concealed forced-air heater, Navajo eye-dazzler rugs in reds, greens, and browns, and a rough-hewn table surrounded by chairs with thick woven cushions.

I took the head seat, the only chair with arms, at the long oval table. I couldn't decide if it was real wood or merely a clever facsimile and was saddened that I could no longer tell. The chair was deceptively comfortable despite its rustic look and I leaned back gratefully.

"A small glass of Scotch with some ice," I told the tablemech. Hypos had lost their appeal for me long ago and now I preferred to imbibe the old-fashioned way.

A mech waiter brought my cup of cheer, ice tinkling, in a sturdy, hand-blown glass.

"Happy days." I toasted my brother's ghost.

The Scotch was cool at first, then warm as it went down, depositing strength and even a bit of courage. A good thing, too, because Alanna was suddenly in the room, her boot heels ringing loudly against the floor.

She wore emerald-green silk robes that whispered when she moved and she had two young nonmutant men with her. Between them stood a secmech.

"I thought we agreed to meet alone," I said.

She glared at me, a flash of gold. "Wait outside, boys."

"Take that mechanical secretary with you," I said.

The secmech rolled out behind Alanna's henchmen and Alanna joined me at the oval table. Oh, so carefully did we avoid each other's eyes, until she tired of the standoff.

"You broke years of silence. Begged for this meeting," she said. "I made a special trip. Now will you deign to tell me just what the emergency is?"

I looked at my sister, envying her eerie youthfulness—was she using antigeriatric treatments? I have turned silvery and pale, neither fleshy nor spare. But she was smooth-skinned, elegant, almost unchanged. Her hair was dark save for a spray of silver at the temple.

I gave her a grudging compliment. "Aging well may be the best revenge."

"I certainly hope so," she said. "How are you feeling these days?"

"Who feels all right when they're seventy?"

"No complaints?"

"None that matter."

"Well, then, what *is* the matter? I thought you were on your deathbed."

"Is that why you raced out here? To gloat?"

"Don't be silly." She paused, eyeing me suspiciously. "I swore years ago that I would never speak to you again."

"Understandable."

"You'd know that more than most."

"Touché." I stared at her. She was ageless, magnificent even when poised in opposition against me. "I can't get over it, Alanna. You really look fine."

"You've already said that, and with the same degree of chagrin. Please, Julian, don't start to tell me how good it is to see me after all these years. I'll give you five minutes to tell me what's on your mind. Get started."

"I don't know where to begin—"

She made a long-suffering sigh. "I can't believe I was so stupid."

"Beg pardon?"

"I can't believe that I actually fell for your ploy."

"What do you mean?"

"There's no emergency, is there?" Her eyes flashed. "You just wanted to drag me out here. This is just one last power play to amuse yourself. You've resorted to false alarms in your dotage." She began to rise out of her chair.

"Sit down," I said. "Oh, sit down, Alanna, for God's sake. I'm sorry, all right? I'll get to the point."

"Good."

"I'm afraid that I'm losing control of Better World."

She sat down with a thump that must have rattled even her well-preserved bones. "What makes you think that?"

"It's pretty obvious: a lot of decisions are made first and

then I hear about them. Discussions around me. Meetings without me. I don't like it, not at all."

"I can see why that would trouble you. But you shut me out so long ago," she said, "why come to me now?"

"I think the only way to beat this is a united effort by the two people who knew Rick best."

Alanna didn't move, didn't flinch, didn't give any sign that the mention of our brother's name caused her the slightest bit of discomfort. The years seem to have worn her smooth as a river-washed stone. There was no flaw, no place on her for me to grab hold of and gain a footing. She merely sat there, staring at me.

Her lack of reaction infuriated me. "Aren't you concerned? Losing Better World will destroy everything we've worked for."

"Calm down, Julian, you're getting hysterical." Alanna was placid, almost amused. Her words were cool, her face composed. But plunging through her mind I spied the image of Better World burning like a comet, crashing, falling into a thousand pieces on the floor of some terrible canyon. What's worse, I sensed her pleasure at the image. She wanted it to crash, crash and burn.

Alanna selected an apple from the basket on the table and sat before me, calmly peeling it with her sharp telekinetic skills. The fruit bobbed between us in midair, shedding its red skin in lazy whorls to reveal crisp ivory flesh beneath. Alanna took a bite, chewed carefully. And as she chewed, a tiny smile curved her lips upward.

I imagined the grinning skull beneath her skin. Grinning as it sat on a shelf in a museum. "A fine example of a late twenty-first-century carnivore," the mechcurator would say. "The only type known to devour its own kind." The skull smirked at me and I wanted to knock it from the shelf, to smash it into a thousand bone fragments.

Delusional thinking, a quiet voice in my head informed me. A clear sign of stress.

In real time an eternity of seconds ticked loudly in the silent room as I stared at Alanna.

"So you'd murder the whole thing by neglect, wouldn't you?"

Alanna stopped smiling. "What did you say?"

"I didn't realize that murder was a trait that ran right through our family."

"Have you lost your mind?"

"I've misjudged you completely."

She stood. "I'm going to call the medics and get you a sedative."

"And just maybe the dosage will be too strong?" I cast a mental image at her of vidnews headlines: *"Desert Prophet's Brother Dies. Foul Play Suspected."* "Is that really what you want?"

"Stop it, Julian."

"I just want you to be honest with me."

My sister's face was livid, her calm assured mask ripped to shreds. "How dare you probe me! Stay out of my head. This is the second time you've accused me of murder."

"Don't you give a damn about Better World?"

"It's too late," she said. "You should have come to me years ago. I don't want to have anything to do with the church now. I can't help you, Julian. And I won't."

"Is this revenge, Alanna? For my cruelty? My ruthlessness?"

But even that failed to prick her. She gave me a sad, tired smile. "Oh, stop playing games with me, Julian. I'm no longer so ambitious. I've gotten older, too, don't you see? I just plain don't care."

"I don't believe you."

"Believe whatever you wish. I don't care about *that*, either."

Before I could blow upon the faint ember of her disdain she was on her feet and at the door.

Desperately, I tried to stop her. "Don't you think Rick would want you to help me?"

"Please don't mention him to me again." Her voice was husky, almost a whisper, and her glance convinced me that she really, truly hated me. But she mastered herself quickly and the heat receded from her gaze until all I saw was lukewarm dislike glazed with gold.

"Goodbye, Julian," she said. "I suppose I should wish you luck. I think you'll need it." And with that, my sister left me to the comfort of the lonely room, the flickering holo fire, and the company of old, old ghosts.

In the days that followed I could not work, could not sleep. Old memories and doubts I had long thought dead rose up to torment me.

Although I've often considered myself a patient man, now I grew restless and irritated. I scheduled extra sharings to relieve the stress, but even that comfort was only fleeting, and I was getting too old, too tired to hold more than three sharings a week, regardless of my need.

Age surprises everyone with its gradual limitations. I've tried to tell myself that I've grown accustomed to the shortened attention span, limited energy, and unreliable memory. But one can never quite grow accustomed to the machine running down and beginning to fail. I've tried to take it gracefully. I haven't always succeeded in the attempt.

One of the greatest frustrations for me was the effect of age on my memory. I've found gaps where formerly there were solid walls. And so, if, occasionally, I've reframed a sequence or missed a beat, it was only because the fugitive data winked, teasing me. But the past provided consolation, yes it did. I returned to my memories eagerly.

ONCE I KNEW WHERE RICK WAS, my twinsense itched and ached like a sprained muscle. I stayed away, though, buried my head in routine, and tried not to think about him. Not that I didn't see Rick. Oh, I saw him all right.

One evening I got home early, popped the top on a self-cooling red jack, turned on the vid, and leaned back on the floatsofa.

The vid, set to random dial, scrolled through the channels. Suddenly a familiar image flashed by.

"Stop!"

A man with a dark beard, desert tan, and long hair pulled back tightly behind his head was facing the camera and speaking seriously, earnestly. It was Rick. He was dressed in white and his golden eyes were hypnotic, like huge pools of light.

"Friends," he said. "Strangers, everyone who can hear me. I bring you joyous news."

What in hell was he up to?

"Each one of us has felt lonely," Rick said. His voice was

silky, embracing. His eyes stared intently out at me, at everyone. "Abandoned and afraid. Let that be the foundation of our commonality. Let us share our experiences with one another. With wisdom. With compassion. With healing intent. This is an invitation."

My brother was doing more than talking. I could feel the waves of empathetic energy flowing from him, flowing out of my screen and into my nervous system. As well as I knew him, as closely linked as we had been, I nevertheless fell completely under his spell. It was as though he were speaking directly to me, and me alone. Was this happening in every place where a vid screen was tuned to Rick's message? Was every viewer personally communing with my brother? Was it really possible?

Rick drenched us in ease, empathy, and goodness. "Join with me," he said, and his voice was a soothing, compelling caress. "Become a friend. We are waiting for you. I am waiting for you."

He nodded and his image slowly faded, to be replaced by golden, glowing holo letters that seemed to jump from the screen. Behind them, the camera panned over the Sangre de Cristo mountains at sunrise while a gentle mellifluous voice told me all about Better World.

"Help yourself. Help those you love. Comfort and understanding can be yours. New friends await you in an atmosphere of support and acceptance. We're here for you. Help yourself and help others through Better World, a service organization." A fax and phone number followed.

The glow of good feelings persisted long after the letters had faded from the screen.

Then the scene shifted to a white room without windows in which a man sat facing the camera. He had gray hair and a well-baked reddish-brown tan. He twisted his hands nervously as my brother walked into camera range.

Rick leaned over the man in the chair, talking quietly, and coaxed him to stand. As he rose to his feet I could see he was tall and sharp-featured, with all the stigmata of the seriously disturbed. He seemed nervous, even agitated, hands fluttering in tight circles. Rick took hold of the man's shoulders.

I knew that Rick was both calming him and scoping out

the psychological territory with a quick mind probe. The man smiled, closed his eyes, lowered his hands to his sides.

My brother leaned close to the man, frowning. Then he nodded intently. He must have found the damaged areas. I made an educated guess at Rick's approach: he would probably work on the memory first. The key to the chemical imbalance underlying the man's problem might be beyond Rick's analytical skills. But maybe not.

Rick's concentration increased as he went to work. The patient's face relaxed, the jaw went slack, creases at the mouth and eyes were less apparent.

Despite my uneasiness I felt a pang of real envy as I watched Rick. How easily he rewired the synapse paths, rejiggered the neuro-transmission levels, and removed the abnormalities in the cerebral cortex. He probably even erased one or two knife-edged memories while he was at it. Oh, I knew what he was doing—I could almost feel him making each move. Twinsense saw to that.

Rick whispered something that the microphone failed to pick up. Slowly the schizophrenic's face cleared. His eyes, when he opened them, were focused and bright. The haunted, hunted shadows in them were gone. His nervous twitches and tics had vanished. Clutching my brother's arms, he laughed a laugh of liberation.

"God bless you," the man said. "God bless you for what you've done for me. It's like a miracle. You don't know what I've been through, me and my family. You don't know. Thank you. Oh, thank you."

Rick's face glowed with delight. Tears sparkled in his eyes, and in mine as well. For a moment I forgave Rick the peculiar sideshow he had just staged. What he wanted to do was to help, to heal. He was convinced that he could ease others' pain. And, apparently, he could.

But why in God's name had he chosen to do a public healing on the main vid channels? There had to be some other, more dignified way to get his invitation across.

Rick's image faded, and the orange New Mexican sun was back, rising over the dark hulk of the Sangre de Cristos. A gentle voice said that such cures could be found through Better World. Again, the phone and fax number were shown.

Oh, Rick, I thought. Watch out. Be careful. Don't take on more than you can handle.

After my brother's little show, the real fun began. Carmen Ventura, a popular talk-show host, interviewed a therapist, two ministers, a Rotarian, a priest, a rabbi, an abbess, and an imam about what they had just seen. They took considerably more time to fulminate than Rick had taken to cure one entire human being. One measly little five-minute miracle followed by an eternity of reinterpretation by talking heads: it was a synoptic history of organized religion.

Ventura, obviously primed and looking to stir up controversy, began her show practically salivating with anticipation. "You've seen the miracle," she said. "You may have heard about the group of true believers who follow this man, almost worshiping him out in the desert. Is this just one more trend or is this Rick truly a miracle worker? What do you say, Rabbi?"

Judith Katz, rabbi of Temple Beth Shalom in Miami, frowned at the camera and said, "This seems like some sort of circus trick to me. I refuse to give him or his group credence. He's a performer, pure and simple."

Ali Haddad, first speaker of the Center for Moslem Studies in New York: "This is evil, ungodly, he will be struck down. No one may masquerade as Allah's divine healer."

Said Dr. Irena Strugatsky, "It was a fascinating demonstration of healing—if that's what actually took place. I'd be interested in studying this further."

Elder Robert Martin of the Church of Jesus Christ of the Latter-Day Saints in San Diego: "We're uncomfortable with the implications of this man's actions and are investigating the entire group carefully."

Sister Catherine was the only dissenting speaker. "If he did help that man, isn't it amazing?" she said. Her eyes glowed with wonder. "How marvelous to think that such powers exist and can be used to heal people."

For the most part, those interviewed seemed to be united in their sense of uneasiness—even fear—and mistrust. Who could blame them? Rick offered new and different miracles. Wondrous stuff. How could their religions, their therapies and disciplines, hope to compete? And could they afford to look foolish, publicly applauding the acts of a possible charlatan? No, no, it was much more prudent to condemn first and, if necessary, endorse later.

And then the calls started—I never knew how the reporters had gotten my phone number. Probably Metzger had given it to them. In any case, I quickly found myself uncomfortably spotlighted as a leader of the loyal mutant opposition to Rick.

"Dr. Akimura? This is Tom Quinas for Eye-Five Vidnews. I understand you represent a group of mutants who are actively opposed to the efforts of the Better World group. Would you care to comment on the healing that the man some are calling the Desert Prophet just effected?"

"How did you get my number?"

"Dr. Akimura, why are you and other mutants so opposed to Better World's stated policy of community service?"

"I don't know that I can speak for other mutants," I said carefully, feeling pangs of ambivalency. "I know that some mutants feel this group has all the earmarks of a cult and they're uncomfortable with the potential for extreme behavior that's usually associated with cults."

"You're a psychiatrist and healer, isn't that so?"

"Yes, that's right."

"In fact, you specialize in combining mutant and nonmutant healing techniques in the psychiatric therapeutic process, isn't that so?"

"Yes, I try—"

"Isn't that the same thing as what this Desert Prophet is doing?"

"Not at all. As far as I can tell he isn't trained as a healer. Not even remotely. I question his credentials. And his motives." I hoped that Rick was hearing this. Perhaps I could encapsulate my own message to him within my public pronouncements.

"Do you deny that he helped that man?"

"I have no way of telling what actually took place without physically examining the patient."

"Why do you think they televised that event?"

"To publicize Better World, of course. And to draw others into its embrace."

"Which the majority of mutants do not support, despite

the presence of a mutant at the helm of this Better World group?"

"I would prefer to say that a large group of mutants doesn't feel comfortable with it. I don't think anyone, anywhere, is ever entirely comfortable with the formation of a cult."

"Thank you, Dr. Akimura."

THE NEXT CALL AFTER THAT was from Joachim Metzger.

"I saw that live feed just now," he said. "A good beginning. But you must be firmer. More insistent."

"Perhaps you'd like to write me a script?"

He chose to take that as a joke and smiled broadly. "You seem to ad lib well, Julian. But remember that you represent more than yourself when you speak."

I answered irritably. "Yes, yes, of course. The Mutant Council. Mutants in general."

"And me," he said. "Don't ever forget that you represent me."

AS I HAD SPECIFIED TO METZGER, the reporters had no idea of my real relationship with Rick—I can only imagine the fine time they would have had hounding my parents, Narlydda, and anybody else they could ferret out of the genetic records. But Rick remained something of a mystery man—where had he come from? Who was he? I certainly wasn't saying. All I *was* saying was, "This must be stopped. This is no good. This is dangerous." I was becoming a sort of negative shadow of Better World, dogging reports of their activities whenever they appeared on vid.

Which is not to say I was comfortable with my new prominence—not in the slightest. And I began to see that Joachim Metzger wasn't much happier—perhaps he resented my public stance as a mutant representative when I was not even a Book Keeper. But hadn't he enlisted my support? I would happily have relinquished my role as media contact and mutant talking head in a moment, but that was not to be.

Finally, even my mother called me. Either she had forgiven my intransigence against Rick or just decided to overlook it. "Julian," she said, "I saw you on the vid."

"I thought we weren't talking to each other."

"You take what I say too seriously." She smiled. "You're pretty good, you know? But you ought to even out your complexion with some foundation before each broadcast."

"I'll try to remember that. Did you call to advise me on my makeup?"

"Don't be silly. Have you talked to your brother?"

"Not recently."

"Well, good luck if you try. Julian, believe it or not, I have to get on a waiting list to talk to my own son."

"Be glad you're not working the anchor desk for vidnews," I said. "You could probably get an exclusive with Rick, but you'd be ninety years old before you reached him."

"Don't I know it," Mom said. "But if you do get through to him, Julian, tell him to call me. Remind him that even the Desert Prophet has a mother."

6

BY THE TIME OF Rick's next vidded miracle, I was a seasoned media performer, able to provide an extemporaneous sound bite without batting an eye.

When the first reports came in, no one seemed to know where the fire had started at the Grande Gorge Theater in Taos, New Mexico. Perhaps some wiring had shorted out. Perhaps it was arson. The flames spread with frightening velocity until half the theater was ablaze.

Members of the Taos volunteer fire department raced to the scene but they were too late. Some of the support structures in the walls were old, made of a ferro-ceramic manganese, and there's nothing a manganese fire likes more than water. When the internal sprinkler system came on it spread the fire quickly and efficiently to the other parts of the building. The volunteer firemen just made it worse. Other structures nearby were in real jeopardy and there was the clear threat of a major catastrophe if the fire could not be contained.

Regardless of the size of the blaze, this was a news item that would scarcely have merited a quick mention in the morning national news roundup if not for Rick's intervention.

The local Albuquerque vidnews team had caught Rick's arrival as he teleported almost directly into the inferno, a strange, dark silhouette poised against the flames. He sized up the situation, teleported everyone else out of there, including all the firemen, then closed his eyes and did something to smother the flames. In ten minutes, the theater was a smoking ruin, but the fire had been extinguished. Rick vanished and the tape ended.

A white-haired reporter stepped in front of the camera and said, "Later investigation revealed that the molecular structure of the surviving manganese wall supports had been disrupted to prevent them from igniting. Fire officials speculate that the oxygen in the station was somehow converted to carbon dioxide, smothering the fire. The New Mexico Movie Company that owns the theater is offering a reward to the mysterious mutant known only as Rick who evidently halted this fire single-handedly. Anyone with information on this man is asked to please contact the New Mexico Movie Company and/or New Mexico state troopers."

"This isn't miracle-working," I told the vid reporters when they called. "Any reasonably talented telekinete could have accomplished what that man did. He's simply using mutant powers."

"But, Dr. Akimura," said Tim Walters of Vidnews Too, "what about the disruption of the manganese structure? How do you explain that?"

"Easily," I said. "Any telekinete who knew what he or she was doing could handle that task. We're dealing with a heroic deed here. But not a miracle."

"But if what you say is true, then why don't other mutants come forward to aid their communities?"

I scented smoke here: the first tinder catching in a backlash of resentment against selfish mutants hoarding their skills. "No," I said quickly. "I want to emphasize that not every mutant can do these things. Our skills vary. But this man is not some avatar. He's just a very skilled mutant employing his talents for the good of others."

A WEEK LATER, Rick really outdid himself.

My brother went down to Mexico City to help battle a cholera epidemic. The vid report I saw was not of first quality—apparently the tape had come from some amateur vid jock's hand-held rig. Although the color and sound wavered from time to time the action was clear enough.

My brother was standing in the midst of what looked like an International Red Cross hospital tent as a tall, blond-haired doctor glared at him.

"How did you get in here? Who are you?" the doctor said. "Get away from that patient."

"Is this a terminal case, Doctor?"

"What are you doing?"

"I think I can use microkinesis to save her," Rick said. "At least I'm game to try."

A short, gray-haired woman in a Better World jumpsuit moved into view. She had the no-nonsense air I've always associated with nuns and medical professionals, and she ignored the sputtering doctor as easily as Rick did. "We've got to deal with the dehydration," she said to my brother.

"What about the bugs?" Rick asked.

"The antitoxins will get them. It's the fluid loss that's killing these people. Probe her bloodstream. Look for white platelet clumps. Wherever you find them, reinforce the cell walls nearby to increase fluid retention. And scan for ruptures. When you find them, try to repair the cell walls so we can stabilize the osmotic pressure. Got it?"

"I think so." Rick frowned, leaned down over the woman who lay, unconscious, on the cot, and closed his eyes. "Okay, here we go." Sweat began to pour down his face.

"Now wait just one frigging moment here," said the Red Cross doctor. He reached out to grab Rick's hand—and froze in midgesture. Rick had trapped him in a telekinetic field. The doctor's eyes roved back and forth in obviously mounting frenzy but otherwise he was completely immobilized.

Yet Rick seemed oblivious to him, eyes tightly shut, all his will focused on the dying woman.

She stirred once, moaned softly, strained for breath, then her labored breathing eased.

Rick opened his eyes. "There," he said. The tension went out of him; he stood up, breathing heavily, and swung his arms back and forth.

The Red Cross doctor gasped and took a staggering step or two. "What the hell was that?" He rubbed his fingers and arms, concentrating on the tricep muscles. "Jesus, I ache all over."

"That's because you fought me," Rick said. "You shouldn't have strained so hard. You probably gave yourself a pretty bad charley horse."

The doctor glared at him. "What have you done to this woman?" The color drained out of his face as he examined her. "My God," he said. "My God, I don't believe it."

"What's wrong?"

"Nothing. Absolutely nothing. Her fever's broken. She seems to be in a light sleep instead of a near-coma. All other bodily functions seem to have returned to normal. Fluid balance is fine." He gazed up at Rick in wonder. "Did you cure her just like that? Can you really do that? I mean, I've heard of mutants having unusual talents, but—"

"Let's just say that I'm more unusual than most," Rick said. "Yeah, I guess it worked. Is there anybody else around here I can help?"

The doctor rubbed his jaw. He seemed to be turning things over in his mind, and then turning them over again. After a long moment he said, "I don't know. It's irregular as hell just letting you waltz right in here and go to work on people. But on the other hand, we've got terminal cases I can't help. You might as well take a whack at 'em." He grabbed Rick's shoulder. "Come on. This way. Hurry."

Rick moved from cot to cot and the camera followed him. The work was draining, and under his desert tan his skin grew pallid and waxy, but he refused to rest. In his wake, patients breathed with renewed vigor, sat up, and a few of the strongest even attempted to walk.

All afternoon he worked on the most critical cases and a quick, clumsy montage showed that within hours Rick had cured most of the patients within the tent city.

"What's next, Doctor?" Rick said. A tremor ran through his body but he seemed not to notice.

"Don't you want to rest?"

"Please, Rick, listen to him," said the short, gray-haired Better World staffer. "You nearly passed out after curing that last patient."

Slowly, stubbornly, my brother shook her off. "No, I've got to keep moving. There's too much work to do."

"Here." The Red Cross doctor began to press a hypo

against Rick's arm. Rick jumped away from him as if he had just tried to bite him.

"What the hell's in that thing?"

"A vitamin-B booster."

"*You* take it. I don't need anything. I'm fine."

"Can't hurt," the doctor said. "Especially if you want to keep on going."

"I told you, I'm fine." Rick's left eye twitched in an odd tic. "Where to next?"

"Well," the doctor said, "if you're absolutely set on running yourself into the ground, there's an auxiliary tent hospital set up in the Galeria Plaza. I'm sure they could use help there. And if you've got any energy left after that, try the city hospital near Reforma at the corner of Sevilla and Ocampo. That place has got to be a nightmare."

"I'll bet." Rick took several steps, staggered, stopped. "Y'know, on second thought, maybe I will have the hypo after all." He held out his arm and the doctor pressed a small syringe against it. If he felt the sting of the injection he didn't show it. "Thanks."

His stride lengthened as the serum took effect and he moved quickly out of range as the film faded, blurred, and ended.

I was deeply alarmed by this particular vid and not only because it showed my brother mucking about in international health crises when he didn't have any sort of medical training to begin with. That was bad enough, but I was even more concerned when I saw Rick nearly faint from exhaustion. Oh, yes, he had made a lightning-quick recovery, but I knew that something had gone wrong, and *that* frightened me more than anything—and hardened my determination to head off Rick's juggernaut. What if he, himself, couldn't control it any longer? Who could?

His intervention in the cholera epidemic made headlines, of course. He was both anointed and vilified by the usual chorus. Loudest among his critics was the ever-vigilant, ever-hysterical Roman Catholic Church, which ceaselessly warned him to stay away from its precious flock. But the AMA was right behind them, cautioning against public sanction of untrained miracle workers.

Theirs were voices in the darkness and they went largely

ignored. A letter of commendation arrived from the Secretary General of the United Nations. Rick was even invited to dinner at the White House. And, of course, after a while, he seemed to take all the kind words a bit too seriously. At least, that's how I saw it. So once again I added my voice to the refrain.

"Of course he helped the medical teams," I said to the reporters. "But I can't believe that one man alone was responsible for chasing cholera out of Mexico City. He merely has a very efficient P.R. staff. They're exaggerating. He's a glory hunter, pure and simple."

THEN CAME THE PLANE CRASH. Or, let me rephrase that, then came the near-miss.

It was a night of uneasy dreams for me. If, in fact, they were dreams at all.

I was standing with my brother outside the main building of Better World. Rick held me in an affectionate embrace.

"Little brother, I wish you were here with me," he said. "I need your help so badly. Why do you insist on rejecting me? You're a part of me. Why do you stay away?" He hugged me tightly against his rough wool shirt and his eyes were suspiciously bright, as though he were fighting back tears.

I returned the embrace happily until his grip changed and I began to have trouble breathing. "Rick," I said. "You're hurting me. Let go."

He didn't seem to hear. With punishing fingers he held my arms and his eyes were wide and unfocused and horrified.

"Oh, oh God," he said. "They're going to hit. All those people, the little children. No, no, I can't, I—" He grabbed his head with his hands as though rocked by some terrible pain.

"Rick, what is it? What's wrong?"

He ignored me, lurched backward, and vanished.

For a moment I was dumbfounded. Then, somehow I saw it also. Two planes were taxiing down a runway toward each other in the twilight. Red lights blinked secret messages from the wings and tail, freezing drizzle fell gray from the sky in the winter dusk. Ice-slicked runways reflected the lights, making ghost patterns of shadows as I watched the slow-motion ballet performed by the elephantine flying machines. In silence they met, metal on metal, and in silence came to pieces. In silence the lights flashed, the bodies fell, the people screamed and screamed and screamed.

No—no, wait. It wasn't that way, not at all. No one was screaming, no one was dying. The planes floated toward each other and passed smoothly, silent metal birds on separate and safe trajectories. There was no crash. No death. None at all.

Then I saw it yet again, faster this time, and even more terrible. The planes raced toward each other, engines screaming. They hit, they hit, they hit. Oh God, the blood, the sounds, the horror of it. I covered my face. Please, don't make me see it anymore, please, I can't bear it.

As if a film were being rewound, the images reversed, planes re-formed, disengaged, pulled back and away from each other. They moved forward, then pulled back. Forward, then back. My vision looped around and around, finally catching and holding on the image of a young woman's face frozen in midscream.

Julian?

The vision shattered into splinters of color and light. My twinsense twinged, a maddening subcutaneous itch I could never reach, never scratch. I saw a figure, head down, shoulders slumped, standing in the midst of a gray and endless void. I knew before I had even seen his features clearly. It was Rick, and I sent him a query in private mindspeech mode.

Are you all right?

No answer. Couldn't he hear me?

Rick? Answer me. What happened?

Still no response. I was really worried now.

RICK!

I hear you, for God's sake. I hear you. Yes. I'm all right. Brother, let's walk.

Before I could assent I was in a dark, chaotic place, tumbling end over end, stomach rebelling. Then I was standing, shivering, on a high cliff, the wind was blowing fiercely, and my brother stood beside me. He seemed reinvigorated, almost exhilarated by the icy wind.

"Where the hell are we?" I said between chattering teeth.

"Mesa Chivato, near the old Zuni-Jemez trail," he said. "Sorry for the quick trip but I had to get us out of there, away from the confusion. And besides, I like it here."

I stared down at the tormented landscape far below us. Rick *would* like it here, I thought. And why not? It suited his nature. He could range throughout the roughest, wildest spots in New Mexico. Or anyplace else he desired.

"What happened?" I said.

"I dunno. Guess I didn't get to the airport in time. But it was so close—" His voice, already hoarse, broke and for a moment he said nothing.

"You mean the accident had already occurred?"

"*Was* happening," he said. "As I arrived. I was too late. So like an idiot I tried to t-jump back five minutes to see if I could divert one of the planes off the runway."

"You tried to jump in time?" I gazed at him in amazement. "But I didn't think that was possible."

"Oh, it's possible, all right," Rick said. "But it's hard, even for me. And the displacement of energy really screws up the sequence of events. Not to mention my head."

I laughed. "If you think you were confused, you wouldn't believe what I saw." Quickly I told him about the conflicting visions that had so astounded me.

Rick whistled. "You, too? I don't know, Julian. Maybe that twin link leaves you open to leaks." He nodded. "It wouldn't surprise me. Nothing would, anymore."

"Hey, at least you managed to prevent the crash."

"Took everything I had. I got into the cockpit of the 987 and grabbed the pilot in major coercive mode. Made him pull to the right as fast as he could. Jesus, it was hard. I thought I was going to have a stroke or something. And as it was, I couldn't quite hold it long enough. I could feel it slipping, getting away from me: felt kind of like I'd pushed an elastic band a little bit and then let go. That's when the plane hit that shack."

I saw tears in his golden eyes.

"But you did save most of the passengers," I said. "Gods,

Rick, you practically worked a miracle. There were only twenty casualties. If you hadn't tried to intervene, seven hundred people might have died instead of twenty."

Rick shrugged and wiped his eyes. "Yeah. But try telling that to the families of the casualties."

I grabbed him by the shoulder. "Rick, don't do this to yourself."

"Yeah, yeah, okay. Spare me the therapy, Doctor." He shook off my consoling grip. "Y'know, when I first had that vision of those two planes hitting, I couldn't tell when it would happen, or if it *was* happening in real time, right then as I watched. All I knew was I had to get there. For all the good it did."

"Stop it, Rick. You're only human."

My brother smiled at me oddly. "Glad you're so certain, kiddo." Then he faded, faded, until all that was left of him was a smile against the tormented clouds in the New Mexican sky. Even after I awoke I could still see his smile against the clouds.

That morning, I heard about the near-miss at the Albuquerque airport as I dressed for work. Twenty-seven people had died. But a major disaster had been averted.

The phone began ringing immediately and for once I let the answermech take it.

"This is Channel Two. We would like a reaction from a mutant spokesman to the rescue at the Albuquerque airport. Officials at the Mutant Council gave us this number."

"Chris Rossfeld, Independent Vid, and I'm calling about the miracle in Albuquerque."

"Dr. Akimura, this is Clayton Pierce. Will you comment?"

"The miracle man of New Mexico—"

"Do you still think he's a fraud?"

"We need a reaction shot—"

The dream was still too fresh in my mind and my doubts were overwhelming. Had Rick just barely managed to save those two planes? Was he in any way responsible for the deaths that had occurred? And what had I seen? Was my unconscious mind somehow tied into Rick in such a way that I received visions from him? For the rest of that day I didn't return any calls.

*   *   *

RICK'S MEDIA EXPOSURE increased threefold. He was peripatetic: curing people, extending his hand in friendship, pouring out good vibes to everybody within the sound of his voice. And his miracles just got bigger and better. If they cost him more in energy, in concentration, in all the tiny special areas that he relied upon to work his magic deeds, he carefully shielded his weakness from the view of others. On video, at least, he was strong and splendid, a demigod for all seasons.

The mountain rescue he performed in the Canadian Rockies made for extraordinary video and he followed that up with a midair levitation and t-jump of survivors from a shuttle crash. Then there was his nifty trick at the Houston Spill, the recovery of the neutronium shipment lost between the Gulf of Aqaba and Dakar, and his plugging of the hole in the seawall of Pacifica II, thirteen miles off the big island of Hawaii, saving the sea colony. As if that weren't enough, he even extinguished the fire storm on the French/Saudi orbital platform. By then he was famous. And not merely for his heroics.

Word of Rick's wondrous sharings had spread throughout the nonmutant community and people were intrigued—and attracted—and most eager to experience the healing qualities of Rick's special magic. Apparently, a few members of Better World had talked to the vidnews, describing their experiences as transformational, empowering, and even more enjoyable than sex.

Needless to say, Better World was besieged. Half the people in the Western Hemisphere seemed to want to have a transformational, better-than-sexual experience as soon as possible. And each one of them sent money.

I watched these developments with a certain sour uneasiness. Was I jealous? After all, I wasn't the brother for whom people clamored. I didn't draw crowds, didn't trail vid cameras behind me for a block, didn't require a security force to protect me from the people who loved me. But no, no, I don't think I was jealous, exactly. More likely, I felt disappointed with Rick for falling under the spell of it all and allowing a documentary crew to accompany him wherever he went.

Everyone seemed to embrace my brother's philosophy of support, caring, and comfort. The Public Vid Service rushed through a four-part documentary series on Better World narrated by one of the youngest, most sincere, most popular actors in the business.

Hollywood loved Rick. So, too, did politicians, students, and white-haired old grandmothers. Why not? H was the perfect hero for a nation starved for icons. Best of all, he had answers. He provided solutions.

Rick easily drew people to him. Originally, Better World had been a loose affiliation of about two dozen folks—ranchers, mostly, some ski bums, a couple of boutique owners, and a miscellaneous handful of ragged homeless folk who had followed Rick in out of the desert.

They were indefatigable do-gooders, and their numbers spread quickly, into the schools, the neighborhoods, the isolated mesas and arroyos, on mountainsides and along river valleys.

At first there had been little evidence of their activities outside of local events: standardized test scores began to go up among the New Mexican schoolchildren. There were fewer petty crimes and much less vandalism in the schools and streets. The sight of a broken-down skimmer was infrequent, a shattered store window even rarer.

Less tangible but more important, the sense of community seemed to improve and flourish: people passing on the street waved, called to one another, were kinder and more thoughtful. Everybody was far happier. Who wouldn't be, with a private superman and his merry band of helpers always available, always on call? I imagined that this was how the early Christians might have felt and behaved when they began to gather in small, hidden rooms and whisper to one another about a powerful, wondrous savior.

It all worked splendidly for a while simply as a private nonprofit loosely run volunteer service benefiting whoever sent up a distress signal. But word spread quickly.

What had been a ragtag assortment of trailers and campers gathered around B.W. headquarters coalesced into a neighborhood of sorts. This community was codified even further when, through donations, Better World acquired a nearby property: a defunct recreation area whose existing buildings and facilities seemed ready-made for Better World's needs.

The faithful adapted the place and began to plan more structures. A merchant or two moved in to supply food and other basic necessities. Rick seemed pleased. "That's the way," he said. "We'll take care of ourselves and each other."

Word of the burgeoning community spread from coast to coast throughout the enclaves of the homeless and disenfranchised. All, all of them, flocked to Taos much to the displeasure of the governor, the mayor, and assorted city officials.

Those immigrants who agreed to participate in Rick's sharing sacrament were welcomed and few among them saw reason to refuse. The population of Better World swelled. More buildings were needed. More services, supplies, and merchants arrived.

Rick began to see that if he was going to help even half of the people who had already petitioned him for his aid, then he had to do it in a standardized, systematic way. Which led to the official incorporation of the Better World, a privately held service organization.

Its canonization by the media—and its excoriation by all organized religions—is nearly legend now. The Roman Catholic Church, the Mormons, the Moslems, the Protestants, the Jews, and a whole host of various other sects—all complained mightily, noisily, and regularly that Better World was plundering their ever-thinning ranks. The AMA rattled the bars on its cage, citing Rick for practicing medicine and healing without a license. The politicians courted Rick for the votes represented by Better World membership. And, of course, Better World flourished. It was on the cusp, just beginning its flamboyant and astonishing metamorphosis from community group to international cult. Who could have suspected how huge it would become? No one but me and Joachim Metzger, and I hoped that I was wrong.

The demand for seats at Rick's sharings became so great that he was forced to hold them in huge sports arenas and theaters. Rick suggested that half of the proceeds from ticket sales be put toward various charities and the rest used to help Better World pay administrative costs. He even designed a subscription series for people who couldn't get enough of him: five sharings in five cities. The best seats sold out in two hours. After each sharing spectators would come away glowing, satisfied, having gotten their money's worth and much, much more.

People flocked to the sharings, scalpers made new fortunes, and the public's appetite for Rick grew. As for Rick, well, I'm not exactly sure how he felt, what he got out of the sharings—perhaps some momentary relief from the guilt that he carried. Certainly each sharing seemed to take more than it gave, extracting a physical toll from him that could be seen in the new silvery strands glinting in his beard and ponytail, and in the whittling down of his muscular frame to sinew and bone. I told myself it was nothing, that my brother was just one of the lucky ones who would only become spare and wiry as he approached middle age.

When I first learned of the plans to dedicate Better City I decided that I had to make one last direct personal appeal to Rick to cease, to desist and go away. Since I lacked farspeech I had to call him, and his line, of course, was busy, so I set the phone to auto redial. The screen glowed red steadily—busy—but ten minutes later it switched to blue and the electronic cricket-cheep told me that my call had gone through.

A familiar measure from an orchestral passage tootled pleasantly, redolent of synthesized clarinets. It took me a moment to recognize the tune: it was from a piece my father Yosh had written in honor of my birth and Rick's. "Dual Sonata," he had called it. A playful, spritely work. The music cut off and the screen was filled by a muscular young man with a squarish head, wide neck, and hardly any cheekbones. I couldn't tell if he was a sim or for real.

"Better World," he said. "How may we help?" His voice was high and surprisingly gentle. A former fullback who sang countertenor in his spare time?

"I want to talk to Rick."

The fullback smiled patiently. "Of course you do. Unfortunately, Rick is very busy right now. Perhaps I can help you."

"Look, I'm his brother."

The smile broadened. "We're all his brothers and sisters."

"No, really. I mean it." Irrationally, I wanted to wipe that contemptible look off his face and I scrabbled in my pockets, searching for my hospital identification. I had holocard in hand when the screen image dissolved into jagged lightning bolts before re-forming around my brother's face. He looked a bit three-dimensional, as though his screen were transmitting in holovid.

"Little brother!" Rick smiled broadly. "What's up?"

His eyes were bright but there were dark circles under them and his face was thin, even drawn. He looked ten years older than when I had last seen him. I suddenly remembered the vid image of him stumbling in Mexico City and I was more worried than ever.

For a moment I was so stunned by his appearance that I couldn't speak. Then I found my voice. "My God, you look like a wreck."

"Just tired," Rick said. "Nothing that a good night's sleep won't fix."

"Bullshit, Rick. You look absolutely depleted. When was the last time you had a checkup?"

"Hey, did you call to play doctor? Don't waste your time or mine."

"Rick—"

He turned away from the screen as if to go.

"Wait—"

"What is it?"

My concern flipped over into anger. "Just what do you think you're doing, Rick? Running yourself into the ground with televised appeals and documentaries on your healings? And now you're building a city? Even God rested on the seventh day, you know."

"Whoa, now cool down, Julian."

"No, I won't cool down." My hands were shaking and so was my voice. "Do you realize the risks you're taking? The furor you've created?"

"Sure. And I also noticed that you've been one of my loudest critics, Dr. Akimura-of-the-mutants." His smile was suddenly gone but his tone was still light, almost playful.

He was treating me with a certain indulgent fondness that I found completely maddening.

"Do you blame me? You're out of control, maybe even irrational."

"Oh, so helping people is crazy? Since when?"

"How much of what you're doing is helping and how much of it is ego gratification, Rick? Sheer grandstanding just for the hell of it."

"Don't be ridiculous." My brother sounded just the tiniest bit impatient. "We've been all through this, Julian. You, of all people, should understand. You know why I'm doing it."

"Not why you're suddenly publicizing every move you make. When do we get a peek at 'Rick, the Bathroom Tapes'?"

"Look, did you call just to do a comedy routine with me or was there something you really wanted to talk about?"

"Rick, please, you must stop. Abandon this plan to build a city. You're getting too ambitious, drawing too much attention to yourself. You don't know the kind of trouble you're making for yourself and the other mutants."

"Trouble? As far as I can see, it's just the opposite. A bonanza. Everybody wins."

"The nonmutants don't really understand you. They expect all mutants to have your powers and are furious that we all seem to have been withholding our secret talents from them."

"Well, in a way, haven't we?"

"Meanwhile, the government, various organized religions, and the American Medical Association have been putting a lot of heat on the Mutant Council over you."

"Good."

"Rick, you don't know what you're saying. You've almost doubled the population of this area. You're stretching the available resources too far too fast."

"We can take care of ourselves, Julian. You're the one who seems confused. If you would only come out here and join us, then you'd understand why this construction project is so important—so crucial to my plans."

"But an entire city, Rick? Where are you getting the money? The materials?"

"We're using what's already here. And we get a lot of donations." He winked smartly. "We've got international interest in our efforts, little brother. Which translates directly into eurodollars."

"Are you kidding me?"

"Of course not. And I don't see why the mutants are so upset with me. They won't be satisfied unless I let them run things, which I can't do. So they've refused to participate as equal partners. Too bad. Let them take some heat. What are they going to do about it, little brother? Send a couple of first-level telepaths after me? I can hold them off in my sleep."

"Rick, this might be construed as counterphobic behavior. Are you trying to rub their noses in what you're doing?"

"No, of course not. I don't have energy to waste on petty vendettas, Julian. The time was right for this expansion. Do you know that as a result of our vid broadcasts we've gained an extended membership base of one hundred thousand?"

"My God," I said. "Are you serious? Can you actually deal with that number? Across the country?"

"*Internationally.* Of course we can. Compared to the big boys and girls and their official churches it's doodly-squat."

"Churches? Wait a minute, Rick. I thought Better World was a secular organization."

"It's whatever anybody needs it to be: secular, ecumenical, holy, free lunch, whatever." He seemed to be spectacularly unconcerned.

"You know that some people are calling it a cult."

"And if they feel better treating it as a cult, what do I care? Especially if it enables me to reach and help more people."

"Rick, I thought you wanted this to be a small, grassroots organization."

"Things change. They grow and change, Julian."

"Into an entire community?"

"Why not? As soon as Better City is finished, we'll be able to accommodate three or four times our current membership."

"Are you telling me you intend to house the entire membership?"

"As much as we can. Julian, many of them have nowhere else to go. Better World just fits in where the state and federal safety nets unravel. And it's amazing what happens to someone who's been down on his luck when he's given shelter, regular meals, and work to do. It's like magic."

"Your followers are building you your own personal Xanadu?"

"It's not for me, Julian. It's for them. And they're good workers, too."

"I don't believe it."

"I wish you would. I need your help more than ever, little brother."

"You know how I feel about Better World. I've shot my mouth off all over the vid as standing firmly against you."

Rick waved away my arguments. "I don't pay any attention to that, Julian. You have to do what you feel is right, I know that. But there'll always be a place here for you, little brother. You're my flesh and blood."

"Please, Rick," I said. "Won't you stop this foolishness before it all falls in on your head?"

"Sorry, little brother. You know *I* can't do that. But take good care of yourself. And call anytime. You know where to find me."

SPRING TURNED INTO SUMMER, bringing the usual malaise of warm weather. Boston is a city well suited to spring or autumn, the transitional seasons. It even has a certain chilly appeal early in winter when the Charles is thickened with ice and the brick row houses near the harbor wear neat caps of new-fallen snow. But summer leaves the city limp and steaming, draws the life out of it, and sends residents scuttling for deep shadow and beach cottages. Half a century ago, city planners had spurned requests for climate-control domes, arguing that such urban improvements would destroy Boston's unique character. At the moment I would have settled for a bit less character and a whole lot more comfort.

I tried to ignore my misgivings about Better World with the distraction of work, and was even somewhat successful. I sweated my way through the days and stumbled home at night, exhausted. But at night my dreams were filled with strange scenes of Rick moving mountains, floating through space, even walking on water. The worst dream of all was— well, I hoped that it *was* a dream. I told myself it was but I'm still not sure.

I dreamed that I had slipped into a bottomless, dreamless slumber, falling and falling, but at some hour before dawn I awoke in the dark with the breath caught and sticking in my chest. Someone was in the room with me. I reached out, tapped the bedside module, and the small, round lamp came to life, casting a yellow glow across the room.

Something golden sparkled by the door. Golden eyes fixed upon me the way a jungle cat stares down its prey.

I must have jumped almost a foot into the air; the jellbed sloshed as I bounced down against its pliant surface. "Jesus Christ, Rick! What are you doing here?"

My brother was silent, motionless, leaning against the blue paneling of my bedroom wall like a waxen doll. He appeared dazed, perhaps even hypnotized. Only when I moved did he blink.

"Hi," he said. His voice was weirdly furry, so remote that he might have been speaking from another room.

"It's two in the morning," I said. "I thought you were in New Mexico. Are you all right?"

"I'm hiding."

"From what? Whom?"

"Alanna."

"Oh." I lay back against the pillows, momentarily at a loss for words.

"I'm not kidding, Julian!" He could barely get the words out. I realized that he had been crying. But why? And were they tears of rage? Desire? Regret?

The healer in me took over right away. "Easy, Rick. Take it slow. Deep breaths. Tell me what's happened."

He rubbed the back of his hand against his wet cheeks. "I never asked—didn't expect—didn't want her back," he said. "But now she's here." His eyes met mine and there was an unspoken plea in them. "Damm it, Julian. I still love her. I still want her. I know I should send her away. But I can't. I can't!"

"Are you crazy?" I said, abandoning in that moment any

role but that of brother. "What do you mean, you still want Alanna? It's impossible and you know that."

"Yes, I know." His voice was rough, tortured.

"What did she tell you?"

"Oh, something about believing in my cause. Respecting Better World and wanting to work with it. I told her no, leave me alone. Go away. But then—"

"Maybe you'd better tell me what happened right from the beginning."

He shot me a sharp look. "Well, she stared, I stared, a Tchaikovsky love theme resounded in the room, and we ran, slow-motion, into each other's arms."

"Rick, I can't help you if you don't tell me what really went down."

"Okay, okay. She made a couple of attempts to reach me but I gave all sorts of excuses. I didn't want to see her. But she kept on, persisted, and finally, just to get rid of her, I said yes, come over. We just shook hands, both of us kind of stiff and clumsy. I asked her to come upstairs to take a look at the place—Betty nearly had a fit that I was wasting my time on this visitor when we already had an entire tour-guide system set up. But I gave Alanna the whole tour and she did the usual oohing and aahing. Everything was fine—awkward but okay. Just friends, right? Until she was standing by the window, looking out at the mountains. She was so beautiful, you know? And I started to think about how much I'd loved her. Thinking about all that we'd been through. How often, alone, at night, in the desert, I had thought of her. And then I wanted her. Dammit, Julian. I wanted to hold her, wanted to kiss her so badly I nearly went crazy, and well, you can imagine the rest." He shrugged with actual embarrassment. "It was like she could read my mind. And I'm the one with telepathy, remember? She just turned and held out her arms. It felt as if we'd never been apart for a moment."

"And now what?"

"She wants to close up her house in California and move out to New Mexico to be with me."

My heart sank. "And what do you want?"

My brother shook his head in bewilderment. "I don't

know. One minute I want to run, get away. And the next, I can't wait to get back to her."

I hate tilting at windmills, but I decided to make at least one valiant effort to deflect what seemed to be inevitable, so I said, "Let me give you some brotherly advice, all right? Send Alanna home, as quickly as possible."

He stared at me, speechless. Then he shook his head. "Can't do it. I just can't."

"Rick, I've got a terrible feeling about all this."

"I know, Brother. And you're probably right. But I still can't do it."

"Fine." I was suddenly angry again. Didn't the fool know what he was doing? "Then go ahead and make your own mess, Rick. It's not my problem."

"Hey, come on, Julian. Don't be that way. Don't be angry. You know I trust your judgment. Even when I decide to ignore it." He smiled his crooked smile at me and once again I was reminded of our biological father.

I waved my hands in defeat. "So Alanna'll stay?"

He nodded.

"What about Better World?"

"She says she wants to be a part of it."

"What about her money?"

"Are you suggesting I'm manipulating her for Narlydda's loot?"

"Just probing the possibility."

"Save it for the lab, Julian. Alanna's money is her own."

"Okay, so she moves in here and starts working for B.W. What about the staff? Betty?"

"They'll all love her."

"What about Betty? She seemed pretty jealous of her prerogatives."

"Are you kidding? She'll love Lanna once she gets to know her. It'll be somebody else for her to mother. Somebody who's close to me."

"And Mom? She might not love this quite so much."

"If she comes out to New Mexico and makes trouble I'll send her off on a field trip. Maybe let her open a branch of Better World in Nepal."

"I see you've got it all figured out."

Rick hesitated and a look of helpless confusion, perhaps

even self-loathing, contorted his features. His eyes, when they met mine, were pained, pleading for an answer, for an absolution that I couldn't provide.

"I don't know," he said hoarsely. "Maybe it's not right. I don't want to hurt Alanna again. I always thought I was dangerous to people I really cared about."

I touched his shoulder gently. "Intimacy can sometimes seem dangerous. But that doesn't mean you carry some sort of curse, Rick."

"No?" The last traces of easy confidence fell away from him and I saw just how singular he was, how alone and terribly, terribly different, even from me, his twin. "You know what I am, Julian. Maybe I've been kidding myself, trying to deny it. I thought that if only I help people, try to make things better, use all these strange skills in beneficial ways, maybe I can live among real people." He paused. "I don't want to go back to the desert!"

His desperate cry echoed in the room, tore at my heart. And—God help me—I put my arms around him as he sobbed, hugged him, and gave him my benediction in a choked murmur. "You don't have to go back. You can stay. It's all right, Rick. Alanna will be with you. It'll be all right."

He clung to me, and I to him, two drowning men—Rick, at least, knew it, I think. But I was busy treading water, theorizing and improvising.

Rick squeezed my arm and sat back against the wall. His eyes were clear. He seemed restored, calm and confident once again. "It seems as though everything is falling into place. Thanks, little brother." He grinned rather sheepishly. "Guess I'll let you sleep." And he blurred, became a smoky outline against the wall, and was gone.

Two days after I had this dream, I learned from Joachim Metzger that Alanna had indeed moved in with Rick and I knew that she had won the first round.

7

MONTHS WENT BY, months in which Rick was seen meeting with world leaders, intervening in hunger riots in Brazil, holding a world peace meeting in Beijing, and capturing stray satellites falling from decaying orbits over New Zealand. Everywhere he touched down he left behind the busy seeds of Better World: eager staffers who opened foreign offices and drew excited new members into the fold.

The vidnews called him a man of wonder and "The Marvelous Mutant." The U.S. Government classified him as a resource but also kept an eye on him. Fan clubs sprang up all over the planet for Rick, the Desert Prophet. Every organized religion raised its collective fist against Better World. Rick was discussed, debated, cursed, and acclaimed. Meanwhile, my brother saved thousands of lives and helped cure thousands of people. But, occasionally, he misfired.

Despite Rick's reported last-minute intervention in a bullet train crash in Japan, hundreds of lives were lost. I saw pictures of Rick after that crash—he looked as though he had not slept in weeks, his skin was so gray it was almost putty-colored, and he seemed deeply, deeply dispirited by his failure.

Then there was the tsunami snafu. Rick did manage to divert the tidal wave that had threatened to wash out most of the populated areas of Maui. Unfortunately, he lost control of the wave and it hit part of the Big Island instead. I'm certain that Better World's legal staff put in a lot of overtime dealing with the lawsuits from island developers and survivors of those killed.

For a while that fall we didn't hear a peep out of Better World, until the Mars Colony rescue mission. To give Rick credit, seventy-five percent of the vaccine serum that he teleported *did* arrive intact. Not enough to save every colonist, but as NASA officials pointed out, without Rick's efforts they all would have died. No conventional rescue mission would have reached the red planet in time. Nevertheless, I wondered why the entire shipment had not made it. Was Rick overreaching even his own unique abilities?

Abruptly, I came to feel that I had overreached mine.

The chirping of my screen awakened me at two A.M. Out of bed, quickly, quickly, I snatched up the keypad, my skin prickling with goose bumps in the cold November air.

Who was it? Mother? Father? Agonizing fantasies of compound family tragedies cut through sleep-fog and brought me to full wakefulness. Stop speculating, Doctor, and find out.

"This is Dr. Akimura."

The mechanical voice of the answering service vibrated from the speaker. "Doctor, the emergency room at Mass. General is trying to reach you."

"Put me through to them. Priority channel."

Gwendolyn Smith, a third-year intern in the psychiatric ward, appeared onscreen. Her blond hair was pulled back into a severe bun that emphasized the sharpness of her features. Her gray eyes were bloodshot with exhaustion and overwork. "Dr. Akimura? One of yours was brought in about an hour ago."

"Who?"

"Thomas Wyndham. Overdose."

"What'd he take?"

"What didn't he?"

I pulled on my pants. "How bad?"

"He's holding, but I don't know if I can keep him stabilized. Maybe you've got some better tricks up your sleeve." She wiped sweat from her brow as I shivered in the cold air and buttoned my shirt. "Just between us, Doctor, if I were you, I'd get down here as soon as possible."

"Thanks. I'm on my way."

I flagged down a cab and as we raced toward the hospital I mentally reviewed Wyndham's file. Seventh-generation scion of an old, formerly moneyed Bostonian family with genetic ties to early Massachusetts settlers. He had an obsessive/compulsive personality disorder complicated by bouts of incapacitating depression. Medication and deep relaxation techniques had provided some relief but Wyndham had been quite jittery lately. Not so jittery as to indicate trouble, or so I'd thought.

No personal history of suicidal attempts. Schizophrenic aunt, father's sister. Maternal grandfather who had hanged himself. The usual narcissistically involved mother and remote father. Not a great family lineup but not so terrible either: I'd danced around the rim of many a family snakepit that would have made the Wyndhams look positively benign by comparison.

The E.R. at Mass. General was flooded with cold blue fluorescent light. It played hell with optic nerves accustomed to the yellow-green glare of nighttime Boston, and I blinked heavily before I glanced around the room. The usual post-midnight assortment greeted me: gunshot victim bleeding through his bandages as he lay, unconscious, on the gurney, woman with wildly spiked blue hair fighting against her restraints and biting at unseen assailants, heavyset man with florid complexion clutching his left arm and chest as he moaned, teenage girl in ripped bodysuit, her face scratched, staring with dull eyes at her bandaged hand.

Dr. Smith was bending over a young man whose right arm was partially severed at the shoulder. She looked up and over at me as I approached, nodded toward the adjoining room, and turned back to her patient.

Thomas Wyndham lay upon a cot in the far corner of the ward. His eyes were open but unresponsive to light. He'd mixed a witches' brew of antidepressants and stimulants and injected it. Gwen Smith had attempted to isolate each drug but had finally resorted to massive transfusions in an effort to cleanse Wyndham's blood of all the contaminants. He was still hooked up to the umbilicus of the blood bag.

Good red life spilled into him through the clear tube in his left arm as bad dreams drained out through the other hand. But he remained inert, unresponsive. The brain wasn't dead but he appeared to be in shock.

Much as I dreaded it, I decided to attempt direct telepathic stimulation: it was a technique that mutant healers reserved only for grave situations. This qualified.

I settled in a chair next to the bed and closed my eyes, concentrating. His defenses were few and weakened by the drugs. I penetrated his subconscious easily, navigating the eddies and twists in his mental currents as I looked for reasons and solutions.

Why? Thomas, why did you try to kill yourself? Whywhywhywhy—

My own mindspeech came back at me in mocking echo.

I tried again. *Thomas, it's Dr. Akimura. I want to help you. Please, help me to help you. What happened? Tell me what happened to you since I saw you last Tuesday.*

The subconscious mind is not a direct mechanism. Often, I'd thought of it as a storehouse for consciousness: a spare memory kept here, an odd segue over there, the taste of old pennies and tang of salt air from a seaside vacation twenty years in the past stored in the corner next to a stray erotic image of a woman's leg.

Several renowned psychoanalysts would have us believe that these bits and pieces are maddening clues to the puzzle of self, who one is—and was. Perhaps. But I've often thought they are nothing more than debris: misleading fragments that mean less than we know. Crossed wires and missed connections. The human mind is a notorious packrat: nothing ever gets thrown away. My preference was to stay out of the subconscious, both mine and everybody else's, whenever possible. I didn't care for stumbling around in a dark attic—or basement—looking for the light switch.

Unfortunately, Thomas Wyndham's conscious mind was not available to me. As I plunged down into the strata of his subconscious I hoped to quickly find my way and bring him around.

To facilitate the process I projected a template, framing the subconscious within a physically familiar context. I was in a spacious walk-in closet lined with sleek cupboards and drawers. There were meticulously lettered labels over each of the drawers in alphabetical and chronological order: Christmas 2059, Law School, Lost Socks. I traced them until I came upon the section marked June 2064. Grasped the knob and pulled.

The drawer opened. Within it were files, hundreds of them, one for each day. I flipped through them, coming finally to last Tuesday.

Inside that particular file were Wyndham's memories of our counseling session. Odd to see myself through a patient's eyes: kindly, compassionate Doc Akimura, listening carefully, perhaps even wisely. Thomas thought I was well meaning but perhaps a bit pedantic. He was probably right. I hurried through our session, through his dinner later that evening, and through the next several days. Uneventful. Thomas was coping, managing at his programming job, maintaining a long-term relationship with his lover, nothing out of the ordinary here.

I scanned through Wyndham's memories of the past week: a thrashing, gasping copulation, a game of squash, budget meetings at work, an appointment with his accountant. Nothing. I couldn't find any clues to what had precipitated this crisis. All I gathered was a deepening sense of despair, gloom casting a gray wash over everything. If only I could have checked his endocrine levels and each minute adjustment in his brain chemistry over the past six days. But the mind keeps some secrets to itself.

I glanced around the cabinet of Wyndham's subconsciousness one more time and gratefully disengaged. The closet vanished. I was sitting next to Wyndham's cot in the emergency room annex.

Wyndham's fluid levels were balancing out. A mechnurse came in, green strobes flashing, and turned off the transfusion equipment. I double-checked his chart on the wallscreen: he had been given enough stimulants to jumpstart an elephant. Why wasn't he responding?

As I watched, Wyndham's breathing slowed. His life-support scanners flashed a yellow warning. I saw that his autonomic nervous system was critically depressed. The man was dying. But there was no reason for it. No reason at all. The overdose had been caught in time.

I grabbed him by the shoulders, forcing mental contact again, and caught a powerful sense impression of passivity—even eagerness. I struggled frantically to drag him back. But even as I held him and grappled for his life essence he faded until I was forced to flee his mind or risk being taken with him.

Wyndham died in my arms. Smiling.

The mechnurse returned to the bedside. "Cause of death?" it asked in a grinding mechanical voice.

"Despair." For a moment I tasted old pennies again.

"That designation does not register in my glossary."

"Overdose." I touched the still face once and backed away. There were papers to be filled out, notifications to be made. I didn't leave the hospital until well after five. The sun was just rising and the tube was starting to fill with early commuters. I ignored them, intent on my own private failure. For I knew I had failed Thomas Wyndham. He had wanted to die and nothing I had done had changed that. What's more, I felt instinctively that had my brother been at Wyndham's side, the patient would have survived. Rick didn't look for reasons, consult case histories, nor indulge in monitoring bodily fluid levels. He healed. And he was better at it than I was. Much better.

As penance for Wyndham I accepted a substitute shift at the hospital, midnight to dawn in the emergency room. Halfway through I took a break in the cafeteria, hoping for coffee.

"Dr. A." Victor Sanchez, the day chef, greeted me as he unsealed his sweater. "What are you doing here? It's four in the morning."

"Atoning." I raised my cup of coffee. "Cheers."

"Whatever you say." Sanchez walked deeper into the kitchen, muttering. "Crazy doctors here are as bad as the patients sometimes."

I finished the coffee and swung out of the webseat back to my feet. "Vic, let me ask you something."

"Yeah?" Sanchez peered around the kitchen door. His hands were covered with flour.

"Did you see the latest healing on the vid?"

"That guy from New Mexico? I saw a tape of it."

"What did you think?"

"Think? Doc, he's great stuff. My mother would have loved him. She always believed in faith healing."

"And how about you? What do you think of it?"

Sanchez shrugged. "I don't know. He's like, he's a good man. I can tell that. I'm Catholic—although I haven't been to church since Easter, don't call the pope—and to me this guy seems like something straight out of the Old Testament." He smiled. "A mutant messiah? I don't know. It's okay with me. We need help from somebody, I figure. Listen, I got to get back to the baking, Doc. Come in at six and I'll have fresh bread for you."

I threw my empty cup into the recycler and returned to the E.R. The next couple of hours were quiet—a shame, really. I had almost hoped for a collapsed bridge, a tube derailment, or some other big, messy calamity. Something to distract me from the echo of Sanchez's words in my head: mutant messiah. Mutant messiah. Mutant messiah.

When I got home I took a stiff dose of narcolyne. That silenced just about everything for a brief eight hours.

At three-thirty in the afternoon the phone rang. I surfaced from fathoms of drugged sleep, disoriented and barely functional. Missed the screen switch on my first try, nearly knocked the screen over on my second but at least I managed to turn the damned thing on.

"Hello?" My voice was thick, coated with dust.

"We need to meet." It was Joachim Metzger. "Can you come to Philadelphia? I have to attend to Eastern Mutant Council business and I'll be out here all this week."

"I'm not really up to seeing actual people. Will a screen conference do?"

He frowned at what he must have mistaken for levity on my part. "I don't think so, Julian. Several important people have been in touch with me concerning mutant opposition to Better World. They would like to join forces. What we have to discuss is of the greatest importance, absolutely crucial to our efforts. And I don't trust security fields on screens as much as I do a total room shield."

"I assume these are important nonmutant-type people?"

"Of course."

"Joachim, I don't know how comfortable I really feel about locking arms with nonmutants against my brother."

"What choice do we have? Alanna has managed to sway a considerable number of mutants over to Rick's side. She's been holding meetings on his behalf for any mutants who are interested in Better World and her efforts are beginning to pay off. Frankly, I'm afraid we're losing ground. If we want to maintain and improve our position, then it's crucial for us to join with others."

"Just who are these others?"

"I'm not at liberty to say over the screen."

I was in no mood for his cloak-and-dagger maneuvers. "All right, Metzger. All right. I'll meet you. Just tell me where and when."

THE EASTERN MUTANT COUNCIL convened in an old brownstone building in the heart of Philadelphia. The main auditorium was an overly air-conditioned room decorated in the faded post-modernism of the previous century. Gilded columns rose almost to the ceiling but stopped about two feet short. They were topped by cubes of thick gray metal out of which sprang curving shapes recalling the wrought-iron balustrades and railings of the French Quarter in New Orleans. These, in turn, fused with the ceiling in between pink and gray protrusions that might have once held light fixtures.

The room was dim and seemed almost abandoned, as though it had not been used in months. I began to wonder if I had somehow misunderstood my directions.

"In here," called a jovial voice.

I looked to my left past a row of chairs enshrouded by dust sheets. In the middle of a green-patinaed wall a door stood open. Inside Joachim Metzger sat at the center of a small reception room whose rosy walls and recessed lighting provided an air of intimacy. Half a dozen men and one woman were seated around him and there was a convivial air that gave the tone of a cocktail party to the proceedings. But all conversation halted when I walked in.

"Ah, Dr. Akimura, you made it," Metzger said buoyantly. He looked like a jolly host in his purple Book Keeper robes.

"I almost got lost in the auditorium."

Metzger nodded, not really listening. "This place *is* a wreck. We plan to renovate next year if we can find time for it. Have a seat, Julian. Can I get you anything?"

"Thanks, no. I'm on kind of a tight schedule. Can we get down to business?"

"Of course. This is Rabbi Judith Katz of Temple Beth Shalom and her associate, Rabbi Moshe Davidson of Temple Beth Israel in New York, Ali Haddad of the Center for Moslem Studies, Elder Robert Martin of the San Diego Church of Jesus Christ of the Latter-Day Saints, and Bishop John Patrick Sheehan of Boston."

I remembered some of the names and faces from early vid programs that had first raised the alarm over Better World. Most of these people were notorious conservatives and cranks, odd bedfellows indeed.

"Rick has become completely unpredictable, even erratic," Metzger said. "Yet the media glosses over all of his failures—they're forgotten as quickly as they occur. I don't know how he does it." The Book Keeper looked half admiring and half chagrined.

"Nevertheless," said Bishop Sheehan, "he is dangerous and must be stopped. Cardinal O'Hara of Boston has sent all diocesan bishops strict instructions to warn our congregations against attending a Better World sharing."

"Despite repeated attempts by myself and colleagues to contact him, this Rick refuses to grant us even the courtesy of an open discussion," Rabbi Katz said indignantly. "Several rabbis have received tours of Better World, but when we try to engage him in substantive conversations about his organization's goals and philosophy, he just shrugs us off and ends the visit. We would at least like the opportunity to present our reactions for comparison's sake but he makes that impossible."

Ali Haddad glowered from beneath thick, bushy eyebrows. "I can't understand why the young people flock to him. They ignore the teaching of their elders—it's insufferable. Something must be done."

"But what? Freedom to worship as one pleases is one of the essential liberties provided by a democracy," said Rabbi Davidson. "And we're not even certain that Better

World *is* a religion. Whatever it is, it does seem to be meeting some need."

"Oh, I'm convinced it's a religion," said Bishop Sheehan. "A false religion with a false prophet. A blasphemous and terrible thing that must be stopped before we lose our congregations to it and they compromise themselves completely in the eyes of the Lord."

"Is it a mortal sin to join Better World?" I asked. "How do you know? Where does it say that in the Scriptures?"

Bishop Sheehan glared at me but didn't bother to reply.

"I think we're making too much of this," Rabbi Davidson replied evenly. "These cults often collapse of their own weight. They expand until somebody within the organization gets too ambitious and then the infighting begins and brings the whole thing down, fragmenting it beyond repair. We must be patient."

Rabbi Katz frowned at her colleague, openly disapproving. "Patience? Is that all you can say, Moshe? Meanwhile, our young people slip through our fingers. Once they join Better World they're not interested in anything else. Who knows what this Rick really plans to do with them? Steal their money? Brainwash them?"

Davidson shrugged eloquently. "I agreed to attend this meeting because I thought Judith's views needed balancing. I don't think Rick's group is such a bad thing. A little crazy maybe, but their hearts appear to be in the right place. I think a few of us are overreacting to the threat of seeing our congregations melt away. What's so terrible about love and understanding, about healing? As far as I can tell, too many religions only make it possible for people to face death. But Rick seems to make it possible to face life—"

Metzger cut him off. "I'm sure we all agree that love and understanding are desirable qualities, Rabbi. But we are faced here with a growing dilemma. Better World is expanding its membership across the globe. Should we just sit back and watch Rick take over? Does he represent a threat to our various interests?"

"We simply can't compete," Ali Haddad said.

"Why do we have to compete?" Davidson asked.

"Please watch the screen," Metzger said.

A picture of a large building, some sort of headquarters, appeared, taken from the air. As it came into focus I recognized the main building of Better World.

The camera made lazy circles above the compound, pausing to sweep inward until it caught a lone figure walking along a wooded path. The image tightened to show a close-up of my brother. He was whistling something that sounded like the "Ode to Joy."

Rick raised his head, obviously spotting the vid copter. He squinted, then looked directly into the camera and waved jauntily.

"I was wondering when you'd come for a visit," he said. Either the microphone on the camera had been exceptionally powerful or Rick was boosting his voice for the benefit of the tape. "Hi there, all you guys and gals, mutant and non. I'll bet you're real curious about what I'm doing." He chuckled. "Bet you're pissed off, too, because I won't play your little game. Yeah, I know that you're pissed."

He shrugged but I saw the anger glinting in his eyes and I began to be afraid.

"Well," he said. "Too bad. You all hoard your mutant skills like they're some private fortune for the elite to use, but what good are you really doing anybody? Oh, you give a lot of lip service to the needs of the community and all that, but at heart you're misers, more interested in your precious breeding programs and multitalents than in helping people out. I can hear you all yelling in your Mutant Council chambers." For a moment Rick pitched his voice high, mimicking some peckish old lady. " 'He's dangerous. Public opinion won't tolerate him. Terrible, terrible.' Well, bullshit. If you're so concerned about the public, why aren't you up here helping me help them? As for public opinion, hell, they've already voted. This group is full of nonmutants—I must be doing something they like. So if you're not going to help, buzz off and leave me alone." He made an obscene gesture at the camera. A moment later the tape ended.

The room was silent.

I began to laugh. I couldn't help myself: the image of my brother giving the finger to the Book Keeper—and by extension, the entire Mutant Council—struck me as blackly hilarious. Our father would have been proud of him.

"I don't see anything funny here," said Metzger coldly. "We are trying to decide upon the degree of threat this man poses to us. You can see for yourselves his hostility and lack of desire to cooperate with us. Obviously we must watch him closely. If he cannot or will not cooperate with us, then we must have him restrained, by whatever means necessary."

Ali Haddad nodded eagerly. "Agreed."

"I'm getting tired of asking him to talk to us," Rabbi Katz said.

"I think the time to ask is past," said Bishop Sheehan.

As they spoke, a terrible image came to my mind of Rick, drugged and vacant, penned in a cell lined with mental dampers. I looked around the room. These people were all powerful representatives of strong interest groups. In a united effort, they might be able to summon resources that would overwhelm even Rick.

"No," I said aloud, directing my protest to Metzger. "You can't let them do that!"

The Book Keeper gave me a sympathetic, almost pitying glance. "Relax, Dr. Akimura. Not only do we not advocate violence, we also still believe that Rick can be reasoned with. But we need your help."

"What do you propose?" I asked.

Metzger turned to me. "Well, for one thing, we must increase your exposure, Julian. Perhaps provide weekly commentary to counterbalance all the good press Better World gets."

"I don't see how that will help," I said. "Besides, I don't have time to write and present a weekly commentary. I already have a full-time job—"

"Oh, we'll provide your scripts."

I didn't like that at all. "Now wait just a minute. I'm not an actor."

"Do you want to help us or not?" Bishop Sheehan said. "If not, we can find someone else."

"We understand your hesitation," said Ali Haddad. "After all, you *are* related to this Desert Prophet, are you not?"

I was thunderstruck by Metzger's betrayal, but he didn't

even look uncomfortable, merely nodded in concert with the others. He probably saw this as no more than an unfortunate political necessity. Expedient, or some other such adjective that politicians use to forgive their personal atrocities.

"Think how much more effective you could be," said Judith Katz, and she recited an imaginary headline: " 'Desert Prophet's Brother Denounces Better World As A Fraud.' "

"No. Absolutely not. I refuse to cooperate."

"Oh, we wouldn't need your cooperation in order to notify the vidnews of your relationship to Rick," said Bishop Sheehan.

"This is blackmail."

Ali Haddad stared at me angrily and said, "I thought you were with us on this issue."

"Yes, but not at the expense of my family."

"If you don't work with us, we may be forced to take stronger measures," Metzger said.

"What are you talking about?" I said.

Metzger didn't answer me. Instead, he looked down and began to shuffle papers on his desk. I threw all caution aside and ventured a quick mind probe. I sensed real desperation and rage in him, rage hot enough to kill. He feared that Rick's ascendance would somehow affect his own power and political future. Despite all his words to the contrary, he had murder on his mind, pure and simple. Rick's murder.

I could see the intent clearly but apparently Metzger hadn't determined the means yet. He seemed to be alone in his assassination plan, at least for the time being, but I had no doubt that even acting solo, he could arrange it. As I began to probe further he sensed my intrusion and, with a wordless indictment, brought up his mental shields.

Metzger's gaze was ice-cold. "I beg your pardon, Doctor!"

"You'll never get away with it."

"Say one word to your brother or anyone else about this and we'll expose you and give every vidnews service in the world your parents' address." Obviously, Metzger thought he had me. Well, we would see about that.

"Leave my parents out of this," I said. "Or I'll denounce you and your bloody ideas to the Mutant Councils. They'll be only too happy to impeach you."

"No one would believe you."

"Really? Shall we find out? I'm willing to submit to a mind probe by the Council if that's what it takes to stop you."

We glared, locked together in enmity as the others, confused and curious, began to mutter. Metzger broke the stalemate.

"I see we can no longer work together, Dr. Akimura. I'm very sorry."

Without a word, I stood, turned on my heel, and strode out of the room. I might disagree with my brother and his ridiculous private cult but never would I side with enemies who wanted to harm him. Never, never, never.

8

I TRIED TO KEEP an eye on Metzger's movements—and even went so far as to suggest to my parents that they invest in some private security systems—but I was distracted by a call from Lindy Rotstein, head of Psychiatry at Mass. General.

She was a small, round, ebullient woman of about fifty with graying hair and hazel eyes. Usually she was bursting with high spirits and amusing barbed comments. But not today.

"Julian," she said. "Brace yourself. I've got an enormous favor to ask."

"For you, Lindy, anything."

"You may regret those words, my dear. I want you to go to Brazil."

"What?" I stopped smiling and stared at her, aghast.

"I've been asked to put together a special task force for the International Security Agency—to look into the development of a Better World cult in South America. I'd like you to serve on the Brazilian leg of the tour."

"Me? Why not you? You're the specialist in the psychology of large groups."

"To be honest, I'd love to go, but I'm afraid you're better qualified."

"How so?"

"You know more about this Better World organization. You're nationally identified as a critic of it. An expert."

"Doesn't that mean I would be too biased in my observations? Tainted?"

"I think they want at least one cold, critical set of eyes on this job." She paused. "It won't hurt that those eyes are golden, either."

"So I'm to be the sacrificial mutant and fill their quota?"

"Looks that way."

"What about my patients? Consultations? I'm in the middle of research for two court cases—"

"Don't worry, we'll cover for you."

"Lindy, no. It's out of the question. I simply can't do it."

She nailed me with her hazel gaze. "Julian, you've got to. I simply can't afford to have the plug pulled on our research funding here, and if we don't cooperate, well, let's just say it's been known to happen to other departments that don't cooperate with the government."

"Shit."

"My sentiments, exactly. But stop pouting, Julian. After all, this isn't the first time you've been tapped to serve on a special research project: those golden eyes of yours make you a natural candidate. So cheer up. I can think of worse places to go than Rio—I've been to all of them. And pack for summer. It starts to get warm down there in November."

Despite Lindy's resolve, I stubbornly tried to beg off, citing my numerous patients and consultations. I was told, several times, by Lindy, and then by Morton T. Arpel, chief of staff at Mass. General, that I was considered uniquely qualified for this assignment—my familiarity with the Better World issue would prove invaluable. Other doctors would take my caseload and consultations. The I.S.A. needed my help. Case closed.

And so I went to Rio de Janeiro.

I had been there before on holiday and knew it well. Rio is a city of thunderous contrasts: the very beautiful and the very hideous. Wealth and squalor, pleasure and pain. Rio will lull you, lure you, and in the morning you will awaken chastened and changed.

It had that familiar unfamiliar appearance of most third-world cities—Paris after the holocaust. In cities like Rio there was usually a downtown section of nineteenth-century buildings whose graceful iron balconies were spotted red with rust and through whose windows faded gray curtains blew like so many pale tongues. Gaudy billboards lined the roads that led into town. Half-finished concrete skeletons of buildings dominated weed-filled empty lots on the outskirts of the city. Often, these derelict structures were inhabited by squatters whose strings of laundry were the only touch of color in the area. A fine layer of dust always covered everything. The air was filled with a choking mixture of car exhaust, animal dung, and human effluvia.

Only the few hours before dawn yielded any respite from the daily cacophony: the percussion of traffic and unmuffled motorbikes, the honk and wheeze of horns, the bleat of goats being herded through the streets, the overamplified throb of a radio playing the popular music of the moment, the cries of children and their keepers. Strange faces, everywhere. Strangers to whom I was, at best, an economic opportunity and, at worst, a voyeur.

Nevertheless, I felt the usual arrival euphoria: delighted to be off the shuttle and in the taxi, convinced of the driver's kindness, charmed by the unfamiliar landscape, amused even by the chaotic driving habits of those on the road. I knew that within half an hour my amusement would sour and fade, and as my stay lengthened I would eventually long for the hyper-cleanliness and homogenized uniformity of American architecture, the beloved, hateful sameness of it all, and the ease—quickly mistaken for pleasure—of hearing English all around me. The daily struggle, despite my implant, to communicate in a strange tongue left me with a constant ache down the middle of my back, as though every inch of me were straining to listen and comprehend.

Eventually, out of self-defense if nothing else, I would come to see this foreign landscape as normal, even appropriate, and would cease to notice its strangeness. Indeed, home would come to appear foreign by comparison. Therefore I always savored my first day or two in a foreign place before the strangeness wore off. I knew that the mind refused to perceive something as continuously, permanently alien and soon, too soon, began its relentless efforts to assimilate and tame.

Brazil was at its most seductive in what I persisted in thinking of as the winter months: their topsy-turvy summer that dazed a November traveler with its skies the color of turquoise, honeyed sunshine, white crescent beaches, and nonstop tropical drumbeat.

There was always a party, a feast for the senses, on the beach at Copacabana: dark oiled skin and swaying hips, the air scented with perfume and coffee, the sound of samba whispering on the breeze. And there was usually famine to be found only a half mile inland. Closer, if you counted the beggars: the ragged families lying numbly, half-conscious, on unraveling blankets placed over the black and white mosaic pavement. They lay there, quietly dying in the warm winter sunlight as bronzed Cariocas stepped over and around them on their way to business, dinner, love, their own private lives. Ancient Rome, at the end, could not have been much unlike Rio in the late twenty-first century.

Our little contingent of observers numbered five: Paula Tremaine, expert psychosociologist; Yuri Kryuchkov, master of theological philosophy; Margot Fremont-Chai, anthropologist; Katarina Otulji, specialist in cults; and yours truly, Better World connoisseur and mutant point man.

I had met Paula Tremaine years before and had, in fact, enjoyed a brief dalliance with her during an international symposium on alternative techniques for healing. She was a tall, robust woman with auburn hair, blue-green eyes, and an infectious laugh. She greeted me warmly and I was glad to see her.

Yuri Kryuchkov was the very picture of the cloistered Russian academician: dark-eyed, bushy-browed, with a fierce, frowning countenance that kept the rest of us at bay. He let us know right away that he didn't like this Better World, not at all, and saw its spread as a sign of the continued erosion of what passed for civilization in the benighted twenty-first century.

Margot Fremont-Chai I knew of only through her many publications on cultural relativism. She was a dignified woman of about sixty with straight, shining white hair, an unlined face, and cold gray eyes that seemed to take in everything around her and classify it for later use.

Katarina Otulji had the delicate build of a ballet dancer. She was tiny, with intricately coiled golden braids forming a knot atop her head and smooth, coffee-colored skin. She smiled a great deal but spoke little.

As soon as we were settled in at the beachfront Parc Imperium Hotel in Copacabana, our group convened to share notes and suggestions.

"Cults usually penetrate a society slowly," Katarina Otulji observed. "Then, due to some apocalyptic event, they suddenly gain momentum and new converts."

"That certainly fits with what my contacts have told me," said Margot Fremont-Chai. "Apparently, Better World first came to Rio early this year. The Desert Prophet, Rick, appeared here suddenly and performed one of his famous rescues, teleporting three busloads of schoolchildren off a crumbling arm of the mountain road near Corcovado. Then he vanished. But some American tourists recognized him and told the local media about him. The Better World cult began to take root from that moment."

"What is your proof of this?" Yuri Kryuchkov rumbled.

"A vidtape."

Kryuchkov shook his head sadly. "First world countries export their worst and keep their best for themselves."

Paula Tremaine met my glance and rolled her eyes slightly to show her amusement. "Let's not make generalizations too soon, Yuri. We're here to observe, not to judge."

"It will be the same thing in the end."

"Maybe so. But that remains to be seen."

WE WERE KEPT QUITE BUSY: the signs of Better World were everywhere. My brother had ascended to the pantheon of the macumba saints with a boost from a shrewd street merchant. After the school bus rescue, the shopkeeper had designed a batch of idols to look like Rick. These had sold quickly and the crowd had become furious at the man's limited inventory. The police had to be called.

Now Rick was as firmly ensconced in each macumba ritual as Lemanja, goddess of the waters. He had taken his place among the many deities worshiped by the superstitious Cariocas, and the merchant had become a very rich man.

In banks, on the desks of receptionists, in souvenir stands, and on every bar in Leblon, Copacabana, and Ipanema, ceramic effigies of my brother grinned and nodded, casting their blessings. It was startling at first, then almost comical. I began to wonder whether I should purchase one and send it to my mother, but decided against it. I was certain that Dad would find the statuette funny but I wasn't sure that Mom would see the joke.

I quickly came to see that Better World was no joke to the poor of Rio—in fact, it was an absolute blessing, far from the cult of personality it seemed to have become in the States. In Rio I saw the tenets of B.W. at work in the streets, in the miserable hovels and alleys that made up the *favelas* where volunteers knelt in the mud to tend the sick, fed the hollow-faced hungry children, and tried to repair tattered shacks and rusty, outdated vehicles. Everything I saw made my respect for B.W.—and Rick—grow. Regardless of why he had started the organization, it was doing some good right here, right now. How could I argue with that? How could anyone?

We watched, we asked questions, and we listened. We took notes, made vid recordings, debated the cultural implications of Better World's dissemination, and then redebated them.

One night, after a particularly heated discussion following dinner, I headed for the pool on the roof of the hotel. The hour was late and the pool was deserted. Chlorine-scented mist rose in undulating streams, illuminated by the golden pool lights.

I slipped into the deliciously cool water with a sigh of relief. But it took several laps to work off my irritation at Kryuchkov's dour imprecations, Fremont-Chai's smug assumptions, and Otulji's maddening passivity.

A splash and sudden convulsion of the blue-green water announced that I had company. A dark shape moved toward me underwater, stroking powerfully. Then Paula Tremaine broke through the surface, gasping for air, sleek as a seal.

"Can you believe that Yuri?" she said. "He's like some mad monk. And Margot—I'm ready to wrap Katarina Otulji around her neck and tie her in a bow, if only it will shut her up. Who puts these groups together, anyway?"

"If you're planning to lodge a formal complaint, get in line," I said. "But we've been shanghaied by the ISA, remember?"

"Gods, it'll take years to have anything adjudicated." She sighed theatrically. "Never mind."

"Paula," I said. "Tell me truthfully. What do you think—I mean, *really* think—about Better World?"

She smiled wistfully. "I'm almost rooting for them, to tell you the truth. Of all the cults I've seen in recent years, it seems the most beneficial, the most innocent."

"I wish I shared your view."

"And I wish I could see just where the hidden catch in it is, Julian. You certainly seem to know. But all I see is a group of people uniting in ecstatic communion, providing support groups and services where none formerly existed. What's so terrible about that?"

"They have a leader they worship as though he were a god."

"Wait long enough and, most likely, he'll become one. So what?" Her eyes twinkled but her tone was serious. "You're mighty grim about this, Dr. Akimura. Something about Better World touches you right where you live."

You should only know, I thought. But I shrugged instead. "What the hell, enough business. Maybe I'll never understand cults at all."

"Spoken like a true man of science. Come on, I'll race you to the deep end."

For a time we swam, side by side, in companionable silence. Then Paula triggered the null g-field and we floated easily, staring up at the stars.

"I don't know what it is about this place," she said. "I've been in a monogamous relationship for two years now. But here, alone with you, well, I'm sort of tempted to relive the past." She moved closer until she was pressed against me, thighs against mine. I felt a tightening in my groin, and a growing excitement as she rubbed up against me.

"Just like old times," I said, and kissed her deeply. Her

swimsuit was a triangle of netting and it came off with a gentle tug. Mine offered little resistance.

We moved deeper into the water and cut the g-field. I slipped my hands between her legs, brought her up and over me and the two of us were locked together in that blue-green world, floating dreamily as we moved toward blissful consummation. Afterward, we clung together, gasping for breath, listening to the drumming of our pulsebeats as they slowed.

"It's so good with you," she whispered.

"That's because we only see each other every five years."

"You've gotten cynical, Julian."

"Just realistic." I stroked her cheek. "But maybe we should give it a try—"

She pulled back, only half joking now. "You and me? Oh, Julian, not now. Maybe we could have, years ago. But no. You're a cherished friend, and I'm glad we came together again. But let's just stay friends."

I was a bit hurt, and a bit relieved. She gave me a cool, moist kiss and said good night. I did not suggest that we schedule a reengagement.

ALTHOUGH BOTH PAULA and Katarina Otulji had invited me to accompany them on their investigative rounds, I begged off, eager to be alone and free to go and observe where I chose.

It was the decade of hunger riots and each day there were demonstrations by the poor. They marched, a ragged, desperate, defiant mob, to the outskirts of the moneyed districts where the wealthy Cariocas hid in tall, white buildings guarded by dogs and men with guns. The police used tasers, guns, and clubs to beat back the crowds. Each day, people died in the crush, in the screaming dusty pandemonium.

"Estamos com fome!" they cried in hoarse, exhausted voices.

"Estamos doente!"

"Socorro!"

"Esta fudido."

"Dinheiro! Onde fica o dinheiro!"

Their cries of hunger, of illness and misery, were appalling. I began to despise my role as observer and eavesdropper and nearly turned away. Then I saw them. Clean, neatly dressed people moved slowly through the crowd speaking in low, reassuring voices, laying on hands in an attempt to calm the rioters. Somehow I knew that these were Better World volunteers, vainly attempting to stop the bloodshed. They were risking their own lives while trying to save others. They were trying to help in the only way they knew how.

I held my breath, wishing that my brother were there to help the miserable poor. Then I caught myself. Oh ho, I thought. Hold on, now. Was I starting to pray to St. Rick? Would Lemanja be far behind?

Despite the attempts of the Better World volunteers, the mob would not be turned away. A woman began screaming in a high, ragged voice, the crowd surged forward, and then the police moved in swinging their batons.

After each riot came the street sweepers and the medics, counting corpses. For the many consumed by hunger and hysteria, the greatest mercy seemed to be a quick death. Modern medicine has an arsenal of drugs to deal with pain but none yet cured starvation and poverty.

Hope was a different matter, and I discovered that it could be a potent drug in its way, despite the contending forces of disease, malnutrition, and political corruption. Oddly enough, my brother was responsible for teaching me that lesson. My brother and Star Cecilia Nicolau.

I saw her for the first time at an evening gathering in Botafogo. It was at an outdoor amusement park and bar complex bordered by leafy green trees and lofty palms. She was dressed in a flowing white gown that somehow emphasized the slim lines of her body and her golden tan. Oblivious to the people and street noises around her she was leading a group of perhaps thirty-five people through an elaborate ritual prayer that seemed to consist of an elaborate circle dance followed by a group embrace.

The bodies swirled in and out, in and out, feet beating a complicated rhythm as hips gyrated, heads nodded, faster and faster. They all moved in perfect syncopation, all possessed by the same silent beat that they alone seemed to hear. I found my toe tapping to their movement, to the thump of their feet against the bare, compacted soil.

I couldn't take my eyes from the woman in white: while in frenzied motion she managed to give a graceful cast to everything she did. Twirling, laughing, jumping around the circle, she was filled with infectious joy. If she had looked my way I would have joined her in a moment.

This group seemed to be a macumba–inspired crew that had now given over its worship and rituals to "Saint Rick" of the Better World, or Mundo Melhor, as it was called here. Their songs told of his goodness and exalted his righteousness. As I watched the dancers whirl, their elegant leader began to chant an invocation in a resonant alto voice, and the Portuguese implant I had received whispered to me that she was praising Rick's name and asking that the god Exu protect him and honor him.

The ritual ended with a great round of clapping and laughter. Then the celebrants slipped off through the darkness. The woman in white vanished into a sleek pavilion behind the bar and I followed her.

I knocked but there was no answer. Knocked again and then, growing impatient, tried the lockpad. The door was open and it swung easily on greased hinges. I stepped inside, into shadow, and became aware of unusual sounds.

They were intimate, moist, unmistakable. A woman was moaning softly, almost an animal purr that, as I listened, climbed toward a roaring, gasping climax.

I started to back out of there but in the darkness became disoriented and stumbled over something that emitted a great metallic screech as I kicked it.

The sounds of lovemaking stopped abruptly.

"*Porra!*" a woman said crossly. "*Me deixa em paz.*"

My implant cut in immediately, translating: "Dammit! Leave me in peace."

It was unmistakably the voice of the priestess who had led the celebration outside. But she didn't sound very holy now.

"*Disculpa,*" I said, struggling to form the Portuguese syllables properly. "*Voce fala ingles?*"

"Yes, yes, of course I speak English." Now she sounded impatient but curious, too. "I went to school in the United

States because my parents had no faith in Brazilian academies."

And then she stood there, naked and golden, holding a lamp by a silver chain.

"Who are you?" she demanded.

"Julian Akimura."

"American, yes? My name is Star Nicolau, Julian Akimura." She stepped into a pair of jeans, zipped them up, and shrugged into a thin white shirt. "What do you want?"

That was many years and many miles ago. I stood across the room from Star that night as the light snapped and popped in her lantern, and I watched her dress and felt the first faint stirring of what soon would become uncontrollable passion. But I didn't know it then and I assumed my discomfort was due to the singular way my arrival had interrupted her lovemaking.

"I'm studying Better World," I said wanly.

"Not a CIA snoop?" She peered at me, half-amused, half-angry. "No, no I don't think so. Your face is too kind. You were one of those tourists watching us, weren't you? Yes, I think you were the one, the only one, who looked eager to join the dance."

"So you did see me." I smiled.

She gave me a sly, catlike glance that seemed to take my full measure and find me worthy. "Oh, yes, of course."

"Tell me, how do you know of Better World?"

"When I was in the States last year I began to hear about this group and I was fascinated. I went out to New Mexico and spent some time at Better World. But I had to return here because my mother was not well. I brought the Better World spirit back home with me." She slid on a pair of tall brown leather boots with pointed heels and sealed them just below her knees.

A tall figure loomed suddenly, one of the other celebrants. His dark hair was wild and he looked as though he had just thrown on his shirt and pants. Eyes cast downward, he nodded at me as he strode past, but he and Star exchanged a cryptic look before he bolted out the door.

She seemed quite unperturbed and continued to cheerfully interrogate me: How long had I been in Rio? Did I like it? What had I seen? Where had I eaten? Did I know about Better World? Had I ever met Rick? And Alanna?

Her voice sharpened over that name and I began to suspect that Star Nicolau had a bit more than mere spiritual interest in my brother.

"Yes," I said. "I'm quite well acquainted with Better World and with Rick. In fact, he's my twin brother."

I stopped, horrified. What had I done? Whatever could have possessed me to reveal my intimate relationship with Rick to this attractive stranger? Was I hoping to draw her closer, to use my brother as a bridge between us?

As I stood there, mute and red-faced over my blunder, Star moved closer to me and took my hand.

"I don't think you wanted to tell me that, did you?" Her smile was both sympathetic and smug. "Don't worry—I won't tell anyone. But what are you doing here?"

Briefly, I explained the mission of the task force.

"So," she said. "You've come to watch us and report back to your brother's enemies."

"It's not quite like that—"

"No? Then explain it to me. You are his brother," she said. "Yet you stand against him and Better World."

"Well, yes."

"That would never happen in Brazil," she said. "If one brother were venerated as your Rick is, and a different brother chose to turn against him, the family would never forgive the traitor. They might even stone him to death."

Her glance was sly and I wasn't sure if she was joking.

"So tell me," she said cozily. "I would like to know more about Alanna. Why she is so close to Rick."

"Alanna is our—cousin," I said, a little clumsily. Something warned me not to tell Star the total truth. Not yet, anyway.

"Cousin?" Star squinted at the lantern and shook it: the flame within flared, then died back. "You mutants must have huge families, don't you?"

"It's a complicated story. A complicated family."

"I'm sure." Star waited, but I had stalemated her. She would get no more information out of me. She stared, frowned, stared some more. Finally, she began to pace the room. Her boot heels were loud against the floor.

My treacherous imagination substituted her naked body for the jeans and work shirt she wore now. The more I tried to forget what I'd seen the more I wanted to touch her, to lick and tease those small, dark nipples, to have those strong legs wrapped around me, to penetrate and possess this woman completely.

She smiled playfully. "Well, Julian, why don't you tell me this complicated story?" She crossed her arms and leaned back against the doorway as though she intended to block any retreat I might attempt.

I concentrated on the triangle of golden flesh revealed at the neck of her blouse and thanked the assembled deities that she hadn't yet tried to seduce the information out of me: I never would have had a chance of resisting. Instead, I crossed my arms, mirroring her actions. It's an old psychological ploy, intended to indicate commonality. A useful tool when what you want to do is say no.

"Nothing I can tell you," I said casually. "It's really Rick's story, anyway."

"A twin never has his own singular story," Star said. "You know that." She sighed deeply. "I was drawn to your brother as soon as I saw him."

Jealousy pricked me. "That's Rick. He's like a magnet."

"And which pole is your cousin Alanna? Positive? Negative?"

My voice was level, but inwardly I was seething wildly with desire and confusion. I had to get away from this woman before I did something else foolish. After all, I was no lustful boy, inexperienced and naive. But I didn't trust myself alone with Star.

"Let's go back to your hotel for a drink," Star said. "I'll drive, unless you can teleport us there."

"You're talking to the wrong brother."

Her smile stirred me mercilessly. "Am I?" Her dark eyes flickered over me. "I'm not so sure." Swinging her keys, she led me out the door and we squeezed into the tiny cab of her skimmer truck. All during that long, long ride through the streets of Rio I stared out the window at the passing street lamps and concentrated on the white-hot pressure of her leg against mine.

When we arrived at the Parc Imperium Hotel, everything was quiet and the bar was closed. I was astonished to see that it was four in the morning. The desk clerk yawned as he handed me my room key. I turned to Star, reluctant to let her go. "We could have a drink in my room—"

"No, I think not. It's late." She bussed me quickly on both cheeks. "Good night and good morning, Julian Akimura. I will see you again."

"But wait," I said desperately. "How will I find you?"

"I'll find you." She winked and danced away, out of reach, out of sight.

"Damn." I was confused and disgusted. Things had become astonishingly messy for me in no time at all. What did I really feel for Star? Was it lust fueled by fraternal competition? No answers. No clues. The lobby was empty. The elevator flung me upstairs where my lonely room awaited.

THE DAYS THAT FOLLOWED WERE HOT, humid, filled with dizzying images of a dozen ritual celebrations and cult activities. Better World had infiltrated Rio, all right. At least, some of it had, as Mundo Melhor, and had immediately been adapted to suit the primal pulse of the macumba drums.

November turned into December, but although I searched I did not catch even a teasing glimpse of Star again. The drumbeats of samba teams began to echo in the streets near the beaches and my time in Brazil was almost over.

On December second I was invited to attend a small celebration of Mundo Melhor at a fine home in the moneyed suburb of Laranjeiras. I was surprised to see that Better World had been embraced by the notoriously selfish upper echelons of Brazilian society. Apparently where macumba went, Saint Rick and his helpers followed close behind, even into the houses of the rich.

The party began at sundown as the *pandeiros* announced their arrival with a wild eruption of drumming in the garden. The guests hurried out onto the lawn, heads nodding in time, feet tapping. Over here a stately matron was already swirling, eyes closed, her peacock-blue gown's hem whispering around her ankles, deeply immersed in the mysteries.

The hostess, a slender, pale-skinned woman with thin

red hair and huge green eyes, was next, and then the daughter of the house, no more than fourteen but haughty and with a certain precocious sensuality, joined the dance, swaying her slender arms as though she were floating in the ocean.

Soon all the guests were nodding and swaying, chanting exultant phrases, men and women twirling around one another in the humid night until they seemed to blur into one another.

Although I had sworn to maintain an objective distance I found myself caught up in the beat, feeling its pulse vibrate up through the soles of my feet and along my backbone until I could control myself no longer and I was out there on the lawn, nodding, shaking, and capering like the rest of the celebrants.

As the frenzy built I could make out odd bits of chants that translated into "Rick hear us" and "Rick protect us." I began to chant along. Somehow, it seemed reasonable, even desirable, to be praying to my brother in fragmented Portuguese, nonsense syllables, and even some English. Even as I did so, the quiet part of me that always sits back and watches took notes for later review.

I was drenched in sweat, gasping for air, and yet I couldn't stop. A curious yet familiar sensation crept over me—it felt like the preliminary moments of trance that occur in a mutant group sharing. The air itself seemed to shimmer and I felt a transcendent connection to all of the people there. We were linked, each of us, by our common humanity. We were one. We were responsible for each other, rich and poor, humble and great. I knew it, knew and believed it, to the bottom of my soul.

And then I saw Star. I hadn't noticed her in the crowd before, but there she was, serenely swaying not two steps away from me. As I stared at her, she looked up, met my gaze, and smiled.

"*Now* you understand," she said. "Now you are one of us, Julian. You can deny your brother no longer."

The drums urged me toward her. Their steady rhythm seemed to pulse in time with my blood: boom boom ba, boom boom ba.

The primal beat broke through my last reserves of caution, scattered my deepest doubts. Boldly, I danced around Star, defining my territory, hips thrusting, pelvis shaking. We were surrounded by people and yet we might have been completely alone, dancing together. The crowd moved back and away from us, or perhaps we moved away from them. Regardless, all I know is that finally we were alone in a room with a door that locked.

I turned to face her and Star held her arms out to me eagerly. Her lips were soft, her tongue maddening, and I pulled her down to the warm, welcoming cushions of the wallseat.

We came up for air. And submerged again. I yanked off her clothing with furious impatience. Her skin was smooth and warm, a delight to kiss. I spent a long, luxurious time on her breasts, sucking and licking her nipples until she writhed beneath me, moaning. But who was ravishing whom? She had her hands under my shirt, in my pants, teasing and electrifying me.

I floated happily, drowning under Star's sweet weight. After the third time I lost count of our couplings. Somehow, at some time that evening we found our way back to my hotel room, ordered some food from room service, and, after eating, showered together. Then we spent what was left of the night reviewing all that we had learned about each other. Star and I slept happily in each other's arms until late afternoon.

So Star came to me. I don't think I have ever been as happy.

She asked me if I wanted to accompany her to various Mundo Melhor group rites and I agreed eagerly.

Each meeting was a revelation of sorts. I began to see that Better World, in any guise, had a unique power to draw people together. But I quickly realized that while the techniques of Better World had been adapted to the desperate needs of the Cariocas, the Mundo Melhor meetings were more of an excuse for group dances than an attempt to heal each celebrant of their psychic wounds.

At least, I thought so until I took part in one of their ceremonies.

We gathered in a small house in Botafogos. It was a select group of celebrants, perhaps twenty-five in number.

The evening began as it usually did, with the drumming of the *pandeiros* and the chanting of the celebrants. I stood in the back of the living room, watching the Brazilians sway to the beat, nodding my head, sweating, waiting to be caught up by the moment.

"Join hands," Star said.

I felt a strange electric jolt as my hands were seized—I could swear that every hair on my body stood straight up in shock. I couldn't move, couldn't breathe.

Then the buzzing, burning pain and paralysis ended and I was in close, loving communion with Star. I could feel her essence, read her every thought. We were floating together, the two of us, in loving, intimate harmony. The purity of her intention, the dedication of her life to this cause was sweet and intense. She was beautiful within, consumed by the need to help her people. I wanted to tell her that I loved her and would always be by her side.

But before I could do so, a thousand foreign thoughts crowded into my brain, humming and buzzing like a swarm of insects as they filled the space between Star and me, forcing us apart. My language implant struggled with the torrent of Portuguese and for a moment I felt my legs weaken as though I would sink to my knees under the burden of all these noisy minds.

What was happening here? Why had my telepathic barriers been breached? Always, before this, I had been able to screen out unwanted mental contact. Why had my defenses and training suddenly failed?

The celebrants' thoughts reverberated inside my head. I was a human echo chamber, amplifying and distorting the mental signals of all the others in the room. It was dizzying, frightening, and exhilarating all at the same time.

Any moment I expected the entire room to collapse around me, but instead of faltering, the celebration seemed to shift into a higher gear, the dancers moving faster, chanting louder. But I was weakening, growing faint, feeling myself being led around the circle, leaning on people next to me for support. My awareness spiraled inward, inward, and I stumbled through a dark, humid place in which jungle birds chattered, men shouted, and women shrieked.

Somewhere in the distance a soprano practiced scales as her accompanist attacked a mechpiano keyboard.

Something with wings, unseen, brushed the top of my head. I ducked, stared, but saw nothing. Behind me, the growling, screeching chorus continued, growing louder with each moment. And a deep, familiar male voice was patiently, hypnotically droning a single thought over and over in Portuguese.

Meu nome e Juliano, Meu nome e Juliano, Meu nome—

The thing with wings swooped down again and knocked me spinning, end over end, and then I knew nothing, nothing at all.

When I came to, I was lying on my back on an old-fashioned, lumpy mattress in a dark room. I could hear people talking outside the door in a low undifferentiated hum, but I couldn't make out what they were saying.

The door opened and Star came in carrying a lantern. Her eyes were glistening and she looked rapturously happy.

"What did you do, *querido*?" she said. "How did you do it?"

"I'm not sure I know what you're talking about."

She sat down next to me and took my hands in hers. "Oh, this was wonderful, the best time of all. A breakthrough. Everybody in the circle felt it, so connected, so enlightened. You are one of the gifted, like your brother. You've brought us his light."

"No, Star, it's not that way, not that way at all." I tried to explain, to tell her that somehow, through some sort of fluke, I had temporarily become a kind of telepathic conduit. There was nothing mystical about it. I was not a seer nor a holy man. But she would have none of it.

"Your coming here is a sign, a gift. Oh, Julian, I'm so happy!" She threw her arms around me, kissing me passionately. And in between each kiss she told me, first in Portuguese and then, again, in English, how much good we would do together.

With Star's help I got to my feet and slowly made my way into the next room. A hush fell over the group as I entered, and then a huge cheer went up: "*Quibungo!*" The *pandeiros* began their drumming. People were hugging me, kissing me, draping flowers over my arms and shoulders. The celebration had been a sign, a signal from Rick that through me he was listening to them.

I resigned from the U.N. committee the next day.

"Don't be ridiculous," Paula said. "You're overreacting."

Margot Fremont-Chai leaned toward me. "Don't you see what a valuable observer you would make? You have the access to these rituals that is denied the rest of us. It's crucial that you remain."

"Wouldn't you say I'm a compromised witness?" I said. "To put it mildly?"

Yuri Kryuchkov let out a huge, bearlike roar that was, apparently, laughter. "But you have been compromised from the beginning, Dr. Akimura. First by your media connections and again by your knowledge of Better World. Now you can tell us about the transformation of this cult from the inside out. You must stay."

Only Katarina Otulji seemed to see my point. "He's right," she said sadly. "If he remains on the committee, he will contaminate our observations." She shook her head. "And if he continues to work with the cult on his own, he will contaminate its development here. Oh, this is terrible. Just terrible."

Well, that set me back a bit. I hadn't stopped to consider how I might alter the evolution of Mundo Melhor if I stayed here. But how could I leave? The people seemed to want my help. And I was in love with Star.

Suddenly I felt as though my life were some eerie parallel to my brother's. It was easy now to see how he had been pulled into Better World, and why he had stayed. The expressions of the celebrants after each ritual was enough to bring me back again and again. How much more potent, more basic an experience it must have been for poor, lonely, desperate Rick. I emphasized with him even as I celebrated his righteousness.

In that moment I knew that I could no longer serve as a critic of Better World. Nor would I spy upon its development in other countries. I wanted to leave my brother in peace. And to give him my blessing as well. After all, he was helping people. If what I had accomplished here was even a microscopic fraction of what he was doing with his extensive powers, then there was nothing wrong with Better World. Nothing at all.

Despite the protests of the others, I was adamant. I wished them good luck, got up, and left the room.

"Julian, wait." It was Paula, pursuing me halfway down the hall. "Please, listen to me," she said. "We're leaving for the States next Friday. It's almost Christmas. Are you certain you want to quit now? What will you do?"

"Stay here."

"What about your job in Boston?"

"I'm already on leave. I'll just extend it."

She looked at me, a mixture of exasperation and concern playing over her face. "Julian, I hope you know what you're doing. Once we leave, you'll no longer have the protection of diplomatic immunity. The Brazilian government isn't crazy about Better World, to put it mildly—they see it as a threat to governmental authority. They're one step away from cracking down on the entire movement. The last thing they want is someone like you—a foreigner—kicking up even more excitement at your girlfriend's little gatherings."

I kissed her on the cheek. "Don't worry about me, Paula. I *do* know what I'm doing. Perhaps for the first time in a long, long while."

THE GODS WERE ON DISPLAY at the Umbanda temple in Lagoas, and the celebrants were stamping their feet, swirling to the drumbeats, flirting, singing, and smoking when the police arrived.

"No permit," said the balding sergeant in his gray uniform. "No permit."

The drums kept beating, The initiates kept singing. No one seemed to have heard. Nobody was listening.

"No permit."

Voices got louder and dancers moved faster but I was getting worried. These policemen wore thick black clubs that swung from their leather belts as they walked. And each man held a blunt-nosed laser rifle.

Star smiled ever more brightly, as though special guests had just arrived. Hips swinging, she sashayed up to the headman and draped a white scarf around his neck. Then she casually lit a cigar and handed it to him. "Welcome to

Mundo Melhor," she said. "Of course we have a permit for this gathering." She held up a holocard, flashing it until it sparkled in the lamplight. Then she held out her arms to the officers. "Come," she said. "Come and join the dance."

The drummers switched into high gear, pounding out a raucous, infectious samba beat.

The officers stared at one another as though looking for someone who knew what to do. Then the youngest officer put down his gun and picked up a pair of maracas. Before I knew what was happening, the policemen had all become part of the celebration. The sergeant was in the thick of the crowd, feet flashing as he made one complicated turn after another, hips shaking all the while. The ceremony went on until dawn, and the police were among the last guests to leave.

When we were alone, I turned to Star in respect and some confusion. "Why weren't you afraid of the police?" I asked.

"Afraid?" Her eyes sparkled. "Why be afraid? Don't you see that people are all the same, *querido*? They just want to be able to enjoy their lives, to have enough to eat, to make love, to laugh, to dance, to have some hope." She kissed me gently. "It's not really very complicated, Julian. You're a healer. I thought you already knew this."

"But they came here to cause a disruption. You know that the government doesn't like Mundo Melhor."

"Because it fears our power."

"For whatever reason. You saw the weapons those men brought. They could have become violent."

"Perhaps in *your* country they would have behaved so. But here we understand things a bit differently. Those policemen were sent to cause trouble, yes, but they didn't really want to do it. The police are always among the first to join the early samba parades on Avenida Atlantico—they love to dance and party. I knew that. Everybody in Rio knows it. All I had to do was help them to become human beings again, to forget their badges and guns."

"What do you mean?"

"By showing them a small piece of paper—their precious permit—I removed the burden of their official roles. They were free to stop being policemen and to become people."

Her smile was beatific. "Not so different from what we do with Mundo Melhor. We're just helping people to feel better."

CHRISTMAS EVE, STAR AND I watched a candlelit procession make its way down Avenida Atlantico. The paraders carried huge papier-mâché effigies of Jesus Christ, Mary, St. Michael, St. Christopher, Exu, Lemanja, a host of other macumba spirits, and Rick. I joined the other revelers and saluted my brother's image with a lusty cry of *"Quibungo!"* After the parade we danced and sang at every club in the Ipanema district.

During the holidays, attendance at the Mundo Melhor gatherings soared. Each meeting we held ended with ecstatic high spirits. I never experienced the disorienting cacophony of that earlier meeting again, thank God, but I had a sense that my telepathic presence was helping to drive the group rituals to an ever higher, ever more passionate level.

Each night, in bed, Star and I would attain a very different but equally satisfactory level of ecstasy. Afterward, she would call me her miracle man. I was pleased and embarrassed and happy, so very, very happy.

By New Year's Eve, I was convinced that I had found a worthy goal, a rightful place, and a partner for life.

Star and I stood on the beach holding hands, both dressed in white, part of the crowd waiting for midnight. Each of us held a white rose, as did everyone else there.

Macumba priests and priestesses cavorted across the sand as supplicants made *despachos*—offerings—to their favorite deities: cosmetics and other niceties for the goddess Yemanja, food and drink for the voracious Exu. But the moment of truth was yet to come.

At midnight, a multicolored waterfall of lights cascaded down the facade of every high-rise building along Avenida Atlantica. The crowd roared with one voice and raced toward the water. The white roses were tossed high into the air, up and over the crowd, into the surf. Every person there watched anxiously to see if the gods had accepted their pleas by taking the flowers out to sea, or rejected their entreaties, returning the roses to the beach.

I was watching as nervously as the others, almost frightened by my wish: that I might continue to help people as I was doing now, with Star always by my side.

The waves swelled, surged forward, crashed, foaming, onto the beach, and with a sigh pulled back.

Not a flower lay upon the glinting sand.

Star gasped. "I've never seen this," she said. "Never before were all the flowers taken, all together. Never. Oh, Julian, it's a very powerful omen. Very strong."

We kissed jubilantly.

All up and down the beach, people were screaming and laughing, hugging, kissing, dancing with joy.

We sang and chanted for hours, first on the beach, then followed the crowd through the streets, blowing whistles and beating drums until dawn.

At sunup, a few revelers still straggled along the sidewalks. Several had bedded down on the beach or under trees. A few were sleeping it off on traffic islands in the middle of Avenida Atlantico.

As we made our way back to my room I combed silver confetti out of Star's hair with my fingers.

"It's magic dust," I told her, then I sprinkled it over both of us, giddy with exhaustion and happiness. Gratefully, we fell into bed and slept away most of January first in each other's arms.

JANUARY SECOND, THE SUN HID away and the day was wet and unseasonably cool.

Family matters called Star away and I had a solo dinner that night. I ordered my favorite Bahian shrimp dish: tiny shrimps cooked with onions in coconut milk until the entire savory mixture was stained pale orange. The olive-skinned waiter spooned a generous portion, steaming and fragrant, from a coconut-hull bowl and spread it over the rice on my plate. After two helpings of that and two *caipurinhas* I stumbled back to my room, warm, drowsy, and vaguely amorous, but to my disappointment Star wasn't back yet.

I sat on the jellcouch and looked around the place fondly. I would miss it when I moved, but the hotel rate was exorbitant. Star and I were planning to rent a little apartment in a less-than-glamorous district near Lagoa.

For a while I was lost in pleasant domestic reveries. Then I saw the message light blinking on my portascreen.

I checked the time and location: a call from California made half an hour ago from my parents' exchange. My head cleared instantly. Both of my parents were approaching an age when I anticipated calls late at night, filled with bad news. Hastily, I dialed their number, forgetting, at first, to include the international phone code.

On the fifth ring, my mother answered the screen. She wore a thick red bathrobe and her glossy dark hair was matted and looked slept upon.

"Come home," she said. Her voice was hoarse from sleep or emotion, perhaps both.

"What's happened? Is it Dad?" I could barely get the words out, so frozen was I with fear.

"No. Your brother. Something very peculiar is going on in New Mexico, Julian. Rick has collapsed. Alanna called me earlier this evening. She's been trying to reach you. Rick is delirious, calling for you. Won't see anyone else."

Rick? Impossible. How could he be ill? "He has trained medics on his staff. Can't they do anything for him?"

"They tried but he won't let them near. Even half-conscious, his powers are too strong for them. Oh, won't you go to him, Julian? Your brother needs you!"

What choice did I have?

As soon as I hung up I began to pack, stuffing clothing haphazardly into a portasac. I heard a noise and turned to see Star standing by the door, still wearing her raincoat. She took in the scene at once.

"Where are you going?" she said.

"Back to the States. It's an emergency." Something warned me against telling Star that Rick was ill. I was afraid of upsetting her, and of precipitating a panic among the followers of Mundo Melhor.

"But—"

"I've got to go, Star. I can't explain it."

"You don't want me anymore?"

"Don't be ridiculous. I love you—"

"No. If you loved me you wouldn't leave. The work we are doing is too important. Too vital."

"You're talking nonsense. I love you and I'll be back in a week."

"I don't believe you."

She stood in the doorway, arms outstretched. "I won't let you go."

"Star, I'm already your prisoner." I held my hands over my heart, pretending that they were shackled together.

She tried to smile and almost made it. Almost. Oh, the wounded look of her, the dark eyes glistening doelike in her lovely face. Before I could stop myself I reached out, wanting to heal, to comfort, to love.

"Star—"

"No, Julian. No." She gave me one last tearful look and backed away down the hall and out of sight. Out of my reach.

I hated to leave Star, especially in that way. But my fears for Rick were too great—I could not linger. The ride to the shuttleport was a blur of neon reflecting off wet streets. If I could have teleported, I would have gone directly to New Mexico. But it took me an hour by conventional shuttle, with three stops in between. And all the while I was tormented with fears for Rick. What had happened? And what could I do?

I refused to think about Star. I would explain it to her later, make up with her, and things would be better than ever. She would understand. Right now I had to concentrate on my brother.

Finally, around dawn, I reached New Mexico.

9

A CROWD OF BETTER WORLD members in their blue and green and red jumpsuits milled around outside of the door to Rick's private apartment. Some paced, others leaned disconsolately against the wall, a few were even sitting on the floor, heads nodding as they dozed.

My overtired mind likened them to a scene out of a Renaissance painting: the courtiers awaiting the death of the king. I pushed my way through them, right up to the door. It was locked so I knocked gently.

"Hey," said a dark-haired woman in green. "You can't go in there."

I knocked again. The door opened a crack and I pushed past the startled guard, coming face-to-face with Betty Smithson.

"No one is allowed in here," she said, glaring. Then her gaze softened. "Oh, God, Julian. I didn't recognize—"

I brushed past her, past the other acolytes, and reached for the still figure in the jellbed.

"Rick?"

He lay there, pale and sweaty, seemingly comatose. But my voice must have roused him and he opened his eyes halfway. When he saw me he smiled weakly and said, mumbling a bit, "I knew you'd come."

"Shh," I said. "Save your strength."

Rick nodded and closed his eyes. I checked his pulse. It seemed a bit slow but regular.

I looked up and noticed Alanna, for the first time, standing on the other side of the bed. For a moment we glared at each other in silence. I had the feeling that she was going to grab Rick's other hand and begin pulling. Between us we would tear him apart like a turkey wishbone.

"How long has he been this way?" I demanded.

"A day and a half."

"And what do the doctors say?"

"We haven't had any doctors in. He wouldn't let us."

"No doctors? Are you crazy?"

"Julian, he doesn't want them."

"What difference does it make what he wants? He collapsed, didn't he? He's obviously in no condition to make decisions about his well-being. He needs medical care."

"We have to obey his wishes." Alanna held Rick's hand with fierce possessiveness. "You just don't understand."

I glanced at the pale figure in the bed. His forehead was coated with sweat. The sight—the result of their negligence—made me furious and I said, "Oh, I understand all right. It's just part of your master plan, isn't it, Alanna? Every religion needs its martyr, doesn't it? And Better World would all be so much easier to control with the maestro out of the way."

"How dare you!" Alanna made a move as though to reach across the bed and hit me. Then she seemed to realize where she was and caught herself in mid-swing. "You son of a bitch, coming in here at the last minute and making terrible accusations. What right do you have?"

"I'm not finished," I said. "Not only do you *want* Rick dead, you're probably in cahoots with Joachim Metzger. What do you intend to do? Divide up Better World between you when Rick's safely out of the picture?"

"Metzger? An alliance? What are you talking about?" Alanna's horrified expression made me realize I had gone too far, much too far.

"Oh, shit." I sank down in the bedside wallseat and rubbed my burning eyes. "I'm sorry. I've been up for over twenty-four hours and I'm just getting crazy because I'm so worried about Rick."

"That's no reason to insult me."

"No, of course not. Forgive me, Alanna. But I still insist that Rick be examined by a neurologist. An internist, too."

"Please," Betty said. "Don't fight. Not here."

I looked at my brother again. His color was a little bit better and he seemed to be sleeping peacefully rather than sunken into unconsciousness. I checked his pulse again and it seemed nearly normal. He was still slightly sweaty but his fever seemed to have eased.

"I want him watched all night," I said.

Betty gave me an exasperated look. "What do you think we're doing here, Julian?"

"Maybe I'm overreacting," I said. "But I want a med monitor attached to his pulse points. If he slows down too much, speeds up, or his fever increases, I want a doctor here, and pronto. Will you do that much for me, please? Otherwise, I'll have him med-evacuated to St. Ignazio's in Albuquerque right now!"

Betty glanced at Alanna for a brief, unreadable moment and then nodded stiffly.

"Fine. I hold you responsible, Betty." I stood up and stretched, feeling a hundred years older. "Now will somebody please give me a bed before I fall down?"

THE NEXT MORNING when I got to Rick's room he was sitting up against the pillows, bright-eyed and alert. Alanna and Betty were stationed like guards on either side of the bed.

"Well, you look much improved," I said.

"Hey, is it time for breakfast yet?" His voice sounded vibrant, even hearty.

"Just lie there quietly."

"Why? I'm fine."

"Rick, maybe you should listen to Julian," Alanna said.

"Don't baby me, Lanna. There's nothing wrong with me that breakfast won't cure. I just needed a good night's sleep. That's all."

"But—"

"No buts." Walking a bit unsteadily, Rick gave us a jaunty salute and sauntered into the bathroom.

"He's fine," Betty said. "I'm sure there's nothing to worry about. A good breakfast will fix him right up."

"I hope you're right," I said. I was so relieved to see my

brother back on his feet that I decided I could relax for a moment and try to call Star.

It was midday in Rio and, of course, she was not home. So I told her answermech that I loved her and needed her, and asked her to call me at Better World as soon as she could. Then I went down to breakfast.

All during the meal Rick was charming and amusing, almost manic. He finished two helpings of everything, eating like a famished man. As I watched him wolf down his food, I told myself that he was fine, only a healthy man could eat like that.

"After breakfast, how about a tour of the city?" he said.

"I don't think so," I said. "I really should get back to Rio."

"What's your rush? Hey, is there something going on down there I should know about?"

I smiled mysteriously, a bit pleased to have my own secrets for once.

"What's her name?"

"Why are you so certain that there's a she involved?"

"Why else would you be so cagey? Now out with it, little brother. Tell me all about her."

"Her name is Star. Star Nicolau. She's working with a group down there that's sort of a hybrid of Better World and their macumba religion. They call it Mundo Melhor."

"Wild. So you met her in Brazil?"

"Yeah. It's a long story." I glanced at Betty and Alanna uneasily. "Maybe I should tell you about it during our tour."

"Great. Let's go."

It was a cold morning but the chill wore off as the sun rose higher in the sky. I was amazed by the progress Rick and his helpers had made: Better City was a splendid mixture of traditional, functional, and fanciful design. Most of the buildings were domelike and round, with adobe-colored walls. But some spiraled upward for several stories, cutting through the air, twisting and turning, revealing unexpected windows and walkways.

All around us were the sounds and sights of a community waking up and resuming its daily business. A woman stood in the doorway of a café, sweeping sand into a neat pile for the streetmechs to remove. She smiled brightly at Rick. "Want some coffee?" The scent of fresh-brewed grounds wafted toward us through the open door. "Thanks, Catarina," Rick said. "Maybe later."

Nearby, a man set up the awning of his small grocery store and began setting out trays of bright red apples. "Morning, Rick," he said. "Beautiful day."

People hurried past carrying building supplies, screencases, and bags filled with bread from the bakery at the end of the street. Everyone who saw Rick smiled and greeted him, and he seemed to know every one of them by name.

The city was laid out in a neat grid spanning several miles, bisected by graceful boulevards that bore signs of fresh landscaping. Workers in yellow coveralls were busily planting rows of yuccas in front of a white-washed adobe bank building. They greeted Rick happily but then got right back to business.

Cars and skimmers puttered up and down the street and occasionally somebody pedaled along on a bicycle. As the sun rose higher in the sky, warming the air, the music of a peaceful and prosperous community could be heard more distinctly; the sound of people laughing, music playing, insects buzzing.

"It's fantastic, Rick." I shook my head in wonder. "A dream come true."

He nodded proudly. "Pretty fine if I do say so myself."

"And nearly finished."

"Oh, it'll never really be finished." My brother gave me a cryptic smile. "But wait until you see the centerpiece." He gestured for me to hurry and we jogged up the street, turned a corner, and then I saw it.

A Roman amphitheater—a three-tiered coliseum—loomed like a piece of the past that had collided with and become embedded in the present. It was an incongruous sight amid the adobe-colored buildings and construction cranes—a stone donut with a bite or two taken out of it. I stared in wide-open amazement.

"Is it for real?"

"A replica, courtesy of the best of late twenty-first-century archaeotechnology." He bowed with a deep flourish. "C'mon, let's take a look inside."

He swung open a tall iron gate and we walked into a tall, arching entryway cast in deepest shadow. We emerged into what looked like the second tier of seats in the stadium.

The walls had the convincing mellowed glow of old marble but Rick told me that they were actually an acrylic epoxy mixed with marble dust and artificially patinaed. An impermeable canopy, self-heating and cooling, automatically emerged from a subterranean gully and enclosed the arena when inclement weather threatened. There were pieces of scaffolding set up on the stage below us, and several rows of seats looked as though they were missing bits and pieces. A lone technician was fiddling with the internal components of one of the seats. Obviously, there was still plenty of work to be done.

"The seats look like stone," Rick said. "But they're really heat-reactive ferro-ceramic. Each seat molds itself in shape to the particular anatomy of anyone seated for longer than five minutes. And once the seats are vacated they flow back to a uniform flatness." He sat down and patted the seat next to him.

I perched on the cold faux marble and felt it grow warm and move beneath me, adapting itself to my body's contours. "Rick, it's amazing."

He grinned. "Nice little piece of work, isn't it? It'll be perfect when it's finished."

"Beautiful. But why a Roman theater?"

"Why not?"

"How did you get it?"

"A group of Korean investors who belong to Better World. But later for that." He draped an arm around my shoulders and gave me an affectionate squeeze. "I thought you were going to tell me about *her*, little brother. Miss Mundo Melhor."

Lulled by Rick's voice, the warmth of the sun, the sound of birdsong echoing through the theater, and the sudden relief of stress and worry, I let my secret escape. Rick listened intently, nodding occasionally but remaining silent until I had finished my tale.

"This sounds like the real thing," he said.

"I hope so."

"Good. You've been alone too long, little brother."

It was my turn to give him a cryptic grin. "Not always."

Whatever he might have replied was lost in a roaring, thunderous concussion that seemed to buckle the earth beneath our feet. I fell to my hands and knees.

"What the hell?" I gasped.

But Rick had completely disappeared. Teleported himself away—but where?

A siren began to sound its shrill alarm, *whoopa-whoopa-whoopa*. The air was filled with dust and a cloud partially obscured the sun. I ran down the aisle and back the way I had come, slamming the iron gate of the stadium behind me.

The streets were filled with people running in all directions, yelling and screaming. A young man in a blue jumpsuit raced by and I grabbed his arm, swinging him around to face me.

"What's happened?" I demanded.

"An explosion at the main building," he gasped. "Maybe more than one."

"What caused it?"

"I dunno. A ruptured gas line, maybe." He wrenched out of my grip and sped away.

A crowd of people had already gathered outside of Better World headquarters. I could see that the top half of the building had been damaged: the green panes of glass were cracked and a wall brace hung away from the building at a perilous angle.

Betty Smithson was ahead of me in the crowd and I fought my way next to her.

"Does anybody know anything about it yet?"

She gave me a wild, distracted glance. "Oh, Julian. That's Rick and Alanna's private apartment. Alanna was in there when the explosion happened. She may be hurt."

Just then, Rick appeared on the front steps, Alanna by his side. She had a jagged cut on her cheek that oozed blood but otherwise she appeared unharmed.

"Betts," Rick said. "Help Lanna get cleaned up, okay?"

As he handed her off to Betty, a group of Better Worlders crowded around him, peppering him with questions.

"Was it a bomb?"

"Where did it go off?"

"Did you catch anybody?"

"Was anyone else hurt?"

Rick held up his hands. "People, listen, we're okay. Nobody else was hurt. Yes, it was a bomb. No, I don't know who set it, but I sure as hell intend to find out. I want a clean-up crew in there, and I want security to look the place over carefully."

I hurried over to him. "Rick, are you okay?"

"Sure. Sorry I bolted out of there, little brother. But I could tell where the blast had originated and I had to be sure that Lanna was safe."

"Any idea whose work this is, or how it was planted?"

"My guess is that some terrorist group infiltrated B.W."

"Could they do that without your sensing it?"

"Maybe," he said. "I've been pretty busy lately, and pretty damned tired, too."

"But why would they plant explosives?"

"We've been getting various threats for almost a year. We scare them out of their birthday suits. Some of them seem to hate us. Some fear us. Others just want our attention, I guess. Or just want to annoy and hinder us."

"Threats? Rick, why didn't you increase security? Contact the FBI."

"And run this place like an armed camp? No thanks. That's not the way I do things. And I don't like to call in outsiders. We take care of ourselves." He took a deep breath and let it out, seemingly invigorated by the crisis. He looked much better than he had even an hour ago: there were only slight shadows under his eyes, and he looked thin but fit and crackling with energy. Where was the invalid who had been calling for me from his bed?

"You've got to stay and help me with this," he said. It was a statement, not a request. I knew I couldn't desert him. And he knew it, too.

"Rick, I'm afraid that Joachim Metzger may be behind this."

"The grand and holy Book Keeper? You've got to be kidding me. What makes you think that?"

"I got a peek into his mind—"

"I thought you were against that sort of thing."

"It seemed like a good idea at the time."

"And you saw him planning this?"

"No. But he was mad enough to kill. That much I saw." I paused as a sudden idea struck me. "Rick, you could go back."

"What do you mean?"

"Time-hop. Jump back far enough to see who set the bomb."

Rick nodded. "Maybe. I could try it. But it's not always that easy to do. I can't control the process enough to pinpoint my landings. I don't know when that bomb was set there. I could land right in the middle of the explosion. It probably wouldn't hurt me, but who knows? And even if I got lucky and arrived at just the right moment, I might not know who the guy was. And I can't communicate with people in the past—they can't see me or hear me."

"But what if it *was* one of Metzger's people?"

"I don't know if it was Metzger, and I don't care," Rick said. "Our work here will go on, even if we have to wear flak jackets and conduct our sharings in underground bunkers." He checked his wristscreen. "And I've got a sharing set for two this afternoon. Care to attend?"

"Uh, no thanks."

He looked so disappointed that I could have kicked myself for refusing. After all, I was there, wasn't I?

"Oh, all right," I said. "Why not?" What the hell—I knew how to protect myself from the more potent hypnotic effects of Rick's powers.

Rick beamed. "Attaboy."

At one-thirty a second bomb exploded in Better City.

The noise this time was terrifying, like a superamplified sonic boom. Smoke and thunder filled the air as a fine mixture of ash and sand rained down. Amazingly, no one was hurt.

The bomb made a substantial crater in the main parking lot and shattered the adobe facade on a nearby building. Seconds after the explosion, Rick appeared and began to yell hoarsely above the din of emergency vehicles. "Joe! Where's Joe Martinez?" He rounded on the security chief. "I thought you told me this area was secured!"

Martinez shook his head in chagrin. "We did a full scan

with heat sensors and mechhounds. There was nothing. Nothing. I don't understand it."

"Then I want hourly scans," Rick said. "Double the security staff if you have to. We lucked out this time. But I don't want there to be a next time."

The third bomb went off in the Roman arena at five o'clock. The explosion sent Rick into a wild fury, rushing around the grounds like a hungry lion in search of fresh prey. "Is everybody okay?" he demanded. "No one hurt? When I find out who did this, I'll hang them upside down from the tail of a shuttle. In orbit."

I began to fear that our very lives were in danger. Whoever or whatever groups were behind this seemed to have access to every bit of Better City.

Heightened security measures were instituted immediately: all incoming mail and visitors were scanned before they were allowed access to Better City or Better World personnel. A plan was drawn up by Rick and Joe Martinez to construct a bunkerlike building in which a bomb squad could open suspicious-looking packages.

Joe Martinez set up regular patrols and guards could be seen standing watch along the perimeter of the city. People seemed subdued, quiet, and frightened, and an air of gloom settled upon Better World. By dusk of the following day, the streets were deserted, save for security patrols.

I holed up in my room and thought about Star. She had never returned my call. All right, I thought. If that's the way you want to play it, hard to get, then I'll just keep calling you. And I dialed her number again.

It was evening in Rio and I hardly expected Star to answer but she did and my heart leaped at the sound of her voice.

"Ola. Quem esta?"

"Star, it's me."

"Julian." She stared at me, mouth working silently as though she were chewing over what to say next. Then she whispered, "I got your message."

"Then why didn't you call me back?"

"I didn't trust myself."

"What do you mean?"

"I was afraid I would start yelling. I was so angry with

you." Tears welled up in her dark eyes and began to spill down her cheeks. "Oh, Julian, why did you leave me? Why haven't you returned? I need you by my side."

"You just took the words right out of my mouth." How I wanted to hold her, to be with her at that moment. I threw aside all caution. "Star, I'm here with Rick. He was very sick, was calling for me."

"Why didn't you tell me?"

"I was afraid it would panic you and perhaps the others in Mundo Melhor."

"Oh, *querido*, you can be such a fool sometimes." The tears began again. "If you can't trust me, who can you trust? I love you so much. So very, very much."

Tears welled up in my eyes. "Star, please, come here. Be with me."

"But my work, the people—"

I waved away her objections as though they meant nothing. "They can survive until we get back. Please, Star. I can't leave right now. There's trouble here."

"What do you mean?"

Paranoia returned with a jolt. "I can't say. But I can't get away. Couldn't you just come up here for a little while? I promise you, we'll return to Rio together as soon as things quiet down here."

"You want me to leave everything for you?"

I took a deep breath. "Yes. Goddammit, yes. I'm not asking you to leave it forever. I love you, Star. I want to be with you. Right now!"

My fervor seemed to impress her. Her lips curved up into a smile. "All right. I'll come. Give me a few days to settle things here and I will come to you, beloved. I can't fight my heart. What will be will be."

We spent the rest of the call whispering endearments to each other in several languages. Brimming with joy, I bid her a temporary goodbye and went back to the chaos of Better World.

Requests for information were pouring in from what seemed like every vid reporter on the planet. Finally, to free up the comboards, Rick called a news conference and announced that Better City was under siege by person or persons unknown.

"This is addressed to whoever out there is trying to blow Better World out of business." Rick stared defiantly at the cameras humming before him. Then his expression changed, softening to a smile. "I don't understand why you want to hurt us. We open our doors to everyone, even you, if you need us. It's not too late to come forward. I know you have got to be hurting. You wouldn't be striking out at us like this if you weren't. Come on. Come to us. Let us help you." He paused, and his grin grew broader. "I'm getting better and better at finding your bombs. Don't you want to come to us before I come to you?"

"Any ideas on the source of these explosive devices?" a red-haired reporter asked.

"Nope," Rick said. "Just from somebody who doesn't seem to approve of helping out other people."

"Do you think this is a terrorist group from an opposing religion?"

"I don't see why. We're all on the same team, aren't we? Supposedly."

The vid jocks began chuckling, all but the redhead.

"Then you don't deny that Better World has religious aspects?" he said.

"It has whatever people want it to have. Whatever helps the most people is all right with me," Rick said. "No more questions, okay? Thanks for coming." With that he disappeared. On camera.

Evidently, Rick's broadcast and improved security measures deflected any other attempts at explosive mischief. The bombings stopped, at least for the time being.

But the explosions had damaged more than stone and mortar. I felt a certain dispiriting malaise and I'm certain that everybody else at Better World sensed and suffered from it as well. The violent attacks on Better City, and our lives, had left all of us shaken and short-tempered. Quarrels began to break out between staff members, and even Betty Smithson, our rock of stability, seemed melancholy and irritable.

Just about the time we began to average an argument a day Rick announced a small sharing just for inner-circle members to try to clear the air.

Twenty of us gathered in a small lounge near the main

auditorium of B.W. headquarters. The seats were deep and comfortable and, for once, everybody seemed relaxed, almost cheerfully expectant. And with good reason. Rick's sharings packed quite a wallop.

Rick walked in with Alanna and made his way to the center of the group. He took a deep breath, closed his eyes, and after a moment he nodded.

Friends. We have been together now for some time. And we have endured both elation and disappointment, fear and joy. The circle remains unbroken.

I felt the rising mental harmonies wash over me as a gentle tide and I welcomed it, leaning back in my seat. Although I missed the thumping, primal rhythm of the *pandeiros'* drums I told myself that soon I would be back dancing among the celebrants. Patience, patience now. Here was love and understanding, warmth and the easing of all pain—

There was a tearing, a terrible rending, and we pitched forward and fell, fell endlessly down a long dark and narrow passage howling with wind.

Just as quickly as it had formed the groupmind fragmented into a thousand jagged, flaming pieces that stabbed and burned as they scattered. Nauseated, dizzy, and in pain, I pulled out of the sharing, attempting to free all the other minds in the circle as well. Apparently it worked, for the room was filled with noise as people cried out in confusion, stood up, holding their heads, or collapsed in their seats, white-faced and silent.

Rick had fallen to his hands and knees, head down, the muscles of his face jerking in uncontrolled spasms. Alanna knelt by his side and I felt a sudden pang that she had somehow sensed his distress before I had.

I hurried to my brother. "What is it? What's happening?"

Rick didn't seem capable of speech. His eyes were open but fixed as though focused on some compelling internal space. Briefly I wondered what he saw and hoped at the same time never to have to see it myself.

"Not again," Alanna muttered.

"What do you mean?" I said. "Has this happened before?"

She nodded, looking miserable. "A half-dozen times, but always before we were alone."

"And you concealed it?"

"He made me do it," she said. "What would you have done, Julian? Announced it? Taken vid ads?" Her eyes flashed. "It seemed the best way to handle it for all concerned."

"Who else was concerned besides Rick?"

I felt for his pulse: it was slow but regular. His muscle spasms were easing but he still seemed locked in that other place. I was terrified of what I would find, unwilling to probe, but I decided that it would be irresponsible of me not to try. I touched his shoulder and, tentatively, mindspoke my brother.

Rick?

Nothing. My mindspeech echoed in the silence—it was like the time I had touched Thomas Wyndham's mind. Quickly I shut that memory off.

RICK!!

This time I heard something. It was not thought, not exactly. More like a child's tuneless singing, random notes warbled in a high, guileless voice.

And I saw us, Rick and me, as young children playing on a lavender rug in a sunlit room while towering adults with familiar voices moved back and forth around us. I heard my mother's voice, playful, teasing. And then, with shock, I recognized the sound of a deep male baritone.

It wasn't Yosh. In fact, it sounded a bit like Rick as an adult. But I knew who that jaunty, robust voice belonged to. At least, I think I did.

"Lydda," he said. "Look at these two playing with your laser-brushes. Melanie, I think you've got a pair of budding Michelangelos here."

Skerry. It was Skerry, it had to be. I was watching a random moment snatched from the past that Rick had retained although I had no conscious memory of it.

"Make that Michael *and* Angelo," Yosh's voice said. "Remember, they're a pair but not exactly a matched set."

Graceful hands with slim fingers and long red nails reached in between us, grabbed hold of Rick and lifted him up, up, swinging into a soft lap. He continued to toy with a bit of screenbrain, unconcerned, as our mother cuddled him protectively and I watched. Already, at that age, I was watching.

"I never worry about Julian," my mother said. "He's tested so well, and he already has his telepathy under such good control. But Rick seems to be a null, just like me." She drew him a bit closer. "I hate to think of what he's going to face."

"It's a different world," said Narlydda. "He won't go through what you did."

"He's a tough little guy," Skerry said. He leaned down and patted Rick on the head. "Aren't ya, champ?" Rick looked up from his tinkering and frowned, then glanced down again, more interested in the machinery than the adult babble.

Narlydda said, "Don't worry about him, Mel. He'll surprise you, just wait and see."

"Besides," Yosh said drily, "I don't think *you* did too badly, Mrs. Akimura. Despite your obvious handicap."

My mother smiled, picked up a purple pillow, and tossed it at my father. But instead of ducking he caught it, put it in his lap, and patted it gently.

"Julian," he said. "Come on up here and keep your poor old nonmutant dad company."

How eagerly I crawled into his arms.

Skerry sat across the room, filling a big purple chair. He winked at little Julian—at me—like a fellow conspirator.

The memory fragmented, a puzzle coming apart into random pieces and scattering across Rick's mind.

Outside noises filtered through and I became aware of the room filled with frightened, concerned people. I was bending over me, looking into my eyes and—

I pulled out of Rick's mind quickly. The parallelism was too dangerous.

"Whew," he said. "That was a wild ride."

"How do you feel?"

"Okay." He got to his feet and sat down. "Now where were we?"

"Rick, don't you remember what happened?"

"I had a vision," he said. "It showed a wonderful thing." His eyes shined and his voice grew buoyant. "I saw a huge sharing taking place in the Roman theater. Everybody was there. You, Lanna. And you, Julian. It was at sunset—the sky was so beautiful. And we were all so happy, together, loving one another."

"That's wonderful, Rick," Betty said. There were tears in her eyes.

I saw Alanna smile with relief. And all around the room people breathed more easily. They believed what Rick had told them. And why not? Perhaps he really had seen what he had described.

But I had seen something else—had somehow penetrated Rick's long-term memory. To Rick, the sharing had been interrupted by a vision. Everybody else in the room seemed happy to accept that. Only I knew differently—at least I believed I did. Perhaps while Rick was coasting on his vision I had gone right past him with my probe. I don't know what he really saw and I never will.

"Lanna, Betts, we've got to get moving on this right away. A massive group sharing in the Roman arena."

"Don't you think you should rest?" I said. "Take a few weeks off, Rick. You look a little pale to me."

"No way," he said. "I never felt better. That vision reinvigorated me. I'm reborn, little brother. Can't you feel it?" And, indeed, he seemed to be sizzling with energy. I couldn't explain it. But then again, I never could explain much about Rick.

Quickly and efficiently, Alanna and Betty went to work on the plans for the enormous sharing. Rick was impatient, raring to go, but the bomb blasts had damaged the exterior of the arena and because of the special materials involved, a delay of several weeks was required before the grand mass sharing could be held.

Tickets sold out within hours of its announcement: the faithful flocked in from as far away as New Delhi, Paris, and Sydney, filling Better City. They came with shining faces, with outstretched hands, with their faith in Rick glowing like a tangible aura of blissfulness.

Lost amid the swelling hordes, I wandered, strangely restless. Rick was in high spirits, anxious to connect with his followers, racing around the halls of Better World checking on every detail of the preparations. I watched him in amazement, envying his resiliency. When would he ever slow down? But then again, why should he? He was the supermutant. I was merely his twin, filled with strange, fraternal misgivings.

10

ALTHOUGH I TRIED TO reason with him, Rick was adamant about holding the sharing as soon as possible.

"The arena will be ready next week," he said. "I'm going to inaugurate it with a bang, just as soon as the paint dries."

"Bang is right," I said. "What if those bombings were a threat to stop the sharings?"

"Then I'd be playing right into their hands if I canceled it, wouldn't I?"

"But suppose there's another explosion? Suppose somebody gets hurt."

"No one is going to get hurt, little brother. I promise you that."

The sharing went on as planned the following week. By nine the arena had filled, and after a final sound and light check, the lights dimmed and Rick made his way out onto the stage. Without music, without fanfare. A cool wind ruffled his hair. I shivered a bit in the breeze.

He stood there, a thin, wiry figure clad in faded jeans, blue work shirt, and boots, unnoticed by the crowd. He watched the people who had come to see him as they chattered, yelled, laughed, ate, and drank. They were lost, absorbed in their noisy private lives and their din filled the old theater.

Slowly the arena darkened until all the lamps were out save for a lone spotlight that fixed Rick in a bright yellow halo. The crowd grew quiet. Still Rick said nothing.

Almost as one the audience sighed, a great outpouring of breath that mingled longing, anticipation, curiosity, skepticism, and even a bit of fear.

And Rick opened his mind to us.

Will you share with me?

A thousand heads nodded. A thousand minds reached out to him eagerly.

Then join hands. We must do it together. Join hands and share with me now.

Rick closed his eyes.

A thousand strange thoughts hummed and babbled in the mix of the groupmind. French, German, and Italian collided and rebounded against English and Spanish. Yet all was understood, all was accepted and known in the sharing. No one was alone. No one would ever be alone again.

The audience sighed once more, this time in pleasure and relief.

The hum of the groupmind modulated to a slightly higher key and intensified. It seemed to vibrate up from the white-hot center of the Earth along each bone bead of every vertebrae of every person in the arena, and out of that ancient stadium up into the clear night sky.

Open yourselves to one another. Open your hearts and your minds. We have all been alone, cut off, for too long. The long wait is over. We are one.

As he mindspoke, my brother seemed to give off a dazzling, blinding light. He held out his arms to the faithful and they leaned forward, eyes closed, swaying in his mental embrace.

I took a deep breath, braced myself against the seatback, and closed my eyes. It was like walking into the ocean: the mental tide lapped at me, flowed over, and swept me up.

For a moment I was lost in the egoless depths, floating happily with the others. I was loved and forgiven, understood and accepted. Cherished. Empowered. Then, somehow, I found the surface and broke through, gasping.

I skimmed from mind to mind, briefly touching an essence here, a strange fantasy there. At first it was difficult. Each ecstatic mind tried to lure me in, hold on, weld me into place within the circuit.

A woman to my left was awash in memories of her first

sexual encounter. All the passionate, throbbing urgency of it, the wonder and pleasure, flowed from her to me in wave after pulsing wave of rapture.

Two rows behind her, an elderly grandmother was lost in a tumultuous rebirth. She was laughing with joy, weeping with awe and fright, and I wept and laughed with her.

Nearby, a young man no more than twenty relived his first snowfall, capering in the midst of a cold, white, marvelous fairyland. His father, beside him, was struck by the first taste of a ripe apricot. I could savor it clearly, the sweet, tart, pulpy goodness on the back of my tongue. Together, we smacked our lips.

Each person was caught up in his or her own transcendent moment, connected and yet engulfed by private dreams.

As I trolled through the communion I accidentally touched Rick's mind. It was brimming with rapturous power as he poured himself into the crowd, giving them everything he had.

I floated on his blissful tide for a moment before I noticed a subtle shift in the grand harmony. Strange minor notes emerged and began to dominate. Slowly the sharing moved along an odd, discordant scale I had never heard before.

Rick's body began to shake and quiver: every muscle stood out as though carved. His lips were drawn back in a horrible grimace. His very head seemed to swell.

I looked into my brother's mind, and screamed.

People around me began to erupt into flame as though they had each been doused with kerosene and touched by a struck match. The human torches filled the night sky with the stench of burning flesh. Black smoke obscured the stars. The shrieks. Oh, God, the shrieks were terrible, deafening, worse than the worst nightmare.

My brother was still on stage, still on his feet, but he was staggering, collapsing to knees and elbows, cradling his head in his hands. Alanna was on stage, too, running toward him. But it was all happening so slowly, so very slowly. I could see her dark hair bobbing in the wind as though it were weightless. But she was taking so long to reach Rick. Hurry, I thought. Help him!

A thundercloud swept up and over the arena and began pelting everyone inside with gusting rain. Flames guttered and went out. Thank God, I thought. Rick has gotten control again. But even as I watched, jagged bolts of lightning etched their way across the sky, thunder roared, and rain turned to hissing acid. Wherever it fell, flesh and stone melted away. Where were the arena's protective canopies, the automatic shields of which Rick had boasted?

"No," I cried. "Rick. Stop it. No!" I tried to reach him with mindspeech but there was too much interference.

Somehow I fought my way to the front of the arena, elbowed and kicked a path through the crowd, grabbed hold of the lip of the stage, and swung myself up onto it.

Alanna knelt, center stage, holding my brother's head in her lap, bending over him as tenderly as Mary must once have embraced Jesus.

Rick gasped for breath, rasping and choking deep in his throat. His arms and legs jerked as though they were being pulled by some cruel puppeteer and his face was deep red, almost purple. Nearby, a medic dug frantically through a green medsac.

I fell to my knees beside Rick, touched his shoulder, and—reluctantly, fearfully—reached into his mind.

Rick? Rick, can you hear me? What's wrong?

At first I heard nothing but an odd, grating mental static. Then, faintly, through the buzzing and humming, I heard Rick respond.

Julian, is that you?

Brother, I'm here.

Help me. My head. Hurts. Hurts so badly. I didn't think it would hurt so much. I can't stop it.

What's happening? What should I do?

I can't. I can't—

His thoughts trailed off into gibberish and more static.

Terrified, I searched for his pulse and counted the sluggish, strangely erratic beats again and again while the doctor in me grimly confirmed what the brother refused to believe.

There was a hollow pounding at the center of his being, a muffled drum slowing with each beat. He was ebbing, whirling down into darkness. Rick wasn't having some sort of seizure or attack. He was dying, his life force swirling away.

For a crazy moment I tried to cling to him, to hold on to his essence and keep him here with me. But even in retreat he was too strong. Even as I clawed for him, Rick pulled farther and farther away, out of my grasp, and I knew that if I didn't release him I would be swept up, too, and carried away in that same awful outflowing current. A sob caught in my throat as I broke free and let my brother go. Should I have gone with him? Sometimes I think so.

I felt something give way inside me, as though a single, keening note had been struck so hard against such a tightly wound string that the string had broken. The echo of it persisted for a moment, then faded to silence.

"Let me through!" the doctor shouted. He shouldered me aside and thrust a hypo against Rick's chest.

"Help him," Alanna cried. "You've got to help him. Oh, Julian, please."

But it was already too late.

Rick was gone, I was still here, and nothing made any sense, nothing. I had let him die. Alone.

"No," Alanna cried. "No!" She grabbed Rick by the shoulders and shook him as though somehow she believed that she could shake the life back into him. "You can't go. Don't leave me here. You promised we'd be together. Rick, you promised!"

Suddenly she stopped, as though the insanity of her words had reached even her own ears. With a convulsive shudder she set Rick down, turned her head away, and was silent although her shoulders shook and shook.

I gazed, disbelieving, into my brother's face. He seemed shriveled and old, so very old. In six months he had aged years, and in death he resembled Skerry, our biological father, more than himself. His eyes were open but no one was in there looking back out at me. I shut them and a storm of despair and grief brewed within me, churned and billowed, threatening to break loose. But I had no time to mourn.

The stage resounded under the blows of the crowd and the walls of the amphitheater rang with their outraged cries and screams. The audience had rushed toward the front of the arena and in a frenzy began to destroy it—and themselves. They tore floorboards loose, flailing wildly around, striking out at one another, breaking anything that got in their way.

"We've got to stop them," I yelled. "They'll kill themselves. Us, too."

Alanna peered over her shoulder at the maddened crowd, stood up, and, like a mech doll, began to take peculiar halting steps toward the edge of the stage. For a moment I wondered what she was about, then I realized that she meant to throw herself from the stage right into their raging midst.

"No!" I grabbed her by the arm and swung her around to face me. "Killing yourself won't solve anything, Alanna. Is that what Rick would want?"

At first she struggled, trying to break free. Then with a convulsive gasp, she collapsed, sobbing, against my chest and I clutched her in helpless confusion. I felt frozen in place as though I would never move again. Any second now the mob would take the stage and probably bludgeon us to death.

Suddenly Alanna stopped crying, raised her tear-stained face, and stared into my eyes. "*You* can save them, Julian. You can do it. Reach out. Reach out with your mind and calm them."

What was she talking about? Had grief completely deranged her? "Alanna, I'm no supermutant, remember? I'm the other brother—a telepath. That's all."

She grabbed both my wrists and shook me furiously. "You can do it, Julian. You're a first-level telepath and I know that you can do it."

Something about her crazy fervor broke through my paralysis and I allowed her to pull me toward the front of the stage.

With Rick's death the illusion of the rain had ceased. Below us the mob was shrieking, baying like animals and tearing at one another. Alanna never stopped staring at me. I could see the blood beating in a vein on her forehead.

"All right," I said desperately. "I'll try." Clutching her hand, I linked up with her. Then, telepathically, I reached out beyond us.

At once I fell into a dark maelstrom, submerged in a massive jumble of sorrow, anger, despair, and terror. I was floundering, drowning, losing myself in the emotions of the crowd. In desperation I pulled free. It was beyond my powers to control them. I wasn't Rick.

"I can't," I gasped. "Alanna, I can't do it."

Smoke swirled around us and her eyes glittered like jewels in the murky darkness. "You've got to try again, Julian. Come on, hold on to me."

I wanted to sob, to cry out, to tell her to stop it and leave me alone. But instead I closed my eyes and reached toward the mob once again.

There. A mindhold. I grabbed it.

Beside me, Alanna poured strength and more strength into me, crushing my hand in hers.

And there, another beacon, another bright and shining mind. I reached for that one, too. And, yes, I felt stronger. Suddenly I could feel their minds glowing, calming, humming in tandem with mine. They were beginning to turn toward me—in wonder, in hope.

Stumbling along I found a receptive mind here, a strong one there, and like a pianist slowly hitting the separate notes of a major chord I pressed upon them all until I heard the right sound, until the animal cries had all died away, the horror had passed, and we were united in our grief and loss, buoyed up above the awful flood.

Grieve with me, I told them. *Hold on to me, hold on to one another. Do not move. Do not think. Share with me now.*

Incredible strength hummed through me: such power as I had never imagined. But how was this possible? A mass sharing like this was something only Rick could have managed, wasn't it?

Gently I probed through the circuit. And I felt a subtle difference in one or two of the connectors. They were mutant minds, I knew it. Powerful telepaths, all. I had no time to learn more, but I knew now how I had managed such a feat.

Together we are strong. We can support one another in our terrible pain and through our dreadful loss. Mourn with me. Mourn with me, now.

Tears ran down my face and I was soaked with sweat. But self-awareness had faded: I only knew that I was a conduit for great energies, and without me, all hell would break loose. Trembling, faltering, I held us all up as together we grieved for my brother. Grieved, and comforted one another as, overhead, untouched and eternal, the stars twinkled and glowed.

11

THAT NIGHT, Better City burned.

Apparently, Rick's death had released all manner of peculiar energies, and one discharge had set fire to a row of apartments. Since there was no one on hand to fight the blaze it rapidly spread until almost half of the city was burning.

As we left the stadium, arm in arm, tearful and pensive, we were greeted by a scene from hell: red sky and black smoke. The alarms sounded, but it was too little, too late. Unfortunately, Rick's planning had not included the need for a complete metropolitan fire-fighting network and we were sadly, tragically underequipped.

Houses exploded into showers of glass, brick, and metal. Embers drifted across the sky, forming temporary nebulae that floated slowly down to earth, scattering fire like bright seeds bringing flames and panic, hysteria and death.

A howling wind rose, scattering sparks and flaming debris across every corner of the city. Trees went up like giant torches, limbs crackling, trunks detonating.

I was frantic, being pulled in a dozen directions at once, trying to cope with the fire, deal with my own grief, and help coordinate rescue efforts in Better City.

Perhaps the hardest thing I did that awful night was to call my parents. My mother responded to the news with remarkable self-control. Her face was a pale, shocked mask and tears glittered in her eyes but somehow she didn't crack. It was Yosh, my father, who cried, and I allowed myself a moment of relief, crying with him briefly, before I pulled the grief back inside. I choked out a farewell and promised to call the next day.

Next, I tried to call Star. At first all the circuits were busy. I tried again. There was no answer, and no message mech. A third try netted a "Temporarily Out of Service" notice. I couldn't even leave a message.

Desperate to escape my own pain, I roamed through the deafening, smoke-filled inferno of Better City, throwing myself into relentless motion. I tried to help rescue victims of the fire, organize emergency services, comfort people wherever I could. Despite rescue efforts, at least seventy people died in the flames and smoke and there was nothing, nothing I could do about it. I was a level-one telepath, true, but there were limits to my abilities, and I felt them severely that night.

As I groped my way through the city, probing the ruins of buildings for any sign of life within, I was almost grateful for the urgency, the exhaustion, and the fear that blotted out everything else. Only now and then did a thought, sharpened by grief, manage to penetrate the protective layers of my weariness.

Rick. We came so close together. Why did you leave? How could you die? Just when I was beginning to understand . . .

But there was no answer coming and there never would be.

Near dawn, I stumbled back to the main building of Better World. Miraculously, it had escaped the inferno, untouched. I found an empty couch, curled up on it, and fell into exhausted, dreamless slumber.

I AWOKE TO THE SMOKING RUINS of Rick's dreams. The media descended upon us with frightening swiftness and I was only too happy to use my telepathic skills against them. But they were everywhere, poking through the smoking ruins like starved hyenas scenting fresh kill, finding their meal and surrounding it.

"Dr. Akimura," they barked. "What now? What do you see as the future of Better World?"

"Dr. Akimura, you took control when the Desert Prophet died. Are you a prophet, too?"

"Weren't you against Better World? What made you change your mind?"

"What are your plans?"

"There have been reports of rioting in other cities at the news of Rick's death. How do you intend to stop the violence? The self-mutilations?"

"Can we have a statement about the hundreds of deaths around the world?"

"No comment," I said. "No comment, no comment, no comment." And I backed away from them as fast as I could. Luckily, I kept going until I ran smack into Betty Smithson and Joe Martinez.

"Joe, Betty, we've got to keep those reporters out of here. Give them some sort of statement. Find Alanna—she can help you with it."

"Of course, Julian." Betty's voice held a note of respect and awe formerly reserved only for my brother. "Whatever you say. Whatever we can do to help."

Joe Martinez nodded as well. His ruddy face was streaked with soot and he looked exhausted but he stood there as sturdily as a rock. "We'll see to it right away."

A splinter group of fanatics immediately claimed that Rick's emergence and death was a sign that the world had entered its last days. There were spontaneous riots in New York, St. Petersburg, Rio, San Francisco, Paris, Berlin, and Beijing. I received reports that violence was erupting in every city where there was a sizable contingent of Better World followers. They had lost their idol and were hysterical with grief and fear. The vid images were graphic, unimaginable.

But that wasn't the worst of it. Not yet. After one of several forays I made into the ruins of Better City the day after the fire, I returned to B.W. headquarters and found an urgent message to call home, immediately.

My father answered the phone, pale and distracted. "Julian, thank God." I had never seen him look so disturbed.

"What is it?" I said. "What's happened?"

"Your mother . . ." His voice quavered, choked off.

I couldn't bear it. Not another loss. No, no, no. In icy

terror I begged, pleaded, and finally cajoled the story out of him: Yosh had found my mother in the kitchen at three that morning, covered with blood, weeping, incoherent. In her hand was a golden ceramic blade with which she had managed to slash one wrist. He had pulled the knife away from her, put a pressure bandage on the wound, and called an ambulance. She had received a transfusion at Cedars of Lebanon hospital and was sedated, under observation.

"The doctors say she'll recover."

"I'm sure they're right, Dad."

"Can you come out here? I could really use your help."

I felt a stab of guilt. "I don't know. Things are so chaotic right now and I don't think I can really leave it all in Alanna's lap." I was beginning to feel light-headed and unhinged. Too many demands were being made. But how could I say no to my father? I had always relied upon him to be the strong one, the one able to cope. Now that he needed me, I was useless, no help to him at all.

The expression on my face must have said it all.

"That's okay, son. I understand." And, before my eyes, the father of my childhood, of my heart and dreams, reappeared, steadfast, understanding, able to shoulder unimaginable burdens with a gentle smile and a shrug. "Come when you can."

"Dad," I said, "I love you." I almost couldn't get the words past the lump in my throat.

"And I love you, Julian. Never forget that. I'll expect to hear from you soon. I hope you'll try to call your mother later if you can." And with a smile he was gone, returning, alone, to his own private emergency.

The vid trumpeted the news of Rick's death at full volume:

"Miracle Man Dies Before Thousands."

"The End of Better World?"

"Rick, We Barely Knew Ye."

"Mutant Messiah Stricken During Show. Followers Riot."

After the first night I refused to watch the news. I couldn't bear to see Rick dying over and over again, to see the city burning and hear the people screaming.

"Close Better World immediately," was the immediate command of the Mutant Councils.

"Close Better World," said the governor of New Mexico.

"Shut it down," said the FBI, and every concerned citizens' group with access to a screen and our fax number.

Well, I had certainly intended to close B.W., hadn't I? And wasn't the very means to end it right there in my hands? But I hung back, hesitating, for I knew human nature, had traveled its back alleys and byways. If I abolished B.W. now I feared that worse hysteria and mayhem would result than had already taken place. Better to leave it open, inactive and benign. Wouldn't the faithful eventually lose interest? Without the dynamic allure of Rick, Better World would become a quiet, relatively inert charitable organization. No doubt even such fierce champions as Betty and Alanna would find fresh distractions now that Rick was gone. By the time I shut it down, in a year or two, no one would even notice. Such was my plan.

I slept badly in the days that followed and took to walking through Better City, past encampments of the faithful where campfires gleamed, past darkened hulks that had once been shops and cafés. Occasionally, during my nocturnal prowling I encountered a fellow telepath. I realized that these mutants must have been the same ones whose minds I had encountered in the stadium and used to build my magical circuit after Rick's collapse. So Rick and Alanna *had* managed to draw a few mutants to them before the end. A good thing, too. Without them, I never could have gained even temporary control over that crowd.

Finally all the anger and sorrow turned inward. The maddened crowds quieted and disbanded, the faithful wept and mourned in private, the dead were buried, and the healing process began.

Late one night as I sat in my room, sleepless and grieving, the screen rang. I almost let the answermech take it. Then, on a whim, I answered and my heart turned a somersault of joy. It was Star, safe and sound.

"Oh, *querido*," she whispered. "Finally. I have tried and tried to get through."

"You and me both."

"I've been so worried. So terribly worried for you."

"Never mind about me," I said. "What about you? I heard about the horrible riots—"

"Fine, fine. The people went crazy at the news. You can imagine." Her eyes held mine for a moment. "How can he be dead, Julian? I can't believe it."

"It was awful, Star." And I told her about that night in the amphitheater. At first I gave her the barest of outlines but she urged me on.

"Don't try to spare me, Julian. I must share this with you. Tell me everything." With gentle goading and mock scolding she drew the story out of me, piece by agonizing piece. By the time I had finished we were both in tears.

"I wish I could be there right now," she said. "But you must understand how demoralized everyone is by Rick's death. I can't abandon them."

"I know. At least, I'm trying to understand. But I need you, too, Star."

"Give me two weeks?"

"All right. Two weeks." I had made it this far. I could wait a bit longer. "But hurry."

"As soon as I can, beloved."

After we said good night, I fell into a deep sleep and dreamed of Star, that she was lying beside me, opening herself to me. I awoke happy and refreshed.

We had closed the amphitheater immediately but that didn't prevent people from leaving flowers outside the walls until the roses and lilies seemed five feet deep. In time, the Roman theater became one of the most important sites commemorating Rick's passage, a venerated memorial.

The official cause of Rick's death was listed as a cerebral hemorrhage brought on by natural causes.

"What was natural about it?" I demanded of the coroner who had come bustling out from Albuquerque.

She was a lean, grizzled woman with close-cropped gray hair and tired gray eyes. "About him?" she said. "Nothing. Your brother—and he was your brother, isn't that correct, Dr. Akimura?—was extraordinary in every way. Unique. But mutants have shorter life spans than nonmutants, yes? And his was shorter than most. My guess is that he tried to put out too much energy at that sharing thing and it finished him. He looked maybe forty outside. But inside he was an old, old man." Her expression softened as she looked into my eyes. "I'd say it was just his time to go. Rick wore himself out. He was never meant to last. The very special ones don't."

For a crazy moment I wanted to believe that she was wrong, that somehow Rick had been assassinated, either by Metzger's people or perhaps by a different bunch he had angered and frightened. But I managed to keep my paranoid theories to myself. This woman had no reason to lie to me and she had impeccable credentials: she knew what she was doing. I had to accept her judgment.

The coroner's words also forced me to face something I had only half suspected: perhaps Rick had wanted to die. Perhaps it had been his intention all along—from the moment he reappeared—to sacrifice himself for humanity and atone, at last, fully, for Skerry's death. That would account for the frantic overwork, the denial of weakness, the overextension of his powers. If Rick hadn't died in that stadium he would doubtless have found another place. The coroner was right. My brother had never really intended to stay. Not at all.

But Betty Smithson was less easily satisfied by medical explanations. "Rick didn't wear out," she said. "He couldn't. He was perfect. He was killed—I just know it. People were frightened of him. We'll find them, those assassins, wherever they are, and we'll make them pay."

"Betts, you don't mean that," I said. Her fierce words and wild-eyed expression were unnerving.

"You'll see, Julian." She nodded crisply. "You'll see."

Alanna seemed to accept the coroner's verdict with discomforting ease. She was icily controlled, emotionless, almost robotic. Only her eyes seemed alive in that pale green face. But I had no time to worry about her, either.

Alanna seemed to carve her way through those sad days with ruthless energy. There was a new toughness about her. Her temper flared easily, and she wouldn't tolerate much sentimental discussion of Rick, cutting people off quickly if they didn't take the hint. She devoted all her attention to Rick's funeral preparations.

His funeral was a monumental affair, carried on all the vid channels and attended by an array of foreign dignitaries. He was buried where he had died, in the Roman arena. A marble sarcophagus held his mortal remains, and an eternal flame flickered in a golden urn at the base of his tomb.

A simple phrase, "No One Is Alone," served as epitaph. Alanna had suggested it, and both of my parents endorsed it. I didn't agree with the sentiment—after all, who had been more alone than Rick?—but I saw no harm in using it to honor my brother.

There were speeches by government officials and private citizens, by grief-stricken true believers and glib self-serving politicos.

My mother had not recovered sufficiently to attend the funeral—she was still under heavy sedation. Yosh had stayed behind to be with her, but had shipped me a tape of a poignant, powerful dirge, "Rick's Ode," which he had composed for the event. It quickly became Better World's unofficial memorial anthem.

After the ceremony, the faithful were allowed to approach the grave site. In five minutes Rick's tomb was buried under flowers that nearly smothered the eternal flame. The enrobement of Rick's grave in chamiso branches and white roses became a tradition that persists to this day.

After Rick's funeral, the cleanup process began in earnest and a million questions had to be answered.

"Julian," Alanna said. "We must discuss rebuilding plans right away."

"Who said anything about rebuilding?"

"Don't you think it's time? There's an awful lot of people living in tents out there."

"Well, then, fine. Tell them to do it."

"You don't understand. They want your blessing."

"Why me? I have nothing to do with this."

Alanna's smile was incredulous. "But you're all they have left of Rick."

"They're wrong. There's nothing left of Rick. Nothing at all."

"But—"

"No," I said harshly. "If you want to rebuild and you've got the funds, go ahead and do it. But leave me out of it. Do you understand, Alanna? I want no part of it. Not one little piece."

"Fine," she said. "If that's the way you want it."

The construction crews and aircranes rolled into Better City the next day, without my blessing.

I WAS IMMENSELY BUSY in those days and refused all calls, all messages, fended off anyone besides Star or immediate family who tried to reach me. It was only by chance that Joachim Metzger got through.

"You've got a lot of brass calling me, Metzger."

He ignored my offensive thrust. "I understand you took control of the sharing your brother was holding when he died," Metzger said. "Well done. I'm sure you prevented a great deal of bloodshed. And now that you're running the show, it should be a snap to shut down the remnants of Better World."

I stared at him, completely flabbergasted. "Since you seem to have forgotten our last encounter, let me refresh your memory," I said. "You were considering whether or not to have my brother killed. And there are certain people who are convinced that Rick *was* murdered and would enjoy receiving that information."

"You know I had nothing to do with—"

"I thought I had made it clear that all communications between us were over."

"But, Julian—"

"No buts, Metzger. If you make any further attempt to communicate with me I'll do everything I can to implicate you in the murder of my brother. Is that clear? Goodbye, Book Keeper." I cut the connection, smiling.

The screen rang almost immediately—Metzger calling back?—and I let the answermech take it. Goodbye, Metzger. Good riddance and go to hell.

There was a gentle knock at the door. "Julian," Betty Smithson said. "May I come in?" She held an armful of printouts.

"I'm awfully busy, Betts, can it wait?"

She sat down as though she hadn't heard my reply. "Julian, you were truly splendid that night in the arena. We have you to thank for saving us all."

"Betty, really, I only did what anybody else would have if they could."

"Nonsense. You were heroic, Julian. I can't tell you how much I admire you for that." She was looking at me in a peculiarly intense way, almost worshipful. "And you'll be glad to know we're getting closer and closer to the trail of those who killed your brother. It's just a matter of time before we find them."

Oh, Betty, I thought. If you only knew how close you'd come to having a genuine red herring thrown right down your throat. If you had just stepped into my office a few minutes sooner I could have fed you Joachim Metzger with a sprig of parsley. Aloud, I said, "Betty, you're not serious."

"What do you mean?" Her eyes were clear blue and guileless.

"You're just kidding about this conspiracy theory, aren't you?"

She looked stricken, pierced to the heart. "But I thought you understood. You mean that you don't believe it? You've just been pretending?" Tears filled her eyes.

"Betty, I haven't been pretending anything. You haven't exactly given me a chance to disagree, you know."

"I'm sorry." She stood up, clutching the sheaf of print-outs to her chest. "I thought you really did understand. But you will, Julian. You're of his blood. You'll see."

12

RICK HAD BEEN DEAD for almost a month and I was immersed in Better World business up to my neck. The more I tried to relinquish responsibilities the more tasks seemed to pile up around me. I had taken an indefinite leave of absence from my practice and hospital rounds. My life was on hold, in orbit around Better World. The only thing that kept me going was the thought that Star would arrive any day now.

Once we had agreed that she would wrap up her business in Rio and come to New Mexico as soon as possible, we spent every night on the screen planning our life together. Last night her screen had been busy and I had finally left an impatient message of love, urging her to come quickly. I could hardly wait to hold her in my arms again.

I was working late in the improvised office I'd arranged on the second floor of B.W. headquarters when Alanna came for a visit.

"I can't believe that your door is open," she said. "Feeling unusually expansive?"

"Actually, I was just after some fresh air." I looked up at her warily. All memory of the recent harshness between us seemed to have left her, or else she was repressing it mercilessly. My half-sister radiated good will.

"Oh, honestly, Julian. How about a truce?" She waved her hand in surrender. "You know we've got to talk."

"About what?"

She seemed surprised. "Why, Better World, of course. We have to make some decisions."

"I thought that's what we've been doing."

"Yes, certainly. What I mean to say is we have to talk about Betty and her paranoid suspicions. She's starting to infect people with her conspiracy theory."

"That crazy idea that Rick was assassinated?" I shrugged. "Tell everybody to get inoculations against her."

"I'm not joking, Julian. It's serious to her. I think it's Betty's way of trying to work through her grief and anger."

"Not bad analysis coming from an amateur."

She smiled. "Everybody in this organization seems to be looking for someone to blame. There's already been so much ugliness, so much violence and death. Now I'm afraid that Betty's wild ideas will spread. She'll be leading a mob before we can stop her, chasing down some poor, innocent victim."

"Is it that bad? I had no idea she had gotten so fanatic about it."

"That's why you've got to talk to her."

"Me? Why?"

"You're the only one she'll listen to."

"Don't be ridiculous."

"Come on, Julian. Even you can't be completely oblivious to the way she looks at you. Ever since the night of Rick's death she's developed a huge case of hero worship for you. You're the only one she respects. You've got to make her listen to reason, Julian. Before she becomes a major problem around here."

"Well, if you think it'll do any good I'll go see her." I peered up at the mountain of paperwork on my desk. "As soon as I get a free minute."

I realize now that Alanna wanted me to do more than ease Betty's suspicions. She wanted me to send Betty away. But that wasn't exactly what happened.

The next morning around eleven o'clock I took a break, stretched my legs, and went to find Betty. She was in the library, watching a portascreen. I peered over her shoulder so I could see what she was viewing: it was a tape of that terrible night in the Roman arena that she was running at half-speed, stopping occasionally to make notes.

"A little light entertainment, Betts?"

"Oh, Julian." Flustered, she switched off the screen. "You should have called me if you wanted me. I would have come right away."

"No need. I thought I would come see you."

A look of pleasure, even awe, came over her. It confused and saddened me.

"I'm so glad you were looking for me, Julian. I've never told you adequately how marvelous you were that terrible night—"

"Betty, you've said plenty already."

"No, it's not enough. You just don't know. You don't realize, yet. But you are truly blessed, just as Rick was." She grabbed my hand and, before I could pull away, kissed the back of it. Her eyes were deep blue and as fixed as those of any fanatic I had ever treated.

"Hey, cut it out, Betty. You're embarrassing me. And you're wrong."

I waited for her to chuckle, maybe even blush. But she continued to smile at me with that same fixed, awful look on her face.

"I know that you'll lead us to the assassins, Julian. You'll help us achieve justice. Together, we'll hunt down Rick's murderers and avenge him."

Could this really be the same Betty Smithson who had regarded me with a fishy glare at our very first meeting? I tried but failed to find that shrewd woman in this blissed-out zombie. Betty's delusion about me was as big as the Sangre de Cristos. What could I do? Reasoning was pointless.

Using a telepathic probe, I reached gently into her mind and tried to get some sense of the scale of her obsession. My heart sank as I realized that she was completely lost in her paranoid beliefs. What would Rick have done, I wondered. How would he have healed her? And then I knew.

She thought I was Rick's chosen successor. All right. Fine. She had certainly elected me to that post. Then I would act the part she had assigned to me. In fact, I would go one better. For Betty, I would become my brother.

I intensified the mental connection until I could create an image in Betty's mind. Then I conjured up a picture of my brother and, acting as ventriloquist, had him give her a little talk.

Hello, Betts.

She gasped. "Who?"

Don't you recognize me anymore?

"Rick, is that you?"

Who else? Betts, I can't stay long but I wanted to talk to you.

"Yes, yes, please, Rick. Go on."

You've got to listen to Julian, Betts. He's got your best interests and those of Better World at heart. I don't like all this anger and hatred I see in you. You have to forgive. Didn't I teach you that? Understanding and love, Betts, not revenge. It's the only way.

"But the murderers, Rick—"

There were no murderers, Betts. It was just my time to go. I wasn't assassinated. Do you understand?

"I don't know."

I intensified the connection a bit and inserted a touch of post-hypnotic suggestion.

Betts, that's not good enough. You must accept. Forgive. Let me go. Remember, understanding and love. It's the only way.

"The only way." Her voice was deep and slow, as though she were almost sedated.

Right. You've got it now. So no more of this weird conspiracy shit, okay?

"But . . ."

No buts. Hear me?

"Whatever you say, Rick."

And listen to Julian. He's the boss from now on.

"Of course."

Okay then. So long, Betts. Take care of yourself and have a good, happy life.

With that, I put her into a light sleep and broke the mental connection.

Five minutes later she awoke. The robotic, glassy-eyed fanaticism was gone. In its place was pure, shining adoration. It would have to do, at least for now. I didn't dare fiddle around with her mind any further.

"Julian," she whispered. "I've had a vision, a wondrous vision. Rick was here. He spoke to me."

"That's fine, Betty. What did he say?"

Her eyes glowed. "That you were in charge from now on. That I was to listen to you about everything."

"And do you feel comfortable with that?"

"Oh, yes, yes. Completely." She grabbed my hand, but I pulled away before she could kiss it again.

"Well, that's fine," I said. I was almost amused by my solution to Betty's paranoia. But it saddened me as well. I had lost a friend and gained a worshipper. "I've got to run now but we'll talk later. Do you feel all right?"

"Oh, Julian, I feel wonderful."

As I left the room I could swear that she blew me a kiss.

ONCE BACK IN MY OFFICE, I checked my screen for messages, but there was no word from Star. Feeling a bit put out, I tried her number. No answer. Well, she was probably out holding a healing dance ritual. I admit that I was a bit jealous of the amount of attention she lavished on Mundo Melhor. Well, she would be here soon. Not soon enough, but soon.

I distracted myself with an analysis of my unconventional therapeutic approach to Betty's problem. Not a bad solution, I thought. I was feeling a bit pleased with myself. But when I told Alanna about what I had done, she was less sanguine.

"I suggested that you calm Betty down," she said. "Not buoy her up. Don't you think you went just a wee bit too far with your intervention? She's practically polishing your footprints."

"I can't help that," I said. "Besides, it should wear off eventually."

"No matter," Alanna said. She rubbed her eyes wearily. "In the long run it will be to our advantage, anyway."

"Meaning?"

"Why, the continued health and prosperity of Better World, of course."

"Hey, just a minute here. I thought we were temporarily administering this place until things had calmed down enough for us to shut it down completely."

"Is that what you thought?" Alanna smiled in a condescending way. "I had no idea. How could you imagine that we would ever close Better World? No, Julian, not ever. We've got to manage it as Rick would have wanted it done."

"Hold on, Alanna—"

"Who else is better suited to the task, Julian? We both knew him best. We are both of his blood."

"That doesn't mean a damned thing. I'm a telepath, you're a telekinete, and between us we couldn't cure one leper."

"You'll do it, Julian." Her tone implied that the answer was oh-so-simple, only an idiot like me couldn't see it. "You have to carry on Rick's work," Alanna said. "You're the only one who can do it."

I stared at her. "Me? Why not you?"

"I'm not a telepath or I would. You *have* to do it, Julian."

"Are you crazy, too?" I said. "I can't do miracles. Listen to me, Alanna. I'm the other brother, remember? Just your average mutant. In any case, I don't want to lead a cult. I already have a profession and clientele waiting for me on the other side of this country."

She shrugged off my arguments as though she hadn't even heard me. A strange light burned fiercely in her golden eyes, unnerving me. "You can hold sharings— you've already proven that. And as for the other hocus-pocus, well, we can manage things somehow with some vid magic."

"Fake miracles? Alanna, I'm beginning to believe that you're really serious about this."

"I am, Julian. Deadly serious. What else is left to me now but Better World? It's the only part of Rick that I can still touch." Her voice wavered dangerously, and for a moment her face crumpled in grief. But she regained control instantly and put the steely mask right back in place. "We have to do it, Julian. For Rick. Don't you see that?"

"I see that *you* think we have to do it, for you. And I also see that you've become as deranged by sorrow as Betty has, but you're denying it."

"Don't patronize me, Julian. I know what I'm doing and I want you in on it. Rick would want it, too."

"You know I can't hold sharings," I said. "Not the way that Rick did. To begin with, I would need half a dozen telepaths to assist me. More, if the crowd was really big." I couldn't believe I was actually discussing this. I stared across the table, trying to break through to her. "Alanna, listen to me. This makes no sense, no sense at all. What's more, *I don't want to do it.* I have no intention of doing it. Got that?"

"We'll provide whatever you need."

"You're not listening."

"Julian, we *must* maintain continuity. And control."

"Why?"

Now her eyes flashed. "How can you ask me that? Don't you care about Rick at all? About his legacy?" She leaned closer. "No, I don't think so. In fact, I think you were jealous of him all the time."

"Don't be ridiculous." I was getting uncomfortable with the direction the discussion was taking.

"You're probably relieved that Rick's gone. You can't wait to shovel Better World right after him into the grave."

"That's not true!"

"No?" she said. "Then prove it. Prove that you care about Rick and what he tried to accomplish. Don't make a mockery of his life, Julian. Help me. Don't you want to help people?"

"Of course I do. I'm a therapist. A healer."

"Then heal. I need you. Rick needed you but you turned away. Don't turn away again."

"Forget it, Alanna. You can't run Better World without a resident miracle worker. And I don't want the job."

She shot me a look of pure fury as she got to her feet. "I should have known you'd be heartless, just as you always were in the past. You don't care about Rick, not at all. You never did." And with that she was out the door and gone. But her words remained, etching their way into my conscience.

In those rare moments when I was undistracted by the needs of Better World I tried repeatedly to call Star. She had never returned my last call, and in growing alarm I had attempted to reach her by screen, by phone, and finally by registered letter, but without any luck. She seemed to have vanished completely and I was sick with worry over her.

So when the airmail letter arrived with a postmark from Rio de Janeiro, I tore it open eagerly. Inside there was a packet with a recorded vidnote.

I activated it but instead of Star's familiar features a dark-haired man with a thick mustache appeared onscreen. "I am Dr. Juan Moreira," he said. "Star Cecilia's cousin.

"Amigo, I am terribly sorry to have to tell you this. But my cousin Star with whom you seem to have formed a close friendship was killed by the police during rioting." His large brown eyes stared out at me sympathetically. "As you no doubt realize, there was much violence here after the death of your Desert Prophet. I have sent you the formal death notice, and a picture of my cousin. She was a fine woman. My deepest condolences. *Tem a bravo.*"

The screen went blank. With numb mind and hands I examined the other documents: the packet contained a formal certification of the death of one Star Cecilia Nicolau from a mortal blow sustained while resisting arrest. The date was several weeks after Rick died. Behind that was a holophoto of Star, smiling brightly.

Star dead? I felt as though the breath had frozen in my chest.

No. It was impossible. She was too vital, too beautiful to die. I crumpled the paper in my fist, trying to squeeze the facts into nothingness, into unbeing. Star, please don't be dead. Please. It could not, must not be true. This paper is a lie. Everything is a lie. Only my love for you is real.

I could see her before me, laughing and dancing, naked, in the firelight, alive and fearless.

For a moment I fought to hold on to that vision. Then it faded, and the truth seared me, body and soul. Choking, weeping, I curled into a ball around the pain. Star was gone. I would never see her again. My love, I thought. I abandoned you. And now I've lost you forever.

All these deaths, all this destruction. No, I can't bear it. No more, please. Please.

I ran from the room, from the building, blind with grief, out into the cold night and into the cold city. I wandered through the ruins, lost and soulless.

Chimneys jutted in the gloom like headstones among the ashes and desolated buildings. Deep shadows cut across the streets and crumbling walls, giving the place an almost prehistoric cast. By day Better City hummed with activity, a lively hive filled with eager bees rebuilding their future. But after dark the ghosts came out to play.

I drifted, haunted and shaken, through a gray and hopeless endtime of the spirit, questioning all that I had believed in and valued. Rick was dead, and try as I might, I could deny his loss no longer. It had been a cruel amputation indeed and I was too much of a healer and doctor to deny the trauma I had experienced. The ruse of my busyness had worked for a time but Star's death had forced me, finally, to confront myself.

Beloved, why have you gone? And why am I still here?

My thoughts trailed off into hopeless tears. I was alone, truly alone.

In the midst of my weeping, Alanna's words came back to taunt me. Did I want Rick to be gone and forgotten? Was that what I truly desired? To bury everything that had ever meant anything at all to me?

Yes. Yes, I did. I wanted to run screaming from the past, to pretend that I had been born this very moment, fresh and innocent, without painful memories and poignant ties to other places and people. But at the same time I desperately wanted to preserve every memory, to anoint every scar inflicted by time. To remember Star with love and wonder. To honor Rick. He had been a magnificent anomaly. A miracle worker. A murderer. And my brother.

What, I wondered, do I owe you, Rick? What do I owe to you, to the past, and to the future? Should I tear down Better World or build it up bigger than before?

As I wandered, heartworn, weary, I found myself at the gates to the Roman arena. Slowly I climbed up the center aisle, step by step, until I was inches away from Rick's tomb.

Rick, I'm scared.

All I could hear was the sound of the wind whistling through the stadium and my own blood pounding through my veins. But then I heard something else. It sounded like a rusty voice, whispering from beneath the cold marble.

Scared? Of what, little brother?

Making the wrong move.

That's been your problem all your life, hasn't it? You've clung to your rules and regulations so that you wouldn't have to think for yourself.

And now I don't know what to do.

Do what feels right.

I thought that I should close down Better World. That it was dangerous.

But how do you feel?

As though this place serves a purpose. Everywhere I go I see people working, busy and happy. Better World gives them hope. Someplace to be. Something to do.

And?

Well, isn't that worthwhile? Doesn't it provide something that nobody else can? Comfort. Connection. Better World makes good on that promise, which is more than any three organized religions can say. And there doesn't have to be any incense, any priestly caste. All it seems to take is people.

Now you're talking, little brother.

But, considering what a powerful force Better World can be, I don't know if I can control it. Or if I should try.

Bullshit. There you go with your rules again. Shoulds don't count, little brother. What's important is comfort and connection, understanding and harmony. People don't want that old-time nonmutant religious mumbo-jumbo. And they don't want Mutant Council bullshit either. They need something new. A synthesis of the two. Bring them together, Julian. Bring them home. And heal yourself.

I waited a bit longer but the tomb was silent. Strangely comforted, I rested my cheek against the cold marble. All along the lavender curve of the horizon the stars were winking.

PERHAPS I HAD IMAGINED the entire conversation. Very likely I did. Perhaps it was a delusion born of guilt, or, possibly, love. And maybe, just maybe, I longed to find a safe answer and safer hiding place. What better camouflage than the enormous, obliterating shadow of my brother? And how better to honor Star's sacrifice, and my love for her? Wasn't this one way to hold on to at least a tiny piece of her?

Most probably it was a combination of all of these reasons that made me agree to Alanna's wild plan. But I gave in, yes. In the end I said yes, all right, I'll be a stand-in messiah. I had done it for Betty, hadn't I? Why not for a few thousand more people?

Alanna received the news with a certain calm satisfaction, as if she had known all along I would come around.

"Good," she said. "We can start planning a public ceremony right away."

"Shouldn't we try this on a small scale, first?"

"I don't think so, Julian. So many people need reassurance and comfort. The more we can reach, the better. Maybe we should hold it in the Roman amphitheater."

"No. Not there," I said. "Anyplace but that."

"All right, if you feel *that* strongly. But I think it would be the perfect place."

"What if the faithful don't accept me?" I said. "I can't do miracles. I'm not Rick."

"Don't worry about that." Alanna held up a silvery vid disc. "Here. Study this."

"What is it?"

"*Rick's Way.*"

"Rick's what?"

"It's a collection of quotes by Rick and an overview of his philosophy. I was working on it when he died."

I was both offended and amazed. "You want me to memorize a script? Why don't you just use a vid simulacrum? What do you even need me for?"

"Don't be ridiculous, Julian. I want you to say it in your own words, of course. But you might as well see what we were doing. And it might help you to feel more comfortable."

"I don't know, Alanna."

"Will you at least look it over?" She held the memory disc out to me until, finally, begrudgingly, I took it.

I spent most of that night and a good portion of the early morning sitting by my roomscreen scanning the text. As far as I could tell, *Rick's Way* was one part Eastern mysticism and two parts golden rule seasoned with a sprinkling of mutant aphorisms, good old common sense, and some clumsy poetry. It didn't sound like my brother. Not one word of it.

In the morning, bleary-eyed, I headed for the mechteria downstairs. Alanna was sitting by herself at a corner table, sipping from a mug and staring into a portascreen. Without any preamble I confronted her.

"Funny," I said, "I don't remember Rick as being that profound. Or articulate."

She looked up and a ghost of a smile flickered across her lips for a moment. "He wasn't," she said. "But that's how people will remember him." I stared at her, nonplussed. She had indeed channeled her grief into a raging determination to control every aspect of Better World, right down to manipulating Rick's image, his very words. It was the last vestige of him left to her, and apparently, it was all she thought about.

"Don't you see what you're doing?" I said. "Steamrolling all of your energy into this thing as though it were Rick's child."

"Rick's child *and* mine. That's exactly what Better World is." She gave me a long, cold look. "I'm glad you see that, Julian. It's important for you to understand."

"But isn't this taking advantage of innocent people who believed in Rick—nonmutants who are vulnerable to our sharing techniques?"

"How are we taking advantage of them? They love the groupmind. They need it. We'll just be giving them more of what they want."

"But, Alanna, most of the faithful at Better World are normals. I don't think I can sustain sharings with them. How can I bring normals into a sharing?"

"You did it before."

"Once, under extreme circumstances, and with the help of several other telepaths. Rick was so powerful that he didn't need any help. Ever."

"Of course you can do it. Rick once told me that even normals can become a part of the circuit even though they're poor conductors. You've just got to pair them with stronger minds."

"But that's my point, exactly."

"So in a groupmind you'll need the power of several

combined telepaths to help you create the circuit." She shrugged. "Most mutants are good conductors even if they're not primarily telepaths, and even some normals are tremendously resonant and resilient. I'm sure we'll be able to manage with the people that we already have on hand."

I still had my doubts. But my own grief and determination to maintain some connection with my brother—and, by extension, with Star—pushed me onward. I told myself that if it didn't work, no harm done. I could get out any time. I could still close down Better World.

13

WE HELD MY FIRST official sharing on a Sunday evening in March, in the main auditorium at Better World.

As the hall filled I fidgeted backstage, uncomfortable in my ceremonial clothing. I would have preferred to wear a simple white stretch suit instead of the cowboy outfit Alanna had insisted upon, but she had been adamant.

"Jeans and a work shirt," she had said. "For continuity."

She even attempted to convince me to grow a beard but there I held firm against her.

The hall was filled to the brim with true believers: standing room only against the blue and purple paneled walls. Doubt welled up in my chest as I listened to the crowd chattering.

"We're ready," Alanna whispered. "Get started."

Feeling like some foolish imposter I clomped my way out to the podium. The heavy brown cowboy boots I wore felt uncomfortable and foreign.

There were five hundred seats in the room and every one held a devotee of Better World. Each person sat there, sad, expectant, hopeful, uncertain. Occasionally in the sea of eyes I saw mutant gold glimmering. For one long moment I looked at them and they at me.

Well, I thought. Here goes. Take a deep breath and drop into mindspeech.

Let us form a circle and let us begin.

Everyone linked hands.

Carefully I noted the location of the mutants in the room: two in the back by the main doors, two in the center, three in the front row. And Alanna, offstage.

Join with me. Don't be afraid.

My heart pounded. I closed my eyes and reached out toward them with my mind.

A deep vibration moved up my spine and spread outward from one mutant to another and from them to the others until the entire room was linked. Yes, a circle.

I felt a surge of power, almost erotic in its intensity, move through the core of my being and out into the circuit. I knew all of them, I was with them, I could see into their souls, understand their private sorrows and triumphs. There was no separate being who was Julian or Alanna. We were all Julian, all Alanna, and each the other. It was a moment of supreme communion.

And with the communion came understanding. So many varying tones in this mix but all combined in harmony just the same. Suddenly I knew how badly these people needed this sharing, and saw, too, that they were not alone in their need. I, too, had been a prisoner in my lonely head, rotating in my obsessive grief and isolation. But here was sharing, here was love and relief from isolation. It was good, and better than good. Wonderful.

Together we heal one another. We help one another. Come, touch me, join with me. I'm frightened, too. I need you, too.

I felt a harsh negative surge penetrate the circle and somehow I knew it was Alanna. Instinctively I cut her off before she permeated the entire sharing. Whatever was bothering her, I would deal with it later. I had no time for it now.

The words of sharing came easily. I could almost imagine Rick prompting me. I could hear him, and suddenly I could see him.

He stood upon gray ice in the middle of a frozen pond, one hand above his head as though he had been waving to someone—me?—but had himself been turned to ice or stone in midgesture. Only his eyes were alive. Only the eyes. Golden and glowing, they flashed like miniature suns and left purple-black spots in their wake, purple and black and red on the inside of my eyelids. Their radiance nearly blinded me.

The stone statue blinked and his eyes broke the air between us into a million particles of refracted color: purple, green, blue, red, orange, yellow, white. He blinked again, the ice cracked, and he went crashing through, disappearing below the frozen surface of the lake.

I dived in after him to save him and the water hit me like an electric shock. It was so cold, so pure and cold. And everything around me was white, the burning white of purity, of clarity, of white skirts whirling in a tropical ritual dance as drums pounded. I surrendered myself to the cold, to the burning whiteness, to the pounding of my blood in my ears, and floated there without volition. I didn't need to breathe, didn't need to think. The water evaporated and I hung in space, motionless. But I saw things. So many wondrous things.

A primitive rope bridge spanned a chasm between two cliffs. Rick stood frozen atop one rock face, I upon the other. As I watched, the causeway writhed and spread, fibers forming and re-forming, until it became the connection between us, between our very cells, the winding, twisting umbilicus of DNA that made us, made our parents, and their parents before them, snaking back over the centuries, back and back to the first mutants, the first golden-eyed offspring born after the landfall of those mythic meteors.

It looped around every mutant, stringing us together like mountain climbers as we clambered our way across the ages, up the wall of time. I had all this weight to pull behind me now, so many stone statues sliding up the cliff face catching on scars, on old memories, slowing my pace. I couldn't carry them all, didn't want or need to. I reached behind, slashed at the rope, felt it give, and turned my head to the wall as the past fell away, hurtling out of sight.

Now I raced up the sheer rock, certain of my footing, lighter than the blue sky below and above me. The path was easy, the way clear. Joyous, I stood atop the mountain and saw the millions of upturned faces below, flowers searching for the sun. For me.

And they said, *We need, and we shall always need. Always want, always search.*

And I knew what to tell them.

Yes, we all need, and we shall always need, always want the comfort that seems so constantly elusive. But stay. Stay awhile here with me and let us comfort one another.

Good. We will share with you.

Then I saw them clearly, perhaps for the first time, in every shape, in every color, but identical inside. The same wordless yearning, the same hunger for love and understanding, was felt by the homeless man and the one whose bank account was stuffed with eurocredits, by the mechanic who fixed mechbrains and the engineer who designed them, by the poet and the garbage collector, the husband, the wife.

Need cut across all boundaries, all the jagged lines we had drawn between us. In our need we were equal and vulnerable. Human. Because of it we could love one another. And we did. I did.

For a lovely hour that felt like fleeting moments we all floated together and when I finally dissolved the sharing I knew that, somehow, I would carry on my brother's work.

Go in love, I told them. *Remember what you felt here.*

I had done it. By God, I had really held a group sharing. I was ecstatic—practically floated offstage as the energies from the communion percolated through me. Everyone leaving the auditorium seemed to feel the same way. Everyone but Alanna.

She came storming out of the wings and clutched me by the arm.

"I want to talk to you." There was something at work in her, something that would not be quelled by the mood, the sharing, or even by Rick's memory. I felt my good spirits draining away.

She said, "That's not the way Rick would have done it—"

I cut her off. "I don't care, Alanna."

"What?" She stared at me as though I were someone she had never seen before.

I met her fiery gaze and gave it right back. "Rick's not here anymore, remember? Besides, *you* told me to do it any way I could."

"I thought I told you to read *Rick's Way*."

"I can recite chapter and verse for you, if you like. But I can't run a sharing in any other manner than this."

"Rick healed people," Alanna said stubbornly. "He didn't ask them to help him the way you did. He didn't take as much from them as you did. And he never admitted to being frightened during a sharing. Never."

"So what?" I said. "You saw those folks, their faces. They were satisfied. The sharing was good for them. What different does it make how I achieved it? I don't understand why you're so upset about this."

"Rick went right into them, saw the hurt, and fixed it."

"Fine," I said. "Then get some other mutant who can do that, Alanna. I don't need this. I can go right back to Boston and pick up my practice there." I was bluffing. At that moment I could not have given up the pleasures of the groupmind even at gunpoint. But I knew that Alanna had no one else. Silently I dared her to try and bulldoze me again.

We stared at each other and I began to fear that things were going to get out of hand. But Alanna turned suddenly, hair flying, and walked out, slamming the door behind her.

AT FIRST, over the months that followed, Alanna and I made every effort to deny that there was renewed tension between us—we tried to get along and pretend that nothing had happened. With Alanna and Betty, I became a member of the Board of Directors of Better World. We agreed that it would require a vote of two to one to oust a board member or to implement major policy decisions.

We divided up the duties at Better World between us. She and Betty would handle the public relations and routine administrative decisions. I would shoulder the continuous therapeutic casework of Better World's clinic and hold to a rigorous schedule of public sharings.

The ecstasy I felt after each sharing helped to silence the doubts and reservations that pestered me when I was alone. Soon I was completely hooked on the groupmind, looking forward greedily to the next fix, and the next, and the next after that.

I suppose I could have just gone along indefinitely, burying my own losses, holding sharings, and developing healing techniques. But Better World still frightened people, and its many enemies had far more power than I had reckoned with.

In late spring I made a fast trip to Boston to close up my apartment. Alanna was waiting for me at the shuttleport when I returned.

I greeted her in surprise. "A reception committee?"

"Hardly," she said. "But this won't wait." She handed me a portascreen. "You can watch this while I drive."

It was a tape of a young woman with reddish hair and blue eyes, pretty in a sort of empty-headed way. She held an infant on her lap and she was talking rather earnestly to a sympathetic vid reporter.

"Oh, yes," she said. "This is his child. Rick healed me and made me his own."

The reporter leaned closer to the woman. "Are you saying that before he died, the Desert Prophet impregnated you during one of his mystical healing rites?"

"Yes, that's correct."

"And you're certain?"

"Quite certain." She smiled knowingly. "It would be hard to make a mistake about this sort of thing."

The camera moved in closer on the sleeping infant. Suddenly he yawned, squirmed, and opened his eyes. They were bright gold, and as I watched, he gurgled and began to levitate away from his mother's lap toward the camera. She grabbed him and set him down but he fussed and fretted until she started to nurse him.

"She's been on all the major vid channels," Alanna said. "Can you believe it? Claiming that Rick had seduced and impregnated her during a private healing!"

"Well, the child is undeniably mutant."

"So she had an affair with somebody, got pregnant, and had a mutant child. That doesn't make it Rick's child. She's just trying to rip us off."

The report produced hysteria within Better World as well as in the general public: most of the faithful, desperate to have an heir of Rick's body, wanted to anoint both the woman and her child immediately. I tried to convince everyone that the woman was a fraud and demanded blood and DNA tests. But the results were inconclusive and the mother immediately began a lawsuit on behalf of her child, Rick's "true heir," to wrest control of Better World—and its financial resources—from us.

Alanna was especially livid over the woman's claims and instituted a countersuit, charging fraud, perjury, and harassment. Our lawyers counseled us to settle out of court but Alanna refused, demanding legal satisfaction. Eventually we won, but it took months and months of expense and aggravation.

Next, we received a notice from the IRS that Better World's books would be audited. Although our records were up-to-date and beyond reproach, this added to the demands upon our staff and our spirit.

Out of nowhere, a documentary appeared: "Rick, Messiah or Mirage?" Apparently an unknown independent producer/director had somehow located over fifty "former" members of Better World who had suddenly come to their senses and were accusing the Desert Prophet of outright manipulation and exploitation.

Of course, the names of all involved had been changed to protect them, but I had Betty run a voice and image search through our datanet for these supposed former members. Only five of the hundred seemed to have had any connection with Better World, and two of them had been asked to leave by Rick when they refused to submit to healing procedures to cure their antisocial tendencies.

"Let's have our people make a vid of this information," I told Betty. "Distribute it to every major vidnews channel and to all on-line infonets."

"Why are they doing this?" Betty said. "Why don't they just leave us alone?"

"Because we frighten them," I said. "Because they don't understand and so they're scared and want to destroy whatever scares them."

"But they're lying."

I patted her hand. "Of course they are. There are some very powerful people out there who are very frightened of us and of Rick's memory. They're behind this. I'm sure of it. But don't worry. We have very good lawyers and our own resources."

"Metzger," Alanna said. She tapped the green enameled tip of one fingernail against a mound of printouts as if it were the Book Keeper himself beneath her talon. "It's got to be Metzger. He's been after us from the start and these attacks have all been too well orchestrated to be coming from separate sources."

"We don't know it's him."

"But you agree with me, don't you, Julian?"

I nodded. "Unfortunately, I do."

The accusations came thicker and faster and on their heels came a stampede of reporters, lawyers, and private investigators.

Early one morning I awoke in a sweat from disturbing dreams. Star had been here, in Better City, waving and calling to me. I had cried out to her, begging her to wait for me. But the faster I ran toward her, the more quickly she receded, out of reach. She disappeared in a flash of green light leaving me wide awake, staring at the ceiling as tears slid down my face. Despite every meditative exercise I knew, I could not return to sleep. Finally I got out of bed, dressed, and slipped out of B.W. headquarters to wander through Better City.

The streets were empty. It was too late even for late parties, too early for morning-shift workers and merchants, and even the mechs that cleaned the streets were still locked away, inert, in their underground burrows, their sensors awaiting the trigger of sunlight.

My footsteps on the pavement were the only sound besides the wind. But ahead of me I thought I saw a darker shadow crouched in a sheltered doorway. I could almost hear somebody breathing, and for a moment I wondered if it was Star, come back from my dreams to torment me.

A sound: feet slipping against pebbles. The dark shadow moved and shifted. Rationality reasserted itself. This was no specter from my dreams. It was somebody trying to hide.

"Who's there?" I said.

In answer, the shadow got to its feet, took the form of a man, and began running. I sprinted after him for a moment before I grew irritated and weary. I stopped and threw a mindlock on my quarry, freezing him in his tracks.

Who are you? Answer me!

To my amazement, he broke my hold, sent a mindbolt sizzling toward me that I barely ducked in time, and sped away around a corner out of sight.

A powerful telepath! It was an unknown mutant prowling through Better City. Now I was more convinced than ever that Metzger was behind this.

I raced back to B.W. headquarters and buzzed every telepath on the staff. Then I summoned Joe Martinez, the security chief.

"Meet me in the front hall in five minutes," I said. "And hurry."

They appeared in all manner of dress and undress, hair spiky from sleep, eyes heavy, stifling yawns.

"There's an intruder in the city," I said. "He's a mutant, a telepath, definitely a level one. We must find him and capture him immediately. I need to know who sent him, and what the hell he's doing here."

Joe Martinez blinked at me sleepily. "But if he's such a powerful telepath, how can I or anybody else on my staff hope to grab him?"

"I'll give you a temporary mental repulsor field," I said. "He won't be able to touch you mentally, but physically, you'll be able to grab him."

"Why not use it on all the telepaths as well?"

"Because it has the unfortunate effect of dampening the telepathic powers of whoever is wearing the shield. And I need every telepath on staff to sniff him out."

"Is he armed?" the security chief asked.

"Unknown," I said. "In any case, be careful."

He brandished a laser rifle with infrared scope attached. "Is this careful enough?"

We split up into five teams of two, using nightsight goggles for better vision in the predawn murk, and spread out into the sleeping city.

I began scanning for the man immediately, casting wide my telepathic net. Nothing. Either he had left no mental footprint or else he had been extremely clever in concealing it. Beside me, Lynn Goreman, a level-three telepath, had even less luck. She shook her head and we hurried down the street.

As the sky began to redden with dawn, I grew more and more frustrated. Even in a small city, one telepath could not escape from a group carefully searching for him, could he? Unless he had already left the area. I moved faster, convinced that with every step I took I was falling farther and farther behind.

Just as I was convinced he had escaped us completely, a mental cry went up—he had been located and caught near the Roman arena. A drug dart had rendered him unconscious long enough for us to move him to a secured room in B.W. headquarters and it was there that I interrogated him.

He was an odd-looking mutant, tall and thin with long, bony arms and legs, bluish skin, and a bald head that seemed to come to a point slightly right of center. As soon as he began to shake off the effects of the sedative I began to question him.

"Who sent you?" I said. "What are you doing here?"

He said nothing, merely rubbed his neck where the dart had struck him and glared at me.

I tried a mind probe but it was repulsed by a shield of remarkable density. He seemed to be completely protected, impervious to the best of my telepathic tricks.

"What's going on here?"

Alanna stood in the doorway. She looked wide awake and as though she had been up for hours.

"A prowler," I said. "Probably some kind of spy."

She strode over and grabbed him by the shoulder. "Who are you?" she demanded.

He remained silent, staring at the floor.

Alanna shook him angrily. "Answer me, dammit!"

Still the man refused to speak.

"Perhaps he's mute," Lynn Goreman said.

"I don't think so," said Alanna.

Slowly the strange mutant began to float upward, out of his seat. His eyes grew large, almost bulging with surprise.

He floated up, up, up, and then he began to rotate, round and round, end over end, faster and faster, until he looked like a blue-gray blur spinning in the middle of the air.

A thin, gurgling cry burst from him as his velocity increased. It was painful to listen to, much less watch, him.

"Stop it, Alanna," I said. "This is going too far."

"Going too far? I'd bounce him off the four walls of this room if I thought it would do any good in getting some answers. In fact, I still might try it."

"Please," the intruder cried. "Stop. I'll talk to you. I promise."

He clattered to the floor and was violently ill in several directions. A mechmaid rolled out of its cubbyhole to deal with the mess, clucking like a tired charwoman as it vacuumed, swabbed, and dried the floor.

"Start talking," Alanna said. "Unless you'd rather resume spinning?"

I stepped between them. "Would you like a glass of water?"

"Yes. Please."

I looked at Alanna and she frowned, but then a cup in the wallserve filled with water, levitated, and floated over to him.

He emptied it greedily.

I knelt beside him. "Now, you must tell us who sent you and what you were doing here."

He nodded in apparent weariness. "All right," he said. "I can't hide it much longer and I don't want another ride like that." He gave Alanna a resentful glance that managed to be respectful at the same time. "He warned me you would be tough."

"Who?"

"The Book Keeper."

"Metzger?" Alanna said, pouncing on the name.

"Yeah, of course. He's got a whole crew of us that he's sent in here."

"Why?"

"To cause trouble. Disrupt your operations. Spy. He means to shut you down, you know." He smiled wanly, revealing a mouthful of large bluish teeth. "Nothing gets Metzger frothing faster than Better World. Or you, Akimura. He really has it in for you. Thinks you're an out and out traitor to the cause. He can't stand you."

"The feeling could not be more mutual."

"What are we going to do with him?" Alanna asked me.

The mutant shrugged with almost gleeful insouciance. "It doesn't matter what happens to me. Metzger will never stop. That man doesn't understand the meaning of the word no."

"Perhaps if we repeat it to him enough times," Joe Martinez said.

And then I knew. I turned toward Alanna and mindspoke her: *Hold him still.*

She nodded in full understanding of my meaning and as I reached for the man she froze him in his seat. Only his eyes could move, back and forth, back and forth, faster and faster in his growing terror.

The problem for me was to find a way through the man's mental shields. I probed gently, then less gently, and finally at full strength, but I could find no seam, no flaw to exploit. Whoever had put them in place had been a master telepath.

I poked, I pried, I prodded. And then I found a minute defect that allowed me access to the man's subconscious memory.

He had a surprisingly orderly mind and I saw that he had been well educated. I saw, too, evidence of damage—most likely from drugs—to his long-term memory, which was too hazy and indistinct for a man of his age. Certain synapse paths seemed to have been obliterated while others had been streamlined for quicker access, quicker thought and action.

Five minutes in his head was all it took me to become convinced that this man had been trained by Metzger and used in a variety of capacities, none of them legal or remotely savory.

His short-term memory still functioned well, and as I dipped here and there I saw his various disagreeable activities: in addition to thievery and spying he didn't seem to mind committing murder if the price was right. His mind-crimes abounded, and what's more, he was proud of them.

No, I didn't enjoy sharing his mind, not for a moment. But I had to plant the posthypnotic suggestion quite deeply, and there was no way to do it without direct linkage. He was resistant at first, but a jolt to his hypothalamus finally got him quiet and cooperative.

My work done, I withdrew from him gratefully. It had been tempting to shatter his shields from the inside—a few good scary delusions were all that it would have taken—but I wanted him to appear untouched if Metzger probed him.

Okay, Alanna. Let him go.

For a moment nothing happened. Then the mutant tore himself out of the chair, fell to the floor, and began crawling on his hands and knees toward the door before he realized that the force prevailing against him was gone. Once he saw that he was free to move about he stood up, blinked, and rubbed the top of his head.

"What did you do?" he said.

"Nothing much. Just put a patch on a few leaky memories."

He stared at me blankly, uncomprehending. "So what happens next? Whatever it is, I don't want it to include her." He nodded toward Alanna.

"Simple," I said. "You leave."

"You mean you're going to let me go, just like that?"

"That's right."

His golden eyes narrowed in suspicion, making him even uglier. "I don't get it. What's the catch? First you shoot me with a tranquilizer, drag me in here, and have that lady spin me around the room for a while. Then she won't let me move. And now you say that I'm free to go."

"That's about the size of it."

"Metzger is really wasting his time," the mutant said. "You're all crazier than hell."

Alanna took a menacing step toward him. "I heard the man tell you to leave."

"I'm going, I'm going."

"Not without an escort," Joe Martinez said.

"Save it," said the mutant.

Martinez adjusted his sleek laser rifle in its shoulder holster. "No, really, I insist. At least as far as the shuttleport. I just want to make sure you get on a flight for Philadelphia. I know Julian here would never forgive me if I neglected a guest's transportation needs." And with a wink he followed the mutant out of the room.

"Was it such a good idea to release him?" Alanna said.

"What was I going to do, bring him up on charges in front of the joint Mutant Councils and accuse the Book Keeper? Fat chance they would do anything to him. And if

I went through normal channels and had him arrested for trespassing, he'd be jailed, Metzger would pay the fine, and he would go free."

"Tell me why this way is better."

I smiled. "Because this way Metzger will get a few interesting surprises."

"Oh, come on."

"No, you'll just have to be patient, Alanna. Now, if you'll excuse me, it's late—actually, it's early—and I haven't been to bed yet."

THE NEWS REACHED US two days later. The mutant spy had marched right into Metzger's office, delivered his report, then given Metzger a special message directly from me to him: a coercive/corrective mindbolt. Unprepared for the attack, the Book Keeper was wide open with all his shields down—as I'd expected—and his unprotected mind absorbed the full power of the blast. He immediately lost consciousness and was still in a comatose state. The damage to his brain was being analyzed but it seemed unlikely that he would function as Book Keeper again.

Instead of relief I felt shame and horror. What was happening to me? I had been trained to use my telepathic powers for healing, not for aggression, never in direct attack. What I had done went against everything I believed in and had worked for all my life. I felt like a hypocrite and a monster. Although I tried to tell myself that Metzger had declared war on us and in warfare one uses any weapons at hand for protection, I didn't really believe it, and I certainly didn't feel vindicated.

As for the renegade telepath: he was apprehended and sent by the Mutant Council to Dream Haven in northern California where he was shot so full of mind-damping drugs he wouldn't have known which end of a mindbolt to use if he could have remembered how to generate one. He had no memory of our little session with him and little recollection of his visit to New Mexico—my posthypnotic suggestion had seen to that.

MEANWHILE, BETTER WORLD THRIVED. The sharings went on, the towers of Better City rose higher and higher, and for quite a while my half-sister and I seemed to have overcome our differences.

I began to regard Better World as a healing center of the first order, devoted to taking on difficult cases and furthering the study and synthesis of healing techniques. Meditation, psychoanalysis, aromatherapy, altered consciousness, drug therapy, yoga, sensory deprivation, mutant chants: whatever worked was not questioned but rather welcomed as part of a multifaceted, multidisciplinary approach. I envisioned establishing a network of similar facilities in the years to come. We would spread Better World's comfort around the globe and perhaps even off-planet.

I became fascinated by the enormous healing potential of the group sharings: the remarkable effects these sessions had upon both mutants and nonmutants. A plan began to take shape in my mind for a methodical, documented long-term study of the implications of these effects.

The months passed quickly and before I knew it we were facing the anniversary of Rick's death. Alanna organized a ceremony that included a processional and recitation. It was a bit too much like a pageant for my taste but I knew she was still working through her grief and I thought this would be useful therapy.

So the day came and the mechdrums sounded a mournful beat. Slowly we marched into the Roman arena and up to the stage, and assumed our designated positions around the podium. The arena was packed and the audience was hushed, expectant.

Alanna spoke first.

"I remember," she said. "I was standing beside him that night and I remember how he died. I don't want to stop remembering, not for a moment. None of us who truly cared for him will ever be able to shed those memories. Our last glimpse of Rick."

Betty was next. "He was too good," she said. "Too fine to last. But we'll honor his memory and continue our good work. Rick loved us. He saved us. None of us will ever forget him."

I came third.

"My brother was unique," I said. "A marvel. I loved him, loved him deeply, and I can't tell you how I miss him. We all miss him. Please, join hands and share with me now as we remember Rick and cherish him."

I had mastered the group sharing technique by now and slid easily into the calming, harmonious circuit. When we had finished we all had tears on our cheeks. We left the arena, accompanied by the hushed strains of "Rick's Ode." Each one of us, led by Alanna, paused to place a white rose or chamisa branch at Rick's tomb. I have to admit that even I was moved—though a little uncomfortable at the intensity of the Rick worship.

Shortly after that Narlydda died, and Alanna was forced to leave Better World temporarily to see to her mother's estate. Narlydda's reclusive ways, which had only become more pronounced when Skerry died, had in no way diminished her fame as an artist and at her death she was part of the venerated pantheon. Every major museum in the world was vying for the work that Narlydda had left unconsigned. I didn't envy Alanna her task, especially as I was well aware of her complicated feelings for her mother, half admiring, half resentful. Better World was a safe place for her energy, a path her mother would not follow.

And so, I was astounded when Alanna announced that her mother's remaining work would be housed at Better World in a special museum to be built in Rick's honor.

"Using whose funds?" I demanded.

"There's plenty of money from Mother's estate," Alanna said carelessly. "This won't even put a dent in it. Nor will the contest I'm going to announce."

"Contest?"

Her eyes glowed as she told me her plan. "Yes, a tribute to my mother's memory, and Rick. I want to hold a yearly competition for young artists. The subject, of course, will be Rick or Better World. And each prize-winning entry becomes our property, to be added to our collection."

"And the prize?"

"Oh, a couple of hundred thousand eurodollars, I suppose." She shrugged. "There's more than enough."

"Lovely," I said. "Who'll judge this?"

"I will, along with a group of curators and art critics."

"It seems to be a long stretch from healing people to

endowing museums and sculpture competitions in Rick's name."

"I don't see anything wrong with it," Alanna said. "Just different sides of the same coin. We honor Rick's memory by healing, and by providing works of beauty to delight the senses. To me it all seems perfectly connected."

Although I didn't agree with her, I saw very little wrong with her arts competition. It might drain off some of her energy but it seemed a harmless enough way for her to combine her mourning for Rick with her grief for her mother.

By the second anniversary of Rick's death, the museum had been finished, opened, and the first winner of the Narlydda Foundation's competition had seen her artwork enshrined in the main gallery next to one of only two extant copies of Narlydda's famous "Moonstation Merman."

The winning sculpture was unveiled with a bold flourish of mechtrumpets and considerable media fanfare. Clever, clever Alanna! She knew that Narlydda and Rick were both fading a bit in terms of newsworthiness. By linking the two through her annual competition she had ensured an enduring appetite in the press for information from Better World.

The statue had been cast on a heroic scale and reached halfway to the vaulted ceiling of the gallery. It was an idealized portrait of Rick in postcubist/futurist style, coated with a layer of holopaint that provided an ever-changing aura of textures, color, and mood.

"What do you think?" Alanna asked.

"At least he's not holding two stone tablets," I said.

Privately I thought the work hideous. But art appreciation had never been my strongest suit.

The pageant commemorating Rick's death was twice as long and pompous this time and I couldn't restrain my feelings.

"What is this, Alanna? A passion play? If you intend to have this thing expand geometrically each year, pretty soon nobody will be able to stay awake long enough to last through the entire ceremony."

She made no response, merely handed me a white and gold garment that had a strange glow to it and made an odd ringing noise as it moved through the air. "Here," she said. "Put this on."

"What is it?"

"Your robe for the pageant."

"Robe? My regular clothing was fine last year."

"That was last year."

The fabric chimed again in a series of sweet arpeggios. "What's that?"

"Aural fibers. I had them woven in to provide more majesty to the processional. Each robe is keyed to a specific scale integrating into a harmonic series that should create a deeper sense of awe and ecstasy."

"Won't that be noisy?"

"It should be beautiful."

She was right, it was. The robes added an eerie, otherworldly touch to the proceedings that somehow was exactly right.

I hoped that Alanna would now be content to fiddle with her pageant and art collection without inventing new diversions. I was falling behind on my casework and the public sharings were taking a toll on my energy. Perhaps now Alanna would devote herself to the business at hand.

But she had other ideas. And she published them.

The illusion of our truce melted away when the first edition of *Rick's Way* appeared.

It was available on disc or bound printout from Better World Visual Communications, and also in a deluxe, handbound, slip-covered leather and vellum edition for true believers who also had a considerable amount of disposable income.

The hoopla that announced its arrival was completely funded by Alanna and worthy of the Gutenberg Bible.

Rick's Way sold and sold and sold. The literary critics had a feast on its leaden, cliché-ridden prose, but apparently nobody paid any attention to them. A leading movie studio purchased rights to it as the basis of an inspirational film and several well-known actors were said to be vying for the roles of Rick, Alanna, and yours truly. Foreign publishers clamored for translations.

Perhaps I should have been pleased. Instead, I was alarmed and furious. As the Better World faithful had grown accustomed to me, to greet me respectfully and even reverentially, I had begun to think of Better World as mine. I admit it, I was jealous. Somehow, Alanna's actions felt like a complete betrayal. But even more troubling was her treatment of Rick in the book: he was no longer just some unique player upon the mortal stage. Now, apparently, he had become divine, and every utterance attributed to him took on the timbre of holy, unremitting gospel.

Of course, the churches began screaming.

"Blasphemous!"

"They're running a totalitarian organization under the guise of a charismatic religion."

"It's a sham. Blatant exploitation of the needy."

"It's an attempt at mind control. Mutant hypnosis of the masses."

All the outcry only made the book sell faster. It was translated into fifteen different languages and, very quickly, foreign tongues joined the debate. Who could blame all those enraged pastors and prelates, imams and rabbis, deacons and ministers for their fear? Now there was another deity, freshly deceased, competing for the limited attention of their already diminished flocks. Worse yet, he had an indefatigable front-woman of considerable wiles and resources. Alive, Rick had displayed formidable magnetism. Once dead, he became an absolute lodestar. The outrage of the competition was not only understandable but predictable and almost pathetic. In a peculiar way I even felt a bit sorry for them.

Among the faithful, *Rick's Way* became divine scripture in short order. Soon dozens of people were claiming to have been with Rick when he made each historic utterance captured in the book. Alanna had been right. Obviously, no one remembered what Rick had really sounded like. *Alanna's Version,* as I privately called *Rick's Way,* was a top seller. It became a talisman, a piece of Rick to carry around.

My reaction was a bit harder to explain. In Rio I had giddily embraced the idea of Rick as a "pocket deity." Why then was I so angry with Alanna now for elevating his status? Perhaps in Brazil it had seemed less frightening. More important, it had seemed more like a service organization and less a cult of personality. Perhaps I had taken it more seriously. And perhaps I had been so in love that my judgment at the time had been colored by my happiness.

But the times—and I—had changed. I was in New Mexico now, Star was dead, and Rick's deification had to be stopped before it derailed all my plans for Better World. I confronted Alanna in her office and found her sitting by the voiceprinter.

"Working on volume number two already?" I said. "Baking some fresh god-muffins for the faithful to gobble up?"

She switched the printer off, all cool self-control. "What's bothering you?"

"You might have told me about your plans for *Rick's Way!*"

"I thought I had. Come on, Julian. Wasn't it obvious? You knew I had almost finished the manuscript before Rick died. You even saw it."

"But you never said a word to me about finishing it, much less publishing it. I thought that you'd locked it up in your desk drawer—that it was a dead issue. Why didn't you bring it up at the last board meeting? Didn't you want our help? Our input?"

"What was I supposed to do, Julian? Put it up for your vote? I didn't need any help. Or input."

"Obviously."

"I don't see why you're so upset. Perhaps you would have preferred to mothball the entire project, but I didn't think that was the best way to show respect for Rick. And I didn't want anybody else mucking around with it. It's mine. Mine and Rick's."

Her smugness was infuriating.

I said, "Where did the divine aspect come from? I didn't notice it in your earlier notes. When did you put that in?"

"Why, after he died. It just seemed so appropriate, somehow."

"Appropriate?" I stared at her. "It's poppycock. You can't be serious, Alanna. How can you publish this dreck? You of all people know that Rick wasn't divine. Far from it!"

"Do I? Does any of us really know?"

"Stop it, Alanna. Or save it for somebody more gullible."

"What do you think has been going on here?" she demanded. "You saw the agonies at Rick's death, the flowers at his tomb, the prayers of the faithful. Rick is a real spiritual force to thousands of people, Julian. Why shouldn't I deify him?"

"Because he was human, dammit. As human as you or me."

A fugitive smile flitted across her face. "Wouldn't you say he was a little bit more than that?"

"I'm not denying he was special, Alanna. Don't play semantic games with me. Special, yes. Holy, no. And I shudder to think of the consequences of promulgating this idea."

"I really don't see the harm in it."

I leaned toward her. "Are you crazy? Haven't you heard the outcry against us ever since you published the bloody thing?"

"Don't raise your voice to me, Julian. I'm not a child. And what of the complaints? People have been screaming at Better World ever since it began. I'm so accustomed to it that I would think it was odd if they stopped."

"Don't forget the bombings."

"Those were terrible and unfortunate. But there haven't been any since Rick died. Whoever it was has obviously gone away."

"Which doesn't mean they couldn't resume at any time."

She gave me an impatient look. "I wish you had more faith, Julian. It would make you so much happier. So much less paranoid."

"What is this, your sermon on the mount? And what are you working on now?"

"Why, volume two, of course. Just as you said. The first book was so successful that this seemed like a natural progression. It's important to get it out there as soon as possible."

"And how are you going to explain it? Tell people that Rick had a few afterthoughts in the afterlife and came back to discuss them with you?"

She was complacent beyond belief. "I don't have to explain it. The need and interest should be obvious. Besides, I don't understand why you're so upset. Would you feel better if I had called it *Julian's Way* instead?"

"Don't be ridiculous," I said. But she had strayed uncomfortably close to the truth and I began to bristle defensively. "What I object to is your fanciful distortion of a real person."

"I'm sorry you don't like what I've written, Julian. I was going to ask for your input in the next volume but since you're so obviously hostile to this entire project, I won't bother. Now, if you'll excuse me, I've got work to do."

Was anybody, aside from Rick, ever as stubborn as my half-sister?

Aside from outright coercion, I couldn't stop her from finishing the manuscript for the next volume of *Rick's Way*. And I was unwilling to subject Alanna to mind control. Perhaps I was too squeamish. Too ethical. But I wouldn't do it. I turned and walked away from her in silence.

Volume two outsold volume one.

Alanna had done it—won control of Rick's image and, through it, potential control of the entire Better World organization. She seemed determined to return it to its original status as a cult of personality with herself as keeper of the flame. If she was successful, all my plans for therapy clinics and healing studies would perish. I had to stop her before she pushed us completely off-course.

14

I ADMIT NOW THAT THE methods I used to fight Alanna were not admirable. The only excuse I can offer is that I was firmly convinced she was wrong to distort and gild my brother's image, and infuriated by her arrogating areas of Rick's legacy that, rightly or wrongly, I viewed quite possessively as mine alone.

The pageantry, the art competition, the publication of *Rick's Way*, all were intended to deify Rick. But that wasn't what Better World was about. At least, that's what I believed.

Aside from the weekly sharings, where some contact was unavoidable, I shunned Alanna.

On her part, she seemed just as happy to stay away from me, aloof and private in the apartments she had shared with Rick. No doubt she was already busily at work on *Rick's Way*, volumes three through twelve. As the weeks passed, our estrangement crystallized and seemed to become permanent.

Perhaps I had lost perspective. Perhaps I was more power-hungry than I knew. Regardless of the reason, I slowly became convinced that Alanna was an obstacle to the best interests of Better World.

She seemed determined to cram Rick's word—at least her version of it—down the gullet of every person on the planet, and wanted to devote Better World's resources and energy to an enormous outreach program to support her scheme.

But I wanted no more volumes of *Rick's Way* published, no more movies, no publicity stunts. What I wanted to do was help people, teach sharing techniques, and concentrate on the daily business of Better World. I had no more interest in indoctrinating new members than I had in performing lobotomies by brain-burning. As far as I was concerned, the membership of Better World was barely manageable as it was. We had more than enough work to do and we would honor Rick best by doing it quickly and efficiently rather than grinding out endless memorials to him. Alanna's plans threatened to stretch us to the breaking point if not beyond it.

And so, I turned to Betty. Early one spring morning I poked my head into her office.

"Betts," I said. "We've got to talk. Privately."

"Of course, Julian." She shooed her assistants from the room and locked the door behind them. "What can I do for you?"

I settled into a webseat and gazed out the window at the mountains: the faintest hint of green covered them, as though, overnight, some pointillist had attacked with a giant paintbrush. "Remember way back when?" I said. "You had this wild theory about a conspiracy against Rick." I gave Betty a disarming grin. "Surely you remember."

Her cheeks turned bright pink. "Well, it *was* a crazy idea, wasn't it? I'm ashamed to remember how I ranted and raved."

I took her hand and looked deeply into her eyes. "What if I told you that it wasn't such a crazy idea?"

"Oh, Julian, you're teasing me. Stop it."

"No, Betts. Listen to me." I took a deep breath, knowing that what I was about to do was absolutely necessary but hating myself a little bit for it just the same. "I didn't want to tell you this, but I've done some checking around on my own. And I've become convinced that Alanna not only wanted Rick to die but was instrumental in hastening his death."

"*Alanna?*" Betty obviously couldn't have been more surprised if I had suggested that she herself had plotted Rick's death. "Whatever do you mean? I don't quite understand what you're talking about, Julian."

"I know, Betty. It was hard for me to accept, too. At first. But now I'm certain." I leaned closer. "Remember when Rick was so sick that I came back from Brazil to be with him?"

"Of course."

"And remember how Alanna refused to bring in a doctor?"

"But that was because of what Rick had told her."

I nodded gravely. "So she claimed, yes. But did you ever hear Rick say anything like that to her?"

"Well, no, now that you mention it." I heard the first faint hints of doubt enter her voice. "But Rick was always telling Alanna things when they were alone. Everybody knew that."

"Think about it, Betts. Does that really sound like something that Rick would do? When he wanted to help people so badly? When he had so much work left to do? Do you think that he willingly put himself in a position where he could burn out and die? Or was he the victim of a calculated plan to create a martyr for Better World?"

Her mouth worked for a moment and tears glittered in her pale blue eyes. "I always told him that he worked too hard. I was always asking him to slow down, to rest. But he never listened."

"Alanna never let him listen, did she? And you see the success she's had now with *Rick's Way*. Would she have been able to do that if Rick were still alive?"

"No, I guess not. But you can't seriously think that Alanna was egging Rick on, telling him to work harder and harder until he collapsed!"

"I don't know, Betty. I just don't know." But my tone said exactly the opposite: that I was convinced, and if Betty wanted to stay loyal to me she would be convinced, too.

Of course, I could have coerced her by direct telepathic contact and forced her to see my point of view and support my plan. But I didn't like doing something like that to a friend.

Not that I'm proud of the way I *did* handle things— perhaps, in the end, I would have been fairer to Betty if I *had* just hypnotized her rather than lied to her, leading her along a tangled path of reason until she became so anxious about aligning herself with me that she accepted whatever I told her without question. Why is hindsight so clear when it is also so very useless? A friend once told me that it was proof of God's contempt, but I don't think I quite agree. Not yet, anyway.

Step by calculated step I led Betty down the path I had devised until she was as willing to oust Alanna as I.

"I can't believe it," Betty said, chagrined. "To think that I trusted Alanna all along when the proof was there before me the entire time. She pushed Rick right over the brink, Julian. We've got to stop her."

"My thoughts exactly."

The only problem now was how to go about it.

Better World was administered by me, Alanna, and Betty. The only way to force one of the directors out was by direct proof that he or she had acted recklessly or illegally in the interests of Better World. Or a vote of two to one.

A few days after I had spoken with Betty I called a directors' meeting.

Alanna protested that she had too much to do. Couldn't we wait until April or May? I assured her that there was simply too much to be discussed right now.

We met the next afternoon in the small conference room on the ground floor of B.W. headquarters. It was a sunny day in early spring and the sounds of drilling and other noises from construction of a new wing for the museum filtered into the room.

"Well, Julian?" Alanna stared at me pointedly. "What's so important?"

"It's really quite simple," I said. "Betty and I want you out of Better World by tonight. We'd prefer that you go of your own free will, but we are prepared to vote you out, if necessary."

Alanna gasped. Then, recovering quickly, she glared at me in annoyance. "You're joking," she said. "What's gotten into you, Julian? Are you finished wasting my time or do you have any other funny little things that you'd like to share with me?"

Betty said nothing.

Alanna's face turned a slightly deeper shade of green. "You're not serious about this? I don't believe it. You've both lost your minds. Together."

"I'm sorry," Betty said.

"I don't want sympathy," Alanna shot back. "Sanity, yes. Just give me one good reason why I should leave."

"Because of your role in the conspiracy, of course," Betty said.

"Conspiracy? What conspiracy?"

Betty looked pained and confused. She turned to me for succor, but cruelly—out of cowardice, I suppose—I let her deliver the actual blow.

"You know very well," Betty said. "The plan you hatched to let Rick die so that Better World would have a martyr and you could write *Rick's Way*."

"What?" Alanna stood up. She looked astounded, flabbergasted. "Is that what you think? No. No, it's not possible. You can't be that crazy. What *is* this all about?"

"Don't sound so innocent," I said.

"You're really serious," Alanna said, in wonder. "And, Betty, you're in on this, too. I can hardly believe it. Do you actually think I wanted Rick dead?"

"Well, yes," Betty said. "Wasn't I clear on that point? You ruthlessly forced Rick to his death."

"My God." Alanna's eyes were wide. "I'm almost glad Rick is gone. He absolutely would not believe this either."

Feeling like an absolute heel, I said, "Spare me the sentiment, Alanna."

Astonishment flickered across Alanna's face again. "Why are you both trying to do this to me?"

Betty looked momentarily stunned by Alanna's outburst and I decided I had better move matters along. "There's no doubt about it," I said. "It's obvious that you were planning this from the start, undermining Rick's health, encouraging him to push himself without rest, without medical attention—"

"Julian, you know that's not true."

I continued as though I had not heard her. "Without medical attention, working long hours, holding mass healings everywhere."

"This is absurd," Alanna said. "These are insane lies.

Why in the world would you think I would ever do such a thing?"

"To consolidate your power in Better World. And to provide the definitive version of Rick in *Rick's Way*." I stared at her, daring her to prove me wrong. "To control his legacy."

She laughed mirthlessly. "That's it, really. This isn't about my part in some supposed death plot. This is all about *Rick's Way*, isn't it? About control. You can't possibly think I wanted Rick dead. I loved him, and you know it."

"You did, once," I said. "But you also had ambitions of your own that you were forced to abandon for Rick's dream. You wanted to write, Alanna. And now you have an audience of hundreds of thousands for your work."

Alanna seemed struck dumb by this. She shook her head in either disagreement or amazement. "Let me get this straight," she said, after a moment. "I wanted Rick to die so I could take over Better World and resume my aborted literary career by writing *Rick's Way*?"

"You wanted to build a god," I said.

"But Julian," Betty said, "I don't understand. Rick is a god already, isn't he? Yes, of course he is." She nodded docilely, mindlessly, and I restrained a shudder of out-and-out horror.

"That's precisely what he is, Betty," Alanna said. "Never doubt it." She turned toward me. "No, Julian, I won't play by your rules. But thanks, anyway."

Angry words boiled within me, and with them, self-loathing. What role had I taken on here? How could I cavalierly treat friends and family as pawns? I had never intended, never wanted to use people in this way. But the game had gone too far. There was no retreating from my position now without creating a civil war within Better World. Either Alanna had to leave or else knuckle under to my control.

"If you don't clear out of here I'll have you removed by force. Reluctantly."

"You would if you could," she said, crossing her arms. "But would you really care to pit your security people against my telekinetic skills?"

"Alanna, you can wreck the place if you want to, but in the end I'll have you removed, even if I have to put you under direct telepathic control and frog-march you to the door myself."

Her gaze cut right through me. "Oh, I'll spare you that, Julian. I'm afraid that you would enjoy it too much."

"Then let's settle this peacefully, shall we?" I said. I managed a conciliatory smile. "I could see your remaining at Better World in a reduced capacity. I might even agree to additional volumes of *Rick's Way*. Of course, all future versions would have to pass by me before they could be published."

Alanna nodded but I could see the contempt in her eyes. "Oh, you mean if I'm a good girl, then I get to stay?" she said. "And what will you do, issue a report card for me every quarter? Or perhaps you'd rather turn me into a zombie like Betty here. Easier to handle that way."

"A zombie? What do you mean?" Betty said. "I resent that comment!"

"Oh, Betty, don't you see the truth? He's got you completely hypnotized. You, of all people."

"You're just feeling guilty, Alanna," I said. "Stop trying to point the finger at me. My offer still stands."

She shook her head. "No, Julian. No on every count. I won't leave, and I won't turn *Rick's Way* over to you."

With that she turned and hurried from the room.

By that afternoon Alanna had barricaded herself behind several telekinetic fields *and* a layer of Better World staffers who were still especially loyal to her.

It quickly became a war of attrition.

Her obstinacy forced me to cut off her food, water, environmental controls, and access to outside media. For a time she circumvented some of these challenges by levitating supplies through a hole she had made in her own fields of protection. But she couldn't keep up the effort for long, especially once I had put all food within her range under guard. Alanna was a powerful telekinete but she could not teleport objects through solid matter, over great distances, the way Rick once had. She might be able to levitate a *choba* roll up three stories and in through an open window but she couldn't budge an entire locked kitchen.

Finally, after two weeks of this, she emerged from her

barricades, ragged and pale. Her voice was matter-of-fact, almost meek, but fury burned in her eyes.

"You win," she said.

"My offer stands open, Alanna. Let's bury the hatchet and you can remain at Better World."

"Under your control? Forget it. Nothing could get me to stay now. Nothing."

"Alanna—"

"Congratulations, Julian. I hope you enjoy yourself. How thoughtful of Rick—and me—to leave you this lovely toy to play with."

"If that's your attitude, I expect you to clear your personal effects before the end of the day. And I'm warning you, Alanna. Don't try to publish anything else in Rick's name."

"Remember the Bill of Rights, Julian? I'm afraid that freedom of speech outstrips even the rules of your little pocket kingdom. Now that I'm no longer a part of Better World, I'll do what I like. Consider this my resignation, effective immediately." She turned sharply on her heel.

I had to fight the urge to run after her, to beg her to forgive me, to forget all this, to stay.

Instead, I ordered security to provide an escort for her, and to help her clear her belongings from the premises. In effect, I starved and then drummed her out of Better World. Was I proud of myself? No, not even a little bit.

IF ONLY SHE HAD GIVEN IN. Truth be told, once she was gone I almost missed Alanna and our love/hate relationship. For all of her prickly, uncooperative ways, she was still family. And with her no longer there, the only people at Better World who had been close to Rick were Betty and myself. But as the years passed, I grew accustomed to that peculiar loneliness.

Eventually, we hired a bright young man named Donald Torrance to handle public relations. Better World soldiered on, year by year, healing those in pain and experimenting with various healing techniques.

Alanna continued to administer the annual arts competition. There was no way I could have canceled that without enormous public outcry and accompanying media attention.

To my chagrin, Alanna ignored my wishes and went on to publish several more volumes of *Rick's Way,* a critique of the philosophy of Better World, and a dramatic trilogy based on Rick's life. Finally, she had achieved the literary prominence of which she had always dreamed.

I didn't begrudge her the small comfort her success must have provided. Quite the contrary: the more accolades she received, the better I liked it. It enabled me to assuage my own guilt by telling myself that this was the way things had always been meant to be and, in fact, that I had enabled Alanna to achieve her true destiny. Sometimes I almost believed it.

15

WHEN SHE LEFT, Alanna took a splinter group of loyalists with her and I assumed that she would form her own miniature version of Better World somewhere in California. But, to my surprise, Alanna devoted all of her efforts to *Rick's Way*. Anyone who wished to assist her was welcome but if they were looking for other activities, then they were advised to seek them elsewhere. Most of her supporters eventually came slinking back to Better World with their tails between their legs.

Although she had effectively been banished from Better World headquarters, Alanna figured so prominently in Rick's legend that I could neither deny her existence nor keep her away completely. On the anniversary of Rick's death, Alanna always appeared, suddenly, mysteriously, at the Roman theater to lay a white rose upon Rick's tomb, and she was always cheered lustily by the crowds. But our estrangement was complete.

I hated what she did with *Rick's Way*, and still do. But time has a way of encysting old torments until I can carry them along with me and, for the most part, ignore them.

The rhythm of the seasons overtook me, kept the machinery of Better World whirring, the group sharings on schedule, the reconstruction of Better World progressing, and soon Alanna's absence seemed unremarkable, even normal.

I was caught up in the ebb and flow. When my parents

died, my mother first and my father three months later, I had them buried beside Rick, mourned them, and went right back to my work and research.

The casework was especially fascinating: the faithful were so trusting that I could gain immediate access to their minds without spending the weeks—and often months—it had usually taken in standard therapy to win the patient's trust enough to attempt a mindlink.

I encountered the usual narcissistic disorders, horror tales of abuse and deprivation, incest, alcoholism, and drug addiction. Surprisingly, I saw fewer cases of severe depression at Better World than on the outside: especially if the patient had been a regular attendee of group sharings. As I had suspected, the group sharings had enormous long-term therapeutic potential for nonmutants and I was heartened to see my theory apparently being proven before my eyes. I began to organize my notes for a monograph I hoped to publish on the topic.

I saw a variety of mutant patients as well, and although they exhibited much the same positive reactions to the sharings as did the nonmutants, there was a more pronounced physiological effect that I had not anticipated. Cholesterol levels were down, as were blood pressure readings—always a sign of lowered stress. For those mutants who participated regularly in our mixed sharings I found clear signs of a slowing of the aging process. I confess that I had no explanation for it then or now.

Simply put, the mixed group sharings seemed to extend the short mutant life span in a way that the segregated mutant sharings had not.

I wanted to study this more closely but my attention was diverted by a sudden series of alarming delusional cases that began to flood our clinic.

People were claiming to have seen Rick walking the streets of Better City. He occasionally responded to their greetings with a bemused wave. But they could not hear him, even when it was obvious he was trying to talk to them.

At first I ascribed this to too many joysticks on top of wishful thinking.

"Of course you would like to see Rick," I told the afflicted. "We would all like to see him."

"No, Dr. Akimura, really. I did see him standing in the middle of the street. I walked right over to him but when I tried to touch him he disappeared."

I made a quick telepathic probe and saw that, clearly, this man believed that he had seen Rick. He had unshakable faith. And the specter certainly resembled my brother. But how could I trust the memory of an unsettled mind?

The sightings continued and word started to spread of Rick risen from the dead. I began to grow alarmed. What was happening here? Why were so many people hallucinating the same thing? I knew my brother was dead and I didn't believe in an afterlife. What were these people seeing?

Each mind I probed firmly believed that Rick had returned. Each image I saw looked remarkably like my brother. But that was not possible. I refused to believe it.

Even Betty had an encounter I couldn't explain. She awakened me early one morning and I saw that she looked transformed, almost beatific, glowing with excitement.

"Julian, he really is here! I've seen him. Oh, Julian, the stories are true, all true."

"Nonsense, Betty. Get a hold of yourself."

"No, please, Julian, you have to come and see for yourself."

"It's two in the morning. You ought to be in bed."

"Julian, don't you believe me?"

I didn't want to be cruel but I didn't appreciate losing a night's sleep over this foolishness.

"No. I'm sorry but I don't believe you, Betty. My brother is dead and has been for years. I'm sorry but I think there's some kind of group hysteria spreading here. I'll address it at the next group sharing, which is tomorrow at ten A.M. Until then, I don't want to be disturbed." And I shut down the screen in annoyance, turned over, and went back to sleep.

The group sharing the next day was well attended as usual. I was halfway through the process of establishing the mental circuit when I saw something out of the corner of my eye: a strange, dark movement in the middle of the air.

Rick.

My brother. Incorporeal, transparent, but Rick nonetheless.

I was surprised into speechlessness. Was I losing my mind? Falling prey to this group psychosis? Was the group sharing spreading this delusion even to me?

Others in the room saw him, too. Whispers became gasps of awe and wonder. "He's come back!" people began to murmur. "Rick has returned to us."

And then, just as the sharing threatened to dissolve into complete pandemonium, Rick winked out.

Calm yourselves, I told the crowd. *We have seen a miracle, a splendid vision of Rick. There is no cause for alarm.*

But even my mindspeech, coupled with a coercive wave, could not keep the group calm and in their seats. They were breaking from the mental circuit, jumping up and running down the aisles toward the stage. In another few moments I would be swamped.

Gathering all the strength I had, I pressed a mind command upon them to halt, to return to their seats. At first they didn't respond. But as I tapped into first one and then another of the mutant minds in the group, my power increased and bit by bit I turned the crowd back.

We all love Rick and miss him. I can't tell you what has just occurred but I can share my feelings with you. Come. Join with me now.

We resumed the circle, sharing our amazement and joy. I tried not to question what had happened but merely to accept it as a manifestation of faith on the part of so many minds.

But then I saw Rick again, not very long afterward.

I was alone in my bedroom, sleepless and pondering some old screentapes.

There was a dark movement in the corner, a shifting of shadows. At first I told myself that my eyes were tired. It was nothing. I looked again. My brother stood there, gaping at me.

"Rick!"

Wordlessly, we stared at each other.

But it was not the same man I had seen at the group sharing. He looked younger, much as I remembered him from the days when he rode his jetcycle through the tawny hills of northern California, when his mutant powers were first erupting.

But how was this possible? Why was I seeing different visions of my brother?

I nearly fell out of my seat as the word "vision" occurred to me. Of course. Of course. That was it.

Rick wasn't making visits from beyond the grave. Rather, he was making visits to us from the past, from his life.

What we were seeing were manifestations of Rick when he was making his first time leaps and seeing his first prophetic visions years ago. I shook my head in wonder. So he actually *had* moved through time as he had claimed. Some of his visions had come true—had, in fact, been real flights into the actual future. What's more, Rick had said that in the visions he could not communicate, could not connect with anyone he saw. Obviously, that had been true as well. But he had been wrong in thinking that he could not be observed or detected. At least, he could be seen by those who wanted to see him.

Eventually the sightings of Rick came to be considered blessed visitations and piles of white roses marked each spot where a sighting had occurred. For me, the sightings were a reminder of my brother's unique gifts—and they made me miss him even more. Oddly, I was glad that Alanna was not here to see him. I would spare her this, at least.

To my amused chagrin, these visitations merely added more fuel to the ever more widespread belief that Rick had been truly divine. In fact, they seemed incontrovertible proof. There was nothing I could do about that and I suppose I stopped fighting that particular battle after I had seen my brother's "ghost" with my own eyes. Even dead, Rick was unpredictable.

As my attention was taken up more and more by the sharings, I found it expedient to delegate other tasks that drained away too much of my energy. I began to feel empty, unfulfilled, gripped by cascading anxieties in the times between the creation of each groupmind. I added sharings to the schedule, hired more functionaries. Nothing must be allowed to take me away from the sharings.

I began to grow less and less interested in casework, delegating much of it to subordinates. I abandoned any of my cases that did not relate directly to the effects of sharings. Slowly but surely I constructed my ivory tower, furnished it, and locked myself in.

16

I T SOON BECAME OBVIOUS to me that most of the true believers on the staff, while devoted to Better World and possessed of the best intentions, did not possess the organizational abilities to make good administrators. I would have to look outside of our little nest for professionals: a financial officer, a city planner, and a director of therapeutic services.

First onboard was Ginny Quinlan, a smart, no-nonsense young woman born in Maryland and sporting both the fine-boned features and nervous energy of a thoroughbred. She had an MBA from Harvard and extensive experience with multinational corporations. She seemed to be just what Better World needed and promised to keep the corporation's finances in order.

Next came Don Torrance, fresh from a stint as assistant city manager of Peoria. When his friend the mayor lost her job in an election, Don began sending out résumés and somehow I got a hold of one. I had long been convinced that Better City had to be maintained by a professional: the fire that destroyed two-thirds of the city proved to me that we were not managing things properly. Don was young, brash, and ambitious. I assumed that time would erode some of his rough edges and hired him, appointing him city manager and planner, answerable only to me.

Barsi came to us from the Mayo Clinic. She was a psychologist and therapist with excellent recommendations.

Just what the Better World Clinic needed. But at first I rejected her application. Her dark good looks reminded me uncomfortably of Star. Nevertheless, Betty persevered and convinced me to hire Barsi to oversee the clinics. Obviously, she had spied the girl's devoted nature from the start and thoroughly approved of her.

And so, inadvertently, I helped to create the very conditions in which, inevitably, a coup would be formulated to depose me.

Initially, the portents were all to the good. Ginny immediately streamlined our accounting procedures and bookkeeping. She seemed to be able to do the work of at least three people. Meanwhile, Barsi proved herself as a dedicated, patient administrator who untangled snarled paperwork, made intelligent referrals on difficult cases, and even managed to lure me into participating in one or two tricky therapeutic procedures. She was kind, intelligent, gentle, and tactful, and she managed to keep her ambitions completely hidden while slowly and thoroughly enchanting me.

Don Torrance remained a jangling presence but a necessary one: he was full of energy and ideas, and his brashness had to be tolerated in order to benefit from his skills. I reminded myself that Rick had not always been that easy to get along with. And in short order, Don had revamped our emergency response systems, upgraded our water-pumping and energy-generating capabilities, and began to draw up plans for expanding Better City.

Freed from the mundane responsibilities, I could devote my attention to the sharings and my research. It was a most fulfilling existence. The faithful greeted me warmly in the halls of Better World headquarters, in the streets, wherever I went. Of course, I enjoyed all the attention but it was a drain on me and eventually I decided that I had become perhaps a bit too accessible. I had hoped to maintain an open-door policy but that was obviously unfeasible. After all, what doctor can afford to have each and every patient drop by for a chat whenever he felt like it?

When Betty, Barsi, and Ginny approached me concerning the need for my own private residence I initially fought them off. I hated the hassle of moving and was a man of increasingly entrenched habits. Nevertheless, they persisted, and reluctantly I endorsed their plans to build my official residence, replete with guardhouse and secret underground passages leading into Better World HQ. Without realizing it I helped to create the very conditions whereby a coup would become possible: isolate the head of the organization so that, at the appropriate time, it can be cut off without making an awful, bloody mess.

My new digs were luxurious indeed, four stories of graceful rooms and impressive views. The interior walls were whitewashed adobe, the floors were hand-rubbed pine, and the furniture was comfortable, low-slung, and thoroughly unobtrusive. I allowed Betty and Barsi to talk me into a spot of color here and there: venerable Navajo weavings and kilim carpets were scattered over the floors and hung upon the walls. I never tired of their jagged designs and thick textures. I kept a framed picture of Star at my bedside but aside from that retained few sentimental objects. I didn't have time for them.

My favorite moments were dawn and dusk when the changing play of light across the mountains created a thousand moods and colors. I enjoyed fantasizing that I could see Star in the sunrise and Rick at twilight.

I settled happily into my new home, enjoying both its privacy and Spartan beauty. Occasionally, very occasionally, I regretted that I had no one with whom to share it. But my interest in having a regular companion seemed to have died with Star, and most of my erotic energy seemed tied into the group sharings: I had little left to spare. I'm certain that Barsi would have been happy to join me in bed and was perhaps a bit puzzled that she was never asked.

When Betty's husband died she offered the use of her ranch to Better World as a training center and private retreat. It seemed a fine idea to me and in return I suggested that she move into a small house in Better City. I thought that the company of fellow staffers, the weekly get-togethers, the group trips, and the general therapeutic atmosphere would be a boon for her and she readily agreed. Almost immediately she joined a volunteer outreach group that spent part of each month providing services to communities in the remotest areas of New Mexico.

Better City itself had grown both up and out: at night,

when I glanced through the window at the golden lights of the community, I imagined that someone had scattered the contents of a jewel box across the New Mexican desert.

I believed that Better City was a model community and I still do: it was filled with a lively mixture of people, all ages and ethnos, brought together by need, common interest, and belief. Our schools provided first-rate education and our children grew up straight, strong, and committed to doing for others as much as for themselves. Community theater and arts flourished, and Better City's garden club maintained the public areas of the city as well as each member's private garden.

We encouraged participation in team sports at every age level, and one of the favorite annual events was the baseball game between the Better City Little and Senior Leagues.

The years passed, not without controversy and many challenges to Better World, but they passed nonetheless. I didn't really notice that so much time had gone by until Betty died and I woke up the next morning old and alone. When I looked out the window, I saw the earth-moving machines advancing on the area beyond the Better City stadium.

THE KNOCK AT MY DOOR disturbed my morning meditations and I slowly swam upward through the layers of consciousness until I could speak. "Come in."

The door opened to reveal a burly Better World staffer in a green jumpsuit, heavy gloves, and boots. He had a long red pigtail and a full, bushy beard. "Morning, Dr. Akimura."

"Who are you?"

"Mike Barker. I'm here to help you move."

"Move? What are you talking about?"

A cloud passed over the genial face. "They told me you were all set to go. Don't tell me they forgot to call you."

"Who is they?"

"Mr. Torrance. And Ms. Quinlan."

"I see. Well, they were wrong. I'm sorry, Mike. I'm not going anywhere."

"But—"

"I've got to get back to my meditations." I closed the door and locked it.

A moment later the screen began buzzing. I let it buzz. Finally, it stopped. A few minutes later there was a terrific pounding at my door.

"What is it?"

"Julian, it's Ginny. We need to talk."

I glared at the door in annoyance. "Can't it wait?"

"No. Please, Julian. Let me in."

I opened the door to find both Ginny and Barsi waiting for me.

"Well, what is it?" I said.

A silent, determined look passed between the two women. The silence lengthened until I was about to say something. But then Ginny turned to look at me, chin thrust out. "Julian, we owe you an apology. We each thought the other had told you, and it turns out nobody had."

"Told me what?"

"About the plumbing: we've traced a series of leaks to the pipes below your house, and unfortunately, we've got to tear up the floor to get to them. I've arranged to have you move into an apartment next to Barsi until the entire mess is over."

"I haven't noticed any leaks."

"Nevertheless, the pipes must be fixed."

"But I don't want to move."

The two women exchanged nervous glances. I began to suspect that something peculiar was going on.

"Now, Julian," Barsi said quickly. "You know you have to reserve all of your energies for the sharings. And to teaching those among us whom you've chosen to continue the tradition. You can't be at the top of your form if you've got to climb over workers and equipment. Think of the mess and the noise."

She smiled but instead of my usual melting response I felt chilled to the tips of my toes.

"I was just telling Ginny what a fine idea it is to have your apartments moved back into Better World, to the ground floor, next to mine." Her dark eyes glistened with unmistakable invitation but I wasn't buying it. "I'm looking forward to having you as my neighbor so we can work together more closely."

More closely indeed. I forced myself to shake off the pleasant reveries her seductive insinuations evoked. I was a saintly and foolish old man—at least I had to convince them of that long enough to outwit this obvious attempt to put me under their surveillance. And once they had me there, I was certain they would never allow me to return to my own digs.

"Why in the world would I want to move?" I said. "I'm perfectly comfortable where I am. In fact, I've finally gotten my rooms set up exactly the way I've always wanted them."

Another exchange of glances, this time amused and almost condescending. Things were worse than I had thought. Much worse.

"We're glad to hear that," Ginny said. "But you simply must vacate for the time being. We'll try to get this over with as quickly as possible. It's only temporary, understand?"

"Oh, I certainly do understand," I said.

For a moment no one spoke. Barsi and Ginny looked at each other and looked hastily away.

"Good," Ginny said.

We exchanged tight smiles and nods all around, but nobody was fooled. Plumbing, indeed! They had as good as announced their intentions: their coup was under way and I seemed helpless to prevent it.

This was real. Right here—right now—the battle had been forced upon me. Suddenly I had to fight desperately to hold on to the edifice that Rick and I—and Alanna and Betty—had built.

I tried not to panic as I cast about for some way to maintain control. It was not a task I relished, nor one for which I really felt that I had the strength. But I could not allow Better World to fall into strangers' hands. Not in my lifetime. It was a calling, not a business, and I would fight anyone who wanted to use it to maximize profits at the expense of healing the needy.

When Barsi called to reschedule the transport of my possessions to the location they had selected I pleaded indisposition, an upset stomach. It would work, temporarily. But I could not elude them for long.

"Are you ill?" Barsi asked. Onscreen, her dark eyes gleamed with concern and suspicion. Despite my peril and the tension between us I felt a brief, faint throb of some odd, unused feeling—love? lust?—but shrugged it off. For all I knew, Barsi's attraction for me was her faint resemblance to my lost and lamented Star. Whatever the emotion, I didn't trust it and certainly had no intention of acting upon it now.

"I just feel tired," I said. "A little bit dizzy."

Her eyes widened. "I can have healers at your door in five minutes."

"No, no, my dear."

Her worry seemed genuine. Sweet, lovely Barsi. She probably thought that she really did have my best interests at heart even as she conspired against me.

"I'm sure that a little rest will put me to rights," I said. "A bit of sea air. I want to go to our retreat in Mendocino. A good old-fashioned mutant healing session will shape me up in no time at all."

She looked dismayed. "But there's a group sharing scheduled here in four days. I don't see how you can leave."

Yes, that's right. They still needed me for the sharings—at least until my trainees had finished their apprenticeships. I wasn't quite useless to them. But Barsi didn't dare order me to stay here under her careful, devoted scrutiny. Not yet.

"I'll be back by then," I said. "And this way you can get those damned plumbing repairs taken care of without having to move anything. Now, is there anything urgent, so pressing that I need to know about it before I go?"

"No, nothing." She was a poor liar, for which I was grateful. So I knew that their plans to depose me had proceeded, full speed. This gave me pause. Was I really doing the smart thing? To leave when they were strengthening their control could be a poor move, strategically. But if I did not go now I might find myself prevented from doing so later. I could too easily envision a scenario in which I was held at

Better World under house arrest, their captive sage, hooked on group sharings but otherwise incommunicado.

No, my only hope was in leaving and that during my brief absence I could enlist the help I so desperately needed.

THE WOODS OF MENDOCINO were much as I remembered them, dark and wet with gray fog, the scent of wet wood heavy on the chill afternoon air.

I stood outside the towering redwood house, struck by a barrage of memories. I hadn't expected the sight of the place to affect me so strongly. But it was so familiar, every turn, every winding curve of its peculiar design, even after all this time, so very familiar. I could see my father, my mother, even my long-dead grandmother, Sue Li, here. I remembered the sound of song, of laughter, and also the sound of weeping.

I pressed the keypad at the front gate.

"Alanna," I said. "It's me, Julian. Let me in. Please, open the door."

There was no answer. Was she away? I probed telepathically: no, she was in there, all right. I could pick up her angry mental emanations.

"Come on, Alanna. Don't try to hide. I know you're in there."

"Go away, Julian. I didn't ask you to come here."

I rattled the gate. "Dammit, I've got to talk to you! Right away."

For answer she flung a telekinetic wave at me that, despite my attempts to resist, shoved me back toward my blue rental skimmer by a good twelve feet.

Yes, I had lied to Barsi out of necessity. I had never intended to go to Dream Haven. But if Barsi had known I was going on my knees to Alanna she would have found some way to stop me.

In vain I pressed the keypad repeatedly. Alanna was safe behind her walls. Obviously, she intended to wait me out.

The wind came up and I began to feel tired and cold. Skulking about in the damp woods was a task best left to younger men. Somehow, I had to get into that house.

I slipped into mindspeech.

Alanna, please.

No answer. And from this distance I couldn't coerce her. It was a neat stalemate. But one that I had anticipated.

I wished briefly that I had been born a telekinete rather than a telepath. It certainly would have made breaking and entering a hell of a lot easier. I felt in the pocket of my cloak: the sonic disruptor was still there in its sleek black case.

Alanna, don't make me break in.

Now I could hear her thoughts plainly. She sounded calm, even a bit smug.

I'm calling the police now, Julian. Imagine the headlines when vidnews learns that the head of Better World has been arrested for attempted forced entry.

Oh, the spiteful bitch!

My hand closed around the disruptor, and before I had really thought about it, the safety catch had been released and I was pointing it at the gate lock. The device hummed briefly and the lock shattered. I pushed my way through it and hurried up the slate walk to the front door. Again the disruptor hummed and I heard the sound of metal being wrenched from its housing. I shut off the device and put it back into my pocket. The door gave smoothly and then I was inside.

The front hallway was paneled in stripes of wood, from ivory to deepest mahogany. The old lavender rug had been replaced with a deep emerald carpet, and Alanna had had the old screened porch made into a glass-walled greenhouse. I saw exotic plants with large purple blossoms hanging from the rafters and lining the thick glass shelves. Otherwise the house was much as I remembered it when Narlydda and Skerry had lived here long ago. It was still Narlydda's house, and always would be, as far as I was concerned. How peculiar that Alanna had chosen to live here. The therapist in me briefly pondered the psychological implications, but then I simply shrugged at the endless complexity of the human heart and mind.

The ground floor was dark, illuminated only by a skylight. There were carpeted stairs in front of me and I climbed slowly, feeling an arthritic twinge in my right knee.

Alanna was waiting for me in the center of Narlydda's former studio. She sat there, queenly, in a wing-back webchair. Her face was calm but her golden eyes glittered with anger.

"I thought I'd made myself clear when last we met," she said. "I don't want to see you."

"But I need your help."

"Your problems don't interest me, Julian. I assume you'll pay for the repair of both the gate and the door?"

"Yes, yes, of course."

"Good. Then I suggest you leave before the police get here—"

"Wait," I said. "Please listen to me. Give me at least five minutes. That's all I want."

"I don't see where you have the right to ask me for anything at all, Julian. You broke into my house and now you expect me to just sit here quietly and listen to you? Have you lost your mind?"

She stood up, a slim majestic figure dressed in black with one long silver earring dangling like a hinged icicle from her left ear.

"Alanna, I refuse to believe that you don't care about Better World." I pointed at the wall, at a slim, graceful hatrack made from polished brown wood. It was empty save for a battered old black cowboy hat. Rick's hat. During all this time in exile Alanna had kept Rick's hat close by her.

She looked at the hat, colored slightly, but said nothing. As we locked gazes I could hear sirens in the distance, growing louder, nearer.

"Alanna, if not for me, then for Rick."

The screech of skimmers coming to a sudden halt cut through the air. Footsteps crunched over gravel, then over stone. Heavy footsteps sounded on the stairs. A moment later the room was filled with police.

"Don't move," said a strapping blond-haired officer. He put his hand on the holster of his laser pistol. "You reported a prowler attempting a forced entry, ma'am?"

"That's right," Alanna said. "And it's about time you got here. Who knows what he might have tried?"

"Let's go," said the cop, jerking his chin at me. "We'll

read you your rights on the way to the station house." Two of the officers closed in on me.

"Alanna," I said, "don't do this."

"You should have known better than to come here."

My hands were wrenched behind my back and I felt the cool sting of metal as the cuffs were sealed around my wrists.

They jerked me out of the room toward the stairs.

I sent a desperate image at Alanna: that of a recreation park in which an actor costumed as Rick capered and pranced like a trained chimpanzee in front of gawking tourists while souvenir stands hawked masks of Alanna and me.

That's what you'll see. That's what they'll turn Better World into. They'll make fools of us all, Alanna. Destroy Rick's legacy and distort his vision. Do you really want that?

I knew by the stricken look on her face that I had finally reached soft tissue. I pressed harder.

A travesty. That's what they'll make of your love for Rick. They'll sell little hearts with holo pictures of you and my brother in them, kissing. Is that what you want? To become an exhibit in a corporate sideshow to which bureaucrats charge admission and strangers come to point and stare? Think carefully, Alanna. This is your last chance. They're already clearing the land for it. I saw the bulldozers—

"Wait," Alanna said abruptly. "Officers, wait, I've changed my mind. Don't take him away."

The cops looked at her in surprise.

"Let him go," Alanna said. "It's all right. I don't want to make a fuss."

"With all due respect, ma'am, we saw considerable signs of disruptor damage on both your gate and door. Are you sure you aren't making a mistake here? If this man is armed and dangerous—"

"I told you," she said, "it's a misunderstanding. I won't press charges. It's a family matter."

"You mean that?"

"Yes," she said. "Yes, I do."

At that, the man in charge gave her a sour look. "Domestic problems. Nothing I hate worse. Nothing more dangerous for the police." He shrugged. "Let's go."

They released me from the handcuffs and vanished down the stairs. A minute later I heard the sound of a skimmer engine revving and taking off.

In the newly restored silence Alanna had a difficult time meeting my eyes. She sank down into her chair, head averted. "All right," she said huskily. "Make your case."

"Alanna," I said. "I came because I'm desperate. Ginny Quinlan, the chief financial officer, and Don Torrance, the city manager, are pushing me out."

"What?"

"It's a coup. I told you before that they were planning something. And it's happening right now. If you don't help me stop them, I'll have nowhere else to turn." I thought that would please her, and yes, a small triumphant smile crossed her lips for a moment. I was willing to concede her that. "You've got to help me, Alanna."

"I don't see why."

"I know you're angry at me for the way I treated you. And I was wrong, okay? I know that now. I'm sorry. Would it help if I got down on my knees?"

Alanna smiled openly and derisively. "Julian, you could stand on your head for all the good it would do you. It's too late. How can we possibly come to any sort of understanding now?"

"Why did you make the cops let me go?"

"Because you frightened me with your telepathic tricks."

"Bullshit. You rescued me because you knew I was showing you the truth, and you couldn't take it. Despite what you say to me, I know you still care, Alanna. I know you don't want Better World dismembered by a bunch of corporate raiders and accountants."

"You're living in some fantasy, Julian. Better World should be closed down."

"What?" I couldn't believe what I was hearing. "How can you say that? Once you fought like hell to stay a part of Better World."

"Yes, but I was wrong—young and foolish." She waved her hand in some sort of dismissal. "When I realized that I let go."

"If you let go, then why is Rick's hat still hanging on your wall?"

"Allow an old woman some sentiment, Julian. I'm not entirely made of stone, you know."

"No?" I reached toward her, pleading. "Then prove it. Help me save Better World."

"Better World has been a distortion of mutant values, mutant skills, and a source of social discord for generations. The sooner it collapses, the better."

I dropped my hands. Her smugness made me furious. Why hadn't I brain-burned her long ago? If I had kept her under control to begin with I might not be going through this now. But no, I had to remain calm, must not give in to my desire to shout Alanna down, to punish her for this betrayal.

"How does it feel, Julian?" she said, grinning like a witch. "The shoe is finally on your own foot. How do you like it? How does it fit?"

"You're the one who's crazy," I said. "You're poisoned by resentment."

"Look, Julian, I saved you from the police. But if you don't leave of your own accord right now I'm going to throw you out of here. On your head."

"You don't mean that," I said. "Please, wait." I struggled with myself furiously, trying to find an argument that would win her trust, sway her somehow. I knew she cared. I didn't believe her for a minute when she said she wanted to see Better World destroyed. But what would Rick have done? What would he have said? His voice was so faint in my memory. I didn't know.

"You must listen to me," I said. "Please."

"I've listened to plenty already and all I see here is an old man who's frightened of losing his power and prestige. Why don't you just give in, Julian? Why not bow to the inevitable? Retire and write *your* memoirs."

"That's your solution," I said. "You turned your back on us after you couldn't have your own way. Perhaps it was you who were after the glory, Alanna. You were trying to escape the shadow of your mother."

"Don't be ridiculous. That's cheap armchair psychology, Julian. I expect better of you."

"I'm sorry. I'm not at my best right now."

"It's your church," she said. "You wanted it that way. Fix it yourself or lose it."

I slammed my hand against the wall in frustration. "It's not my church," I said. "It's Rick's. And it's yours. *And* mine. It is for everybody who needs it—mutants, nonmutants. Everyone. You can't fool me, Alanna. I just won't believe that you don't care."

"Telepathic eavesdropping, Julian?"

"I don't need telepathy. Just some knowledge of the nature of the human heart. Have you so thoroughly buried Rick that you no longer care what happens to his memory?"

"He was dangerous. An anomaly."

"Yes, of course he was. But we loved him, didn't we? Didn't we, Alanna? Why else have we remained as we are, two solitary figures in our early old age, never marrying, never connecting with anyone else?"

"I've been too busy."

"You haven't been too busy. And neither have I. It's because Rick took all we had to give of love and shaped it into something else. He shaped *us* into something else. Something wild and unexpected that nobody could predict. Something that benefits mutants and nonmutants, that unites and nurtures them. Isn't that what we've been striving toward from the first Mutant Council meeting? From the very first page of the Book to the last?"

Alanna opened her mouth to disagree but I swept on and over her. "Rick gave us something wonderful, something magical, and left us here to tend it, which I have been trying my best to do all my life. I've just done what seemed obvious and natural, trying to ride a tsunami, to steer it whenever possible. I'm not power-mad, no matter what you may think. Please, Alanna. Don't turn away from me. Not now. I need you. Rick needs you. And everyone who believes in Better World. Don't let it become just some corporate monolith more interested in profits and private agendas—another cynical cult milking its hapless members of their savings."

I was winded from that speech. But Alanna, it seemed, was just moving into high gear.

She stood up, her eyes glittered with anger. "Now that

you're weak and old you need me. But you chased me away, before."

"Because I disagreed with what you were doing with *Rick's Way.* Because I feared what you were planning to do. Which was pointless, considering that you published whatever you pleased anyway. You got what you wanted, Alanna."

A flash of real fury hardened her features. "Not what *I* wanted. All I've been is a caretaker, Julian. First for my mother's artwork and reputation, and then for Rick and his words. I've spent my entire life walking around somebody else's museum dusting off the display cases. When I die they'll probably stuff me and put me out with the rest of the relics." She paused and it seemed that her anger lessened a bit. "After all, a museum is just a church for art. And Better World is the museum for Rick."

"That's the way you see it," I said. "And that's what caused the trouble between us, originally. I saw the potential for it to be more, much more: a living institution for healing. That's why I'm fighting so hard for it now."

"That's fine, Julian, even noble. But what about Rick? Don't you, of all people, think you owe Rick anything?"

"Of course," I said. "I loved him. But I won't sacrifice the existing aspects of Better World in order to turn the place into some dead, mummified thing honoring his name. Or into some fun house, either."

"Honor must be given," Alanna said stubbornly.

"And it has, God knows," I said. "Every time we heal somebody, we do it in Rick's name. But tell me, Alanna, if you no longer care about Better World, why have you stayed here, a recluse in your mother's house? You've been independently wealthy ever since Narlydda died. You could have been off in the Bahamas writing poetry or orbiting Mars. So what's holding you here?"

"Don't be a fool," Alanna said. "Don't you think I would have gone if I could have? But he'll never let me go, Julian. Regardless of where I am or what I'm doing." She hugged herself miserably in a rare display of despair.

"Then I guess we're both trapped," I said. For a moment we eyed each other in mute acknowledgment of the truth. "Oh, why won't you help me if you still love my brother?"

"Because of what he did," she cried. "Because he killed my father! Because Better World was based upon that act, upon Rick's guilt. It was always tainted by that. And it doesn't deserve to survive."

I stared at her in amazement. "You didn't always feel that way."

"I do now. It's taken me years, so many years, to realize how I really feel. I loved Rick," she said. "But I also loved my father. He was a wonderful man."

And with those words, she handed me the key I had been searching for. Unbidden, a memory came to me of a Mutant Council meeting I had attended years ago while still in college.

A pompous speaker had been taking up a great deal of time and people were alternately muttering complaints, falling asleep, or excusing themselves from the gathering. Just as I had begun to consider leaving as well, the podium in front of the speaker began to bark and whine. It seemed to rise up and chase itself like a dog chasing its own tail. Then it started to chase the speaker around the hall.

In panic, he turned and fled. Although the Book Keeper reprimanded Skerry, we all had applauded happily and congratulated him on freeing us from the man's speech. Only Skerry had had the nerve, had taken action. He was reckless and unpredictable, but despite his protests, he had always worked for the common good. He was a rebel, incorrigible, a bridge between the old-fashioned fearful mutants and the bolder, more confident, more irreverent generation that had followed them.

A bridge. Yes, that was it. A connection, spanning time, lives, eras.

Silently, I mindlinked with my half-sister and showed her my memory. Her eyes sparkled with amusement and affection.

Then I took her on a brief tour of recent mutant history, beginning with the riots in the 1990s, Eleanor Jacobsen's election to the Senate and her murder, the rise of the false supermutant Ashman and his fall, thanks to her parents and mine. Rick's development from a null into a super-enhanced mutant.

And more: I showed her the various unscrupulous people, both mutant and non, who would have used mutant powers to their own selfish benefit if they could: Stephen Jeffers, Tavia Emory, Ethan Hawkins, and now the troika threatening to displace me and take over Better World.

Do you see it, Alanna? Do you see?

All I can see is my own guilt, the part I played in my father's death.

Flaming in her mind was that awful moment on Ethan Hawkins's orbital pavilion. Alanna and I stood, helpless, as Skerry and Rick battled to the death. Rick had been wild then, almost crazed by his metamorphosis, unscrupulous and out of control.

My fault. Don't you see? It was my fault they fought. My fault that my father died.

So, Alanna, to deal with your own guilt about loving Skerry's murderer, you want to deny all the good that Rick did? Let it disappear? It will, you know.

But it was all my fault—

Perhaps. But don't you see the good you did?

She gave me a confused, skeptical look.

Don't you realize that Skerry's death was a necessary sacrifice? No, don't turn away. Listen to me. Your father's death saved Rick's life.

Now you're playing with me.

Not at all. I'm convinced that had Skerry lived, Rick would have become a thief and a scoundrel, no better than Stephen Jeffers and his ilk. Probably much much worse, given his extraordinary powers.

A thief? Rick?

Absolutely. He was well on the way to taking over Ethan Hawkins's organization, don't you remember? But Skerry's death stopped all that. In a funny way, it redeemed him. In fact it was an essential element in saving Rick.

Now I really don't understand you.

It saved Rick by propelling him into something bigger and better than he was alone. Into someone who cared about other people and could use his superior skills to help them. He felt guilty and miserable and he was desperate to atone for his actions. So he reached out. It was the only thing he could do. The best thing.

There were tears in Alanna's eyes.

I wish I could believe that.

"You have to," I said. "Come on, Alanna. Can't you see it? After all the hiding and breeding and scheming. The phonies and failures. The mutants had been waiting for so long. And finally, one day, the supermutant comes along."

"Rick."

"Yeah, Rick. And he was all they had imagined, and more. But untamed, wild, and uncontrollable. He wouldn't give them a thing—thumbed his nose at them and told them to fuck off. He seemed determined to utilize his skills for his own selfish amusement.

"But then, the one man who might have been able to command his respect—his biological father—confronted him, and was killed in the process."

"Because of me," Alanna said bitterly. "He wanted to protect me from Rick. Daddy's death was my fault."

"But his death turned Rick away from his self-destructive, unlawful path toward his true destiny. Don't you see, Alanna? Skerry's death made it possible for Rick to become the bridge. The bridge between mutants and nonmutants."

"But my guilt—"

"Should be tempered by your gratitude."

"Gratitude?"

"You helped to save Rick, to redeem his life, to transform his work. You were one of the builders of the bridge. And I was another." I wanted to laugh now, it was all so clear. All along I had thought I was working against my brother, struggling to reshape what he had left us. But what I had been doing was working with him. Every day.

Alanna was staring at me, lips trembling, eyes wide.

"Together," I said. "Together *we* made Better World the true link between mutants and nonmutants. We made the way to bridge humankind's suffering and pain, loneliness and guilt, differences and fear.

"What's more, we've taught mutants and nonmutants that they need one another. Through the groupmind we have proved that together we are greater and better than apart and fearful. I'm convinced that there are unusual psychological and physiological benefits that can be derived from mixed group sharings. They have to continue, and I must teach others how to hold them. And that's why we must preserve Better World, maintain it, *and* control it. Surely now you can see that. It's not for my sake, for my own desire for power. It's for all of us. For the sake of the human race, mutants and nonmutants all together."

"But—"

"No buts," I said. "We've stumbled upon the link between us and if we don't preserve it no one else will."

"Yes," she said slowly, her voice thick with emotion. Tears were spilling down her face. "I see. I understand, Julian. I really do see it."

Alanna's thin frame shook as she cried. There were tears in my eyes as well, tears that almost blinded me as I made my way toward her to offer the only comfort I knew: the embrace of her closest surviving relative. For a long, wordless moment we held each other, sobbing in relief and regret.

"Forgive me," I said. "I was wrong to have chased you away. I was cruel and brutal. All this time I needed you and didn't know it. I thought our goals would put us on a collision course. But there's room for every kind of belief in Better World. I should have known that. I know it now."

Alanna was light in my arms. A bird would have weighed more. And yet I was suddenly convinced that, together, the two of us could lick all comers—anyone who threatened Better World—or Rick's legacy.

As I held her I felt a great sense of completeness and suddenly I saw a vision of all those who had come before us, our parents and grandparents, aunts and uncles, and their grandparents, and theirs before them. Every face was smiling, every eye glinted with happiness and approval. And at the front of the group stood Skerry and Rick, beaming proudly.

I WAS IMPATIENT TO LEAVE but Alanna insisted on having a mechbot fix her front door lock and I couldn't really blame her. Luckily, the repair was finished in half an hour. We hurried from the house toward my skimmer. The sun was low in the sky, casting long shadows between the towering redwoods.

I was in the middle of the road when a sudden dazzling

light came out of nowhere and blinded me. I could hear the sound of a skimmer engine growing loud and then louder.

"Julian, get out of the way!"

Colors danced in front of me but I still couldn't see. The skimmer rocketed toward me, faster and faster, engine roaring.

Abruptly, there was the sound of tires skidding on pavement, the screech of brakes, and then an ugly thud followed by an awful crash in the distance. And silence.

"My God," Alanna gasped. "Are you all right?"

"I think so." I shook my head and red spots danced against my eyelids. Slowly, my eyesight cleared until I could see my sister's stricken face. "What happened?"

"That skimmer just came roaring down the road and gunned right for you." She looked at me, pale and shaken. "I used TK to deflect it but I must have used too much force. It went off the road over the cliff."

"You didn't mean to do it," I said. "They were reckless fools. They were going much too fast. You just acted instinctively."

"Shouldn't we see if they need help?"

I made a quick mental scan and shook my head. "They're beyond help, I'm afraid. There's nothing we can do for them now."

"Oh God. I killed them!"

"No, they killed themselves. But we'll notify the police from the car phone. At the very least we can do that. Come on, let's get going."

Somberly, Alanna slipped into the skimmer beside me and we set off into the looming shadows.

17

WHEN WE GOT BACK to Better World it was Thursday, early evening, and the trees were tall purple shapes in the gray twilight. At the front gate I pulled out my ID card. But as I passed it before the scanner's laser eye nothing happened.

"Perhaps it's damaged," Alanna said. "Try it again."

Once more I inserted the card into the slot. A message flashed across the gatescreen: "Invalid."

My gate authorization had been canceled. "I don't believe it," I said. "I'm going to call the security chief." Quickly I punched up his familiar code on the car phone.

"Hello?" said an unfamiliar female voice.

"Let me speak to Joe Martinez."

"I'm sorry," came the prim reply. "He's at the sharing."

"Sharing? What sharing?"

"May I take a message?"

"This is Julian Akimura. I can't get in the gate. Who am I speaking to?"

"Is that supposed to be some sort of sick joke? You've got a lot of nerve, mister, especially today of all days."

"Pardon me?"

"Dr. Akimura was killed in a highway accident. Run down by a skimmer, somewhere in California. We all heard about it only an hour ago. Just about everybody's at the memorial service in the Roman theater. So take your lousy jokes and go to hell."

"But—"

The phone buzzed. She had hung up.

I turned to Alanna, dumbfounded. "I'm dead. They all think I'm dead."

"And you would have been," she said grimly. "If I hadn't deflected that skimmer."

I stared at her. "They must have sent somebody after me who trailed me right to your door and waited." An icy fury ran through me. Murderers! Assassins. Well, I had survived their ugly plot and now they had a few surprises coming. "Alanna, how strong is your TK range?"

She looked at me as though I had lost my mind. "This is hardly the time—"

"Don't argue with me."

"What are you getting at?"

"Do you think you could lift us over the gate and into the complex?"

"Yes, of course. Hold on."

She shut her eyes. Slowly the skimmer rose up over the trees, rocking a bit, higher and higher. We floated over the gate, over the front wall, and settled behind a thick stand of chamisa near my house. I could see that the lights were blazing inside the building, from the bottom floor to the top.

"Careful," I said. "Let's go around the back. Somebody might see us. We've got to get to that sharing before we're stopped."

It was easy enough to stay under cover and unnoticed in the gloom of dusk. Dodging from shadow to shadow, we picked our way to the rear entrance of the Roman arena.

I had hoped to slip in there but guards had been posted at every door.

"Dammit," I said. "Now what?"

Alanna gave me a look that was half mournful and half hilarious. "I know what my father would have done. He'd have gotten himself levitated over the wall and descended in a chariot of fire. With a choir of angels singing alleluia in the background."

I could have hugged her. "That's it. Alanna, it's perfect. We'll knock their goddamned eyes out with our grand entrance. Can you take us up and over?"

"Easy as pie."

"And then bring us down slowly so that we're floating just above Rick's tomb."

Alanna smiled. "I'm almost beginning to like this."

I grinned back at her. "Get us in there, and leave the rest to me."

As easily as if she were floating a feather across a room she took us up and over the antiqued walls, over the heads of the crowd, and into the stadium proper.

As soon as we were over the wall I summoned every ounce of telepathic skill I had to create a massive illusion.

Forming an image for one person is easy but hypnotizing an arena full of people is a different thing entirely. My heart pounded with the strain and my head ached. For a moment I feared I would fail. I gave it everything I had. The crowd looked up, saw us, and gasped.

Encased in a glowing ball of flame, magnificent, stupendous, casting a brilliant red aura that filled the arena, we descended as though borne by angels. True to her word, Alanna brought us to rest just about a foot above Rick's tomb. We hovered gently above the white marble as my psychokinetic flames turned everything below us orange. I held out my hands to the people below and let them have a good, long look.

Somewhere, Skerry was grinning, I was sure of that.

There was a low murmur of confusion and disbelief. It rose from a whisper to a roar and then the crowd went crazy.

"It's Dr. Akimura! He's not dead."

"He's returned! Father Julian and the blessed Alanna!"

"It's a miracle! Rick be praised!"

A wild cheer went up and I waved my arms over my head at the stamping, clapping mob. Just wait, I thought, wait until you see what I've got in store for you.

Red and green and golden fireworks exploded above our heads: molten embers of color, completely illusory and startling to behold. I filled the sky with illusory light, and the air with illusory trumpets and the sound of an entire city cheering at the return of its one true ruler.

Ginny Quinlan and Don Torrance stood onstage, with Barsi just behind them. They gazed up at me and turned to one another, dumbstruck. Ginny looked dismayed but Barsi seemed distinctly relieved while Torrance's expression was one of amazement and chagrin.

Beside them was a golden-eyed young man with curling red hair, a mutant named Matthew whom I recognized from training classes. He had been one of several selected to learn the group sharing techniques. What was he doing onstage? He was a mere apprentice.

Ginny grabbed the microphone. "This is a blessed vision," she cried. "A group sighting of the late lamented. Praise be! We see dead Julian's very image! If only Julian himself were still with us! Let young Matthew here help guide us in our grief." She all but nudged the mutant apprentice forward with her foot.

Alanna muttered, "Who the hell is that kid?"

"A usurper, I think."

"Let us join together to share our feelings—to express the grief of our great loss," Matthew intoned.

The crowd ignored him. Despite Ginny's attempt to divert and mislead they were sure that we were the real thing. People were jumping out of their seats and whirling like dervishes in the aisles. Only a few of the faithful seemed to be even remotely interested in what was happening onstage.

"Join with me," Matthew said.

No, I thought. Join with me. But hard as I tried, I couldn't maintain all the telepathic wizardry, the son et lumière show, and also manage to link with the crowd below me.

JOIN WITH ME!

Matthew's mindspeech was surprisingly compelling. He was far stronger than I'd thought and with dismay I saw a few more of the celebrants turn to face him, glassy-eyed, mouths open. And then a few more. Despite my best razzle-dazzle, I was losing them. More and more of them seemed to be drawn back under Matthew's control as the sharing's seductive effects began to spread.

I tried to infiltrate the mind circle but was rebuffed. Tried again, and again and again, and each time bounced off the seamless wall of many minds locked against me. How was it possible? How could Matthew summon so many to him?

Then I saw the truth: it was not Matthew acting alone, but several mutant trainees—an entire cadré—who had set up a crude but formidable mental barrier. How easy it had been for Ginny and her crew to turn all of them against me! But they were fools if they thought that Alanna and I were nothing more than ghosts or some peculiar psychic hallucination.

Inch by inch I probed the barrier. Ah, there: a flaw in the mind wall. I worried it a bit and managed to enlarge the gap but it was maddeningly slow work. I should have been able to cut right through to the groupmind but I was nearly exhausted after my flaming chariot stunt.

I pushed against the barrier, battering with everything I had until sweat ran down my face.

"What's wrong?" Alanna said. "What's happening?"

"I'm trying to breach their mental defenses," I told her, my breath coming in gasps. "But it's a tough business. I'm not getting anywhere."

Alanna grabbed my hand. "Use me."

"But you're not a telepath."

"No, but in the past you've amplified your own powers by using a mutant mind in concert with your own. Try it now. What have you got to lose?"

I squeezed her hand gratefully and felt fresh energy flow through me. Eagerly, I linked her mind to mine, and shoved once more at the mental wall. Suddenly I could push harder, longer, had energy reserves I hadn't noticed moments before. With Alanna's strength to bolster me I began to crack through and into the sharing. The barrier splintered as I battered against it, and with a prolonged searing blast of mental power I burst past it and into the groupmind.

But something was wrong, very wrong. I could tell in an instant. There were strange mental currents running through the sharing, disorienting and confusing, almost nauseating. As I searched for their source I saw Matthew shudder and clutch at his head in obvious pain. He staggered, fell, struggled to get up, and fell over onto his side, curled into a tight fetal ball on the floor of the stage.

The sharing disintegrated into nightmarish horror that had a familiar and terrible resonance. Malformed fire imps sprang up and capered madly above the crowd. Hideous creatures came roaring up out of their subconscious prisons to torment their creators: fanged eels, spiders whose legs ended in six-fingered hands with curling yellow nails, men with horrible clubbed and boil-encrusted penes, gobbling purple vaginal maws lined with row upon row of pointed, blood-stained teeth. It was a Freudian free-for-all. And I was at the center of it.

People were howling, biting themselves in maddened revulsion, tearing at one another trying to get away from their worst terrors made real.

I swooped into Matthew's mind and saw with sorrow that he had suffered some sort of cerebral accident—perhaps the strain of maintaining the sharing had been too great for him. He was too far gone—there was nothing I could do. I pulled out of him and right back into the midst of the nightmare. All around me were hundreds of minds gibbering wildly. I tried to calm them but it was like grabbing at a thousand flailing ropes and trying to pull them all back together into one knot. And how long could I hold out and avoid being swept up in the brainstorm?

So many minds. How could I reach them all? I felt numb and light-headed. It was hopeless, hopeless. In a moment I would be hallucinating with the rest of them, screaming at horrific images of Rick and Star and Skerry and my mother dancing in a mocking circle around me. Tears filled my eyes and I began to weep helplessly.

"No. Stop it. Julian, hold on!"

Alanna grabbed hold of my arm and shook me fiercely. Pale and horrified, she alone was untouched by the hysteria and I clung to her for sanity, for my very life, it seemed.

"You can do it," she said. "You *will* do it, Julian. They need you. Help them. Help them, now!"

Once more I felt her strength steadying me, anchoring me. My head cleared, and drawing upon every inch of power I had, I reached farther, farther still, grabbed hold of the fraying mental circuit and pulled it to me.

Hush. These are dreams. Illusions. They have no substance, none at all.

My mindspeech seemed to have little effect. The crowd screamed and roiled below me, oblivious.

LISTEN TO ME! We must be strong. Together we are strong. We must be brave. Together we are brave. There's no need to panic. No need to flee. Take your seats. Calm yourselves. I am Julian. Share with me now. I am Julian, alive in your midst and with you now. I will keep you safe, safe from these horrors.

Was it my imagination or were the screams lessening? The struggles becoming less heated?

We will keep one another safe. Take the hand of your neighbor and hold on. Hold on to one another and help one another. Breathe deeply and slowly. We are calm. We will be calm. Now.

And as I mindspoke them in a reassuring murmur, the mob quieted and the hysteria began to pass.

I saw Ginny staring at me, stunned. Beside her, Don Torrance was similarly dazed. Only Barsi was smiling in obvious relief. I would attend to them, soon. But first I scanned the crowd for a doctor and quietly directed him to Matthew's side. Perhaps there was still something that could be done for the boy. I hoped so.

The regal opening notes of "Rick's Ode" burst upon the air as, under Alanna's invisible and inspired guidance, the arena's mechband began to play.

"Set us down," I said.

Gently, Alanna lowered us to the stage and I raced to the podium.

"My friends," I said. "I bring joyous news. Not only have I survived a cruel and treacherous murder plot this very day, but to add to our joy we have among us today one who was dear to the heart of the sainted Rick. As you can see, to join our sharing I have brought Sister Alanna, beloved of the Desert Prophet!"

Cheers and approving whistles rocked the stadium.

Ginny Quinlan broke from her paralysis and began to run desperately for the wings with Don Torrance right behind her. To her credit, Barsi, alone, stood her ground.

Calmly, coolly, as though she were reaching for a cucumber sandwich, Alanna scooped the three of them up in her telekinetic grasp and held them motionless by the edge of the stage. "We'll deal with you later," she said. "After the sharing."

Drawing Alanna to my side, I launched into the traditional steps of the group sharing. "Open your minds," I said. "Open your hearts."

"We will," the group chanted. "We have."

"Share with me now."

The mental circuit sizzled with energy as I hopped from mind to mind, sealing the coil behind me. I felt like a young man again, full of juice and ready for anything. We floated together, all of us, wordlessly, blissfully. The familiar pleasure of it dazzled me and for a moment I was lost in wondrous harmony.

But a gentle mental jab from Alanna reminded me of my serious, primary purpose here. Carefully I moved from mind to mind, healing, soothing. And then I addressed them as though they were a single entity.

Beloved friends, I am back among you, unharmed and healthy. Once again I shall lead Better World, with your help and with your love. Let us give thanks for our deliverance and forgive those who lied to us and misled us. I ask you now to forgive and forget.

No, came the groupmind's response. *They hurt us. They lied to us. We will never forgive them. Never.*

I pushed my point gently but firmly. *If we do not forgive, then we are no better than those who would plot against us. Better World must teach forgiveness, understanding, and tolerance. These are all precepts of the healing way. Embrace them. Employ them.*

We did before, they replied, *and we've been repaid in pain and falsehood.*

There's always some risk in trying something new. We are attempting to chart a new way, a new path. Mistakes may be made. But our successes will outweigh them. We have a great responsibility to share what we have learned here, to offer our comfort to the needy world, to mutants and non-mutants alike. We need one another and we can help one another. Rick has shown us that, together, we are stronger and better than apart. We must open our arms and our minds to one another, as Rick wanted. Sharing is the bridge to greater understanding. Sharing is the only way.

Humanity has been divided for too long between mutant and nonmutant. Let us be the connection, the bridge, the path to one another. This is just the beginning. We have great days ahead of us. We will build upon this foundation, together, sharing and growing. Sharing is the key. We know that now and we will spread the word around the world. Sharing is the only way.

A thousand minds sighed and moved as one as they replied:

Sharing is the only way.

GINNY QUINLAN AND DONALD TORRANCE resigned immediately and Alanna, who had long experience at both public relations and financial management, temporarily assumed their duties.

A contrite Barsi asked for a private meeting with me, and after some hesitation, I agreed. Meekly, she came to my office, dressed in somber tones of green. No bells were in her hair now. She looked subdued and even woeful.

"What do you want?" I said sharply.

"To apologize." Her voice was so small it was almost a whisper. "Oh, Julian, I'm so ashamed. I was a complete fool to believe you were growing incapable of running this place. But Ginny was so persuasive. She'd almost convinced me to act as a caretaker once you'd been dispossessed. I honestly believed we were acting in the best interests of Better World."

I refused to allow myself to soften. "And what about the murder attempt?"

Tears glistened in her dark eyes and she wouldn't meet my gaze. "I knew nothing of it, nothing, until Ginny announced your death. Believe me, Julian. I never could have endorsed anything like that. Never! I was stunned, horrified, when they announced your death. Then I knew that what she and Don were doing was wrong but it was too late and I thought you were already dead. And worse, that in my naiveté, my stupidity, I had helped to kill you." She wept openly.

I let her cry for a while until I grew uncomfortable. "And what do you want now?"

"To stay at Better World, if you'll have me. To gain your

trust again, somehow. I don't care if you want me to scrub pots in the kitchen or shovel manure in the fields. Please, Julian." She clutched at my hand. "Please don't send me away."

I pulled my hand from under hers and turned to stare out the window at the mountains. What was I to do? Was I a fool not to order her out of my sight? Could I ever trust her again?

"If you don't want me to stay, I'll understand," she said. "I even thought of leaving, just slipping away. But I couldn't do it. Not without seeing you and at least asking your forgiveness."

I stared at her sweet face and, for a moment, saw my long-lost Star again. Perhaps I was getting old and foolish— or sentimental. But I relented. "All right," I said. "You can stay. But I'm going to keep my eye on you."

She reached for me as though to hug me but I waved her away. I wasn't ready to resume our old friendship. Not quite yet. Barsi was a sweet and essentially benign person whom I was certain had been influenced by others far more ambitious than she. All the same, my faith in her had been shaken. She would have to win it back. And I suspected that she would.

Despite the best efforts of our healers, Matthew never completely recovered from the sad and dangerous episode in the Roman arena. I blame myself for this as much as anyone else: there were perilous flaws in the training program that I should have noticed long before Matthew's accident.

Today we train our apprentices much more carefully and safely. When I send them forth in teams across the country and around the world to hold sharings I'm confident that they are well equipped to protect themselves and those with whom they commune. In this way we spread comfort, healing, and connection among mutants and nonmutants, true believers and skeptics. And it's no longer necessary for anyone to worship Rick, much less show any knowledge of him at all. The cult of personality is over. What is important is that each member of the groupmind be willing to open, to share strengths, to cherish and heal one another. We are a healing organization.

It quickly became apparent that Alanna was indispensable to Better World, and to my surprise, with little urging, she agreed to move to Better City and, what's more, to occupy the lower floors of my residence. I had begun to find the building a bit large and lonely, and the sounds of another living, breathing presence were very welcome indeed. I've come to enjoy Alanna's astringent humor and rely upon her incisive intelligence. What a pleasure it is, late in life, to have the company of a close relative who is also a friend and peer.

So we live now, peacefully, brother and sister, partners deeply committed to bringing mutants and nonmutants together in happy harmony.

Every now and then the specter of Rick pops in from the past, creating a stir. As recently as yesterday he surprised me in my study as I was preparing for a group sharing. He seemed young, so terribly young—wearing his leather pants and his ruffled white shirt from his wild days long ago.

"Hi, Rick," I said. "Nice to see you again."

Our eyes met and we stared at each other for a moment. Then I said, "Well? How do you think we're doing?"

Of course he couldn't respond aloud, couldn't say a word. And I'm not certain that he really heard me at all. But he smiled. And when I waved at him it seemed to me that he winked. I would swear that he had. Then, with a nod, he disappeared. But I won't miss him. I know that I'll see him again.

We have gone on to great days at Better World. The mutants and nonmutants have been drawn closer than ever as trust builds and grows. I feel certain our combined strengths will benefit humanity in ways even I can't yet imagine. The groupmind's potential is extraordinary. For a moment I yearn to have a touch of Rick's magic, to leap through time and see the years to come.

But no. I'm content to have been here at the beginning, to have provided the linkage and helped to show the way. Never, ever, did I expect to become that linchpin, that intersection point. Nor did I think that my brother, Rick, would amount to anything, much less a demi-messiah. But

I did my best and so, I guess, did he: the changer and the changed.

Am I glad? Yes, yes I am. For both of us. Very glad, indeed. And grateful and even hopeful: for all of roiling, boiling humanity, young and old, male and female, mutant and non. Rick bless us and keep us, every one.

ABOUT THE AUTHOR

KAREN HABER was born in Bronxville, New York, and grew up in the suburbs of New York City. Her short fiction has appeared in *The Magazine of Fantasy and Science Fiction*, *Isaac Asimov's Science Fiction Magazine*, *Full Spectrum 2*, *Women of Darkness*, and *Final Shadows*. Her books include *The Mutant Season* (cowritten with Robert Silverberg), *The Mutant Prime*, and *Mutant Star*. She is also coeditor of the original anthologies *Universe 1* and *Universe 2*. She lives in the San Francisco Bay Area.